THE
FABRIC
OF OUR
SOULS

Also by K. M. Moronova

PINE HOLLOW SERIES

(Dark Romantasy. Gods/Reincarnation. Why Choose?)
A God of Wrath & Lies
A God of Death & Rest
A Goddess of Life & Dawn

ALKROSE ACADEMY SERIES

(Epic Dark Fantasy. Enemies to Lovers. Why Choose?)
Of Deathless Shadows

STAND–ALONES

A Battle of Phantoms and Hope

THE FABRIC OF OUR SOULS

K. M. MORONOVA

FOREVER

New York Boston

Copyright © 2023 by K. M. Moronova LLC

Cover design by The Brewster Project
Cover images © Shutterstock
Cover copyright © 2024 by Hachette Book Group, Inc.

Forever
Hachette Book Group
1290 Avenue of the Americas, New York, NY 10104
read-forever.com
@readforeverpub

Originally published in Great Britain in 2024 by Orion Fiction, an imprint of The Orion Publishing Group Ltd.,Carmelite House, 50 Victoria Embankment London ec4y 0dz. An Hachette UK Company

First Forever Trade Paperback Edition: September 2024

Forever is an imprint of Grand Central Publishing. The Forever name and logo are registered trademarks of Hachette Book Group, Inc.

The publisher is not responsible for websites (or their content) that are not owned by the publisher.

The Hachette Speakers Bureau provides a wide range of authors for speaking events. To find out more, go to hachettespeakersbureau.com or email HachetteSpeakers@hbgusa.com.

Forever books may be purchased in bulk for business, educational, or promotional use. For information, please contact your local bookseller or the Hachette Book Group Special Markets Department at special.markets@hbgusa.com.

Interior formatting by K. M. Moronova LLC
Character art by K. M. Moronova LLC
Stock images licensed through Canva

Library of Congress Control Number: 2024938100

ISBNs: 978-1-5387-7172-3 (paperback), 978-1-5387-7173-0 (ebook)

Printed in the United States of America

CCR

10 9 8 7 6 5 4 3 2

Content Warning

The contents of this book may be triggering and disturbing to some readers. This is a dark romance thriller, so please do take warning that the content is for adults only.

If you are sensitive to the following words and content please do not continue with reading this story: sick, psychopath, crazy, sane, physical violence, explicit sex scenes, morbid humor, hate-fucking, degradation, explicit gore, suicide and the desire to die (explicit at times), self-harm and thoughts of self-harm (masochist, and explicit at times), childhood mental abuse trauma, emotional abuse, explicit death scenes, traumatic therapy sessions, bite kink, pain kink.

Author's Note

This book is not a self-help book. Everything is morally gray and not for those who don't enjoy dark-themed books. This is a deep dive into emotional and mental illness from my perspective. Not everyone experiences depression/irrational thoughts the same.

This book romanticizes rehabilitation centers and mentally unwell people falling in love.

★ ★ ★

For the Suicide and Crisis Hotline: Call or text 988 anywhere in the U.S.

This book dallies with mentally ill characters in a fake unorthodox rehab setting. Bakersville and Harlow Sanctum are fictional places and in no way, shape, or form are based on real life places or institutions.

The characters joke about their illness and make light of their conditions at times. If you are sensitive to this aspect please do not read this book. I am not making light of the seriousness of their illnesses but rather expressing what it is like from my own perspective and experience to have depression and mental illness.

Playlist

"1-800-273-8255"—Logic ft Alessia Cara, Khalid
"Hold On"—Chord Overstreet (slow/reverb)
"Happiest Year"—Jaymes Young (slow/reverb)
"Dusk Till Dawn"—Zayn and Sia (slow/reverb)
"Control"—Zoe Wees
"Not About Angels"—Birdy
"Slow Dancing in a Burning Room"—John Mayer
"The Night We Met"—Lord Huron
"Never Let Me Go"—Florence and the Machine
"Genius"—LSD
"Thunderclouds"—LSD
"London Calling"—Michael Giacchino
"Sirens"—Fluerie
"Nine Crimes"—Damien Rice
"Seven Devils"—Florence
"For the Damaged Coda"—Blonde Redhead

For the broken ones who are in need of something
dark, morbid, and beautiful.

THE
FABRIC
OF OUR
SOULS

Chapter 1
Wynn

I was born with a bad heart.

Literally and figuratively.

I'm the cold-hearted villain in everyone's story, according to most of my loved ones, while ironically also having a heart condition that will eventually kill me. *Lucky me.*

If this is God's great design for me, then I'm good.

I'm tapping out.

The blood runs down my fingertips. It's colder than I thought it'd be. It isn't painless like some people say—no, it very much hurts.

Red drops *tap tap tap* on the tiles beneath me, making it hard to focus. Difficult to remember the good things that are supposedly due to flashback.

Only the bad ones come to mind. The heinous people and all the things they've said; the things I've said too.

Whoever coined the phrase "sticks and stones" is an asshole, don't you think? Words indeed hurt more than stones. Thanks for trying to gaslight me out of it though. It didn't work.

My name is Wynn Coldfox. I'm twenty-six years old and I want to die.

I want *to die.*

There—I said it.

Does it change anything?

Does it shock anyone, the people who secretly knew but continued to call me things like *evil, a miserable bitch, a monster*?

The answer is no, probably not, maybe mildly.

Sometimes the darkness inside me thinks that this is what they've wanted all along—for me to finally give in.

Well, welcome to the shit show.

The curtain is finally closing.

There will never be a way to explain why I am this way. It's something that you endure wholly, entirely. A deep and empty pit inside your flesh that never closes, no matter what you try to fill it with. No matter what thread you try to sew it shut with, it gapes and itches. An emergency exit that waits patiently for any who stray.

My doctor says it's a chemical imbalance in my brain, and fuck, they're probably right. But it doesn't stop the very real, un-chemical, raw *nothingness* that ravages my entire being. The pills don't help, they never have, and none of my therapists seem to understand why I'm so fucked up.

They think I'm faking or something. Let them speculate.

I stare up at the plain ceiling of my hospital room, trying not to look over at my brother. I've been awake for at least an hour now and neither of us has uttered a word to the other.

"Why?" James finally asks with his hands clasped in front of him, knuckles white. His navy-blue suit is sleek. Expensive. The black watch on his wrist is new too. A gift from a new lover? A present to himself for being so successful? I don't bother asking.

"*Don't*, James." I take a deep breath as I sit up in the bed, reluctantly meeting his gaze.

"Why can't you just...not be like *this*?" My brother runs his hand down his weary face. His brown eyes are heavy with grief and anger.

Yeah, because I *asked* to be like this.

"I've tried to explain this to you many times, James. You don't get it—you never will," I mutter unenthusiastically. I used to get upset when he'd ask. But luckily for those who haven't experienced it themselves, it is a hard feeling to understand.

James furrows his brows at me and links his fingers together in front of him again, pressing them against his lips in a thinking posture, his elbows each on a knee as he stares at me from the corner of the room like I'm a disobedient animal. He shakes his head and looks out the window for a few silent minutes, leaning back in the tacky blue chair that looks overused and uncomfortable. I slouch in bed and fist the sheets, keeping my eyes on his so I don't have to look down at my wrists. They hurt, but if I don't look, I won't have to face the disgusting reality. Avoidance has always been my coping mechanism. If I don't think about it, it doesn't matter. My day goes on.

I grit my teeth and try to lift the tension between us. "You didn't need to come all the way here."

James hates hospitals. It's everything about them, I suppose. The overworked nurses, the somber gray rooms, the drab, colorless curtains that drape the small windows, the smell. The deaths that seems to linger in the walls.

More accurately, he's hated hospitals since Mom died.

He stands and walks over to the bedside, and my heart sinks when I realize he's crying. I've never seen him cry before, not once. James Coldfox is a hard man, one who

3

hides his feelings and doesn't show his cracks. He seals himself deep within walls cemented long, long ago. But now his jaw trembles and he grabs my hand gently as his tears crash against my skin.

I avert my gaze to the dull gray floors of this morbid fucking room. I can't bear to look him in the eyes. I *know* what I did was wrong.

But I'm so tired. How do I tell him I want to sleep forever? In a bed of roses or in a goddamn urn, it doesn't matter—anywhere but here will do.

I'm burning inside, and it hurts.

I just want to stop hurting.

I should've built my walls of cement like his. I've tried vulnerability and *stupid*, senseless love. I often wonder if I'd be different if I hadn't. Now my walls are impenetrable— no one gets in, I don't go out.

James's hands are warm and he grips mine affectionately as he murmurs, "Is it work? Did you break up with that asshole Salem again? What's *so* wrong with life that you'd rather die?" He shakes his head and keeps his eyes lowered, and when I don't respond he continues with a shaky voice. "I love you, Wynn. So, so much. I want you to know that, okay? You're all I have left in this world."

Work sucks, yeah. I don't mention that I just quit the third job I've held this year.

Corporate offices are suicide base camps. They shove you in a cubicle the size of a bathroom stall and expect you to thrive. *Add a few plants and family photos.* Hearing people cough all day and looking into their dead eyes day in and day out. Hearing about so-and-so finally retiring after the endless march of devoting their entire life to a company that will replace them in two weeks.

Salem was just an asshole I was having sex with. And the sex wasn't even good. He cheated on me. I didn't care—end of the story with that jerk.

I guess, if nothing else, being all James has left should be a reason to try to get better. But I've tried...so many times and the sadness doesn't go away. The nights I spend staring into the dark don't brighten.

"I want to discuss placing you in a rehabilitation institute." He dips his head as he speaks and my heart sinks.

"You want to put me in a fucking institution?" I try to jerk my hand away but he holds on firmly. I lift my eyes to his, and my anger instantly disperses with the sorrow that radiates from his soul. I deflate. "I'm sorry... You know, I think that might be a good decision." I press my other palm against my forehead to suppress the warring headache that claws at my skull. "I'm just...*so* tired, James."

He sits next to me and shakes his head. "It's not your fault you're like this...We've been through this so many times, Wynn, but you know what?" His voice lifts and he sits straighter. A sickening flicker of hope dashes through his eyes. "This rehabilitation center is going to help you. They have the highest success rate for curing people like you."

Curing people like you. People. Like. You.

My mind is a plague that needs to be cured and people like *me* are damned to chase this mysterious elixir.

Will I be the same when I'm *cured*?

If I get cured.

I nod in agreement, eager to move on to things less depressing, like the weather. Anything to change the subject will do, even James's corporate job that he's *so happy* to have. Anyone can see that his soul is slowly dying. That's what the real world does to us, isn't it? Grind, grind, grind for forty-plus hours a week just to stand at the grocery store and worry about whether you can afford food.

But I suppose he's doing much better than I ever was. Maybe he doesn't worry about those sorts of things. "So, do you think you'll get that promotion?"

"My boss said that it's a sure thing, I'll be promoted in the next month—"

"Hey, man, it's past visiting hours. I'm sorry, but you're going to have to leave." A male nurse interrupts James as he struts in, carrying an IV bag and some white towels. His black hair lies perfectly on his gorgeous head, his jaw is sharp, and his eyes are a very alluring shade of blue.

He's handsome—but there's something about the way he looks at me that puts me off. It's not pity like the other nurses always have pinned on their expressions. His expression is cold, bitter, and maybe a bit curious.

James rolls his eyes at the nurse but smiles at me. "I'll be back tomorrow. I'm staying at the inn across the street in case you need anything, okay?"

I wave my hand at him dismissively. "I'll be fine. It's not like they're going to let me *do* anything in here," I say as a joke but James does *not* find it funny at all. The nurse, on the other hand, laughs coldly as he closes my blinds and sets the towels down on the small coffee table beneath the window.

James and I both snap our heads at him. I'm shocked, but my brother is furious.

"Did you just fucking laugh at my sister's condition? She's *fucking sick!*" he shouts as he backs the nurse into the corner of the room. I nearly fall out of my bed trying to stop him.

"Stop it! I was joking and he laughed; it's not his fault," I plead with my brother.

James fists the nurse's scrubs and looks at his name tag. "Well, I'll be submitting a complaint first thing in the morning, *Nurse Hull*." He releases Nurse Hull and gives me a quick apology and goodbye before storming out, heading toward the reception desk instead of the exit.

Great. Now I feel like an asshole.

Nurse Hull chuckles quietly as he replaces my IV bag and I dare a glance up at him. The bedside lamp lights his face from beneath and his blue eyes flick down to me as he finishes up. I take a deep breath as our eyes connect. He's fucking beautiful. It's hard to believe he's actually a nurse. He looks anything but the intelligent and all-helping type.

He wears black Under Armour beneath his scrubs—to cover his tattoos, I'm guessing by the small thorns that are inked on his wrist. A black cuff crests his ear and behind it is a small tattoo of the Roman numeral II.

"Sorry about my brother, I shouldn't have made that joke. I'm unwell and he's traveled a long way to be here for me." I let my eyes drift to my bandaged wrists. I feel guilty, but not once have I felt like crying about it. It doesn't seem sad to me. My illness makes me yearn for dark things, which is precisely why James is trying to put me in rehab. I *should* be sad about it. But the emotions aren't there.

Not anymore.

What kind of sickness takes your fucking emotions? It's not fair.

Nurse Hull focuses back on the IV and gives me a cruel grin. "Well, *I* thought it was funny—you know, as a bystander who isn't foreign to being *unwell*. Brothers are just overprotective assholes you're stuck with. We'll do anything for our siblings."

I raise a brow and watch him as he circles my bed to the other side, grabbing the towels from the coffee table on the way over. "You're a weird nurse," I mumble, scooting myself back so I can lie down. The drugs are making me really tired, dizzy too. Maybe I can put some makeup on tomorrow and feel like a person again.

He laughs. The sound of his deep voice gives me goosebumps. "Am I? Noted. Miss Coldfox, right? Wynn Coldfox?" He leans over and stares down at me with hooded eyes; darkness lurks there and a piercing, unsettling feeling coils in my stomach. God, he's absolute murder.

"Shouldn't you know who the patient is *before* coming into the room?" I ask, scrunching my brows at him warily. He doesn't fit this role well. I wonder how many complaints he's gotten since working here.

Add my brother to that growing list.

He sets the towels in the cupboard and pushes his dark hair back. His tan skin is a little darker than my own, but not by much. I bite my lower lip to quell the horrible thoughts that my drug-induced mind is trying to think about his taut chest and arms.

"I knew it was you. I'm just trying to make small talk," he says indifferently before clicking off the TV that's been playing the same boring nineties show all day.

I nod and don't bother trying to give him a fake smile. "You suck at small talk, Nurse Hull."

He eyes me with a grimace, calculating something before he leans in close, his face mere inches from mine. He whispers, "Can you keep a secret?"

I take a quick breath of surprise. He's insanely gorgeous, but there's an air of cruelty about him that makes my heart beat faster.

"Sure, I guess."

He smiles and tugs on the name tag pinned to his scrubs. "I'm not Nurse Hull. I borrowed these scrubs."

His amusement is disturbing. I narrow my eyes at him. "What the fuck—why?"

He shrugs and walks toward the door. He flips the light switch and my bedside lamp goes out. "So I don't get complaints from people like your brother." He laughs as the door shuts quietly behind him.

I'm left in the darkness of my room, staring at the tacky tiled ceiling with a stupid grin, wondering who the hell that was.

And if, perhaps, I'll see him again.

Chapter 2
Wynn

James sets a cup of generic coffee down on the white plastic tray connected to the side of my bed. I don't even care that it's not a fancy blend, I just want the bitter liquid down my throat right this second.

"Careful, you're going to burn your hand if you spill," he grumbles. It's eight a.m. and no one asked him to be here this early. Still, it means a lot that he's set aside this time for me. Even if he did wake me up and throw the curtains open without warning, nearly blinding me.

He pulls out his laptop and starts clicking away on it. His boss lets him work from home most days anyway, so leaving Colorado and flying out to Montana wasn't such a stretch for him. Sometimes I think James truly thrives on working, traveling, and being dressed in a suit, even though the only people he will see today are me and the hospital staff.

I still feel awful about it though. It obviously wasn't supposed to end up this way. I was hoping to not be here for the *after*. Still, I'm sorry for my roommate, who's refusing to talk to me now, and to my brother for having to deal with his adult younger sister.

The coffee is bland but my soul reignites a bit as I sip the hot liquid down. I watch him type for a while, missing my own laptop and wondering what I was working on the night I decided to die. Does it matter? I'm still not sure.

Obviously I won't be going back to that life. Rehab is in the stars for me now.

My gaze shifts to the nightstand; there's a black ring next to the lamp. Weird, that definitely wasn't there yesterday. I set my paper cup down and grab the ring. It's cold and matte, nothing special about it, no engravings or marks.

It reminds me of the sort of thing my mom used to leave me on my nightstand when I was a child.

She would bring me crystals from her work trips. The memories of her travel stories and the crystals consume me for a few moments before a dark and looming presence steals them away. My mother was a wrathful, cruel woman.

I was expected to be some sort of prodigy in school. Maybe that's when I first fell sick. I ponder the thought as I run my thumb over the smooth edge of the ring.

"Did you bring this?" I ask as I hold the black ring up to James. He looks up for a brief second before shaking his head and returning his eyes to his screen.

Okay, was it the nurse from last night then? I look over at the door. It's not like I'm forbidden to leave my room or anything. I shift off the bed and set my feet on the cold floor. The chill from the gray tiles shoots straight through my socks and into the soles of my feet, making me shiver and rub my arms.

"Where are you going?" James stops typing and frowns at me. All this frowning is going to cause him some major wrinkles in a few years.

"I'm going to go stretch my legs. Be back in twenty," I mumble as I slip on my white hospital-issued slippers and make for the door. James grumbles but the sounds of his keyboard fill the room again, so I know I'm home free.

Time to find that nurse and maybe grab a snack from the cafeteria. I want to eat something other than goddamn pudding.

Hospitals are depressing.

Older folks walk around with the assistance of healthcare providers, and family members of patients are either waiting for bad news or receiving it. Sobs fill the third-floor lobby, and it fucking sucks. I hate walking through this wing.

I tune out the sounds and focus on finding the mystery man from last night. Some of the female nurses look familiar. They must've helped me in the first few days after I woke up.

Those days are mostly blurry.

"Hi, can you help me? I'm looking for, um, Nurse Hull?" I ask the receptionist sitting at the circular desk in the center of the lobby. There are three more chairs to her side for other staff members. She gives me a flat expression and looks like she could use an extra shot of expresso in her coffee.

"Hull? He's off all week." She gives me another once-over with disapproving eyes. My gaze finds her necklace, a pendant in the shape of a cross, sitting pretty at the base of her neck. Yeah, I suppose I'm pretty low in her view. My pale-pink hair and tattoos probably don't help either.

"Thanks," I say with the fakest smile I can conjure as I walk down the hall opposite mine.

He must be here somewhere. Is he even a nurse at all?

I spend the morning walking aimlessly and finding nothing more than sick people and tired workers. I can't find Nurse Hull anywhere in this fucking place. James comes searching for me after an hour and finds me sharing fries with a nice woman in the cafeteria.

"Do you have any idea how long I've been looking for you?"

I glance up and shrug. "I got hungry. Want some?" I offer him a fry and he scowls at me like the world is ending. "Jesus, just say no. Stop with the faces." I shove a cheese-smothered fry into my mouth. He has that serious look on his face that says he means business and I'm not in the mood to argue. I thank the nice lady for the fries (I didn't bother remembering her name) and walk back to my room with James.

I nearly jump out of my slippers when I see a ghastly doctor waiting for us. He looks decrepit, with glasses from the 1800s or something and an extremely vexed expression that exaggerates all the wrinkles on his face.

I nudge James. "See, that's what you're going to look like if you keep up the scowling."

He bites back the frown that I know is pulling at his lips and furrows his brows anyway. "Wynn, this is Doctor Prestin. He's going to evaluate you for commitment to Harlow Sanctum."

Dr. Prestin extends his hand to me and I shake it with a strained smile. His hands are cold, much like his horrible smile. He smells like peppermint candy and not the good kind. My arm hair raises with goosebumps and my stomach curls.

"Nice to meet you." I force the words to come out smoothly as I pull my hand back and shove it into the safety of my fluffy sweater, desperately wishing I had sanitizer to scrub over my palm.

His dull brown eyes analyze me from behind his glasses. "A delight, Miss Coldfox. Do you think your brother's suggestion is the right choice? I'm curious about your thoughts on rehabilitation."

James looks over at me, guilt ebbing in his gaze, but it's me who should feel horrible. I'm a fucking adult. He shouldn't have to shoulder my bullshit the way he does.

"I do. I'm...not well. I don't expect you to understand but I just don't want to live. Everything sucks, I have no ambitions, nothing matters... *I* don't matter." I say the latter in a hushed tone before firming my resolve and standing straighter. "But I want to."

"I see." Dr. Prestin writes something down in his notebook, snapping it shut after he's done, and assesses me once more with his dreadful gaze. "Well, from your record and my interviews with Mr. Coldfox and yourself, I do believe it'd be in your best interest to receive full-time care in our facilities. I will have the paperwork finalized and at the front desk upon your arrival tomorrow."

My eyes widen. I'm being admitted tomorrow? I thought I'd be able to spend a little more time with James out of the hospital, but I guess it makes sense. He'd just be babysitting me the entire time and he has *promotions* to worry about.

Dr. Prestin takes James out into the lobby as they talk more about the amenities at the rehab and the time frame for my treatment. How are we going to pay for all of this? The doctor may be creepy, but he's dressed in the most expensive suit I've ever laid my eyes on. My insurance policy lapsed after I quit my job...I don't even want to think about money right now.

I let out a long sigh and drop my shoulders in defeat. What was the point of all of this? I am a complete waste of space. All I ever bring to others is pain. If I wasn't so fucked-up, I could've actually pushed myself to kick this relentless urge to stop existing.

THE FABRIC OF OUR SOULS

But whatever will be, will be.

I can't change the past. I can only hope I'll get better.

I open my window and slump into one of the chairs at the coffee table, staring out at the sky as the sun sets across the city. The leaves on the trees are bright orange and red. Fall is heavy in the evening air, and the scent of fresh rain rides the wind.

Closing my eyes, I try to enjoy the moment for what it is. This is my first new day, my second chance, and new beginning.

I *will* get better. I don't have a choice.

"Everything dies in the fall. It's kind of nice, isn't it?"

I gasp and sit up straight at the sound of Nurse Hull's deep voice. He's standing by the window, leaning on the ledge, staring back at me. His blue eyes are calm and assessing. I'm on my feet in seconds, wondering how long he's been standing there looking at me.

"Who are you really?" I ask with a stern look.

He's wearing a black hoodie with a dark gray skull embroidered on the left side and gray sweatpants, not nurse-like at all.

"Are you even a nurse?" I furrow my brows as worry ebbs into me. Why does he keep coming here? He changed my IV out yesterday...Fear dilutes my blood at that thought.

His blue eyes flick back to the window, uninterested. "Does it matter?"

I want to say *Of course it fucking matters*, but I stop and think about his question. Did he hear me speaking with Dr. Prestin?

"I guess not," I mutter, sinking back down into the chair James has been living in for the last few days. "I'd still like to know your name at least."

He sets his elbow on the windowsill and presses his palm to his chin as he gazes down at me. Orange rays of sunlight dapple across his cheeks and his eyes glow with cold fire.

"It's Liam."

Liam...He's easy to get lost in. His black hoodie fits perfectly, showing off his lean arm muscles. My eyes drift down to his junk. I mean, come on, he's wearing gray sweatpants—I can't be blamed for noticing his package.

Fall is gray sweatpants season, after all.

"So, why'd you do it?" His deep voice snaps me back into focus and I find that damning grin pulling at his lips. He sounds curious and taunting, not at all sympathetic.

I set my feet on the seat cushion and pull my knees to my chest, wrapping my arms around them and resting my face on my forearms.

Of course. Everyone wants to know why.

How many times do I have to keep saying the same shit to different people?

"Does it matter?" I throw it back at him and he smirks diabolically at me.

He reaches down to my wrist and I hold my breath as he pushes my sleeve up, revealing the stained bandages. He runs his thumb across the tender flesh and heat rises in my chest. Our eyes meet. The tension in the air is thick between us. His crooked smile sends shivers up my spine and a chill through my veins. He looks longingly at the dried blood and hunger flickers through him at my painful wince.

"I think next time you should wait." He says it coldly as he continues to gently brush against my wound and I'm too stunned to do anything except stare, bewildered, at him. I'm mesmerized by everything about Liam—specifically, the darkness within him. Because who the fuck touches someone like this? And why does the sick and depraved part of me draw closer to it?

"Wait for what?" My breath hitches—my next one rides on what he'll say next.

He kneels in front of me and pulls a little stone from his pocket, placing it in my palm. It's smooth and ebony—onyx? "For anything. Someone, something, *anything*. Wait for a devil like me if you have to."

I narrow my eyes at Liam. He's fucking insane. "I don't know you, I don't think—"

He laughs and covers my mouth with his hand. His scent sweeps over me; his cologne smells earthy, woodsy. "You didn't let me finish." Liam pulls his hand back. "You should wait...and it doesn't have to be for anything specific. I'm just saying—wait for the weight of the world to pass. Wait until the tremors that wrack through your skull drift into the depths again. Wait until the sun rises, and the light makes you feel a little less pointless."

We stare at one another for a few silent moments. I'm speechless because what he said made that wall in my mind crack. I haven't cried in years, nor do I feel the tears now, but his words sink deeper than most have in a really long time.

Almost...like he gets it.

"What if waiting doesn't work?" I whisper.

Liam smiles easily at me. His presence is like an eerie forest. I want to stay for a while and sit quietly in his dreary gravity. "You let me know and I'll hold you until the darkness fades."

Why does he act like he cares about me? "Why would you offer me something like that? Why do you care if

I'm alive?" I furrow my brows at him. Vulnerability tugs at my heart.

His eyes narrow and that taunting smile returns to his lips. "Because it's so much better to watch things squirm in pain than simply die, Wynn. You'll let me know, won't you?" He extends his hand to me with his pinky out. I consider him for a moment before deciding to entertain whatever *this* is.

Almost all his fingers have some sort of black ring wrapped around them, some matte, others glossy. The matte ones look exactly like the ring I found on my nightstand last night. The back of his hand is completely tattooed with simple lines that run over his tendons as if his veins are branches.

This *promise* doesn't mean anything...and I'm going to mini prison tomorrow anyway. So why not have one day of dark fairytale bliss?

"Okay, I will." I wrap my pinky around his, gripping the stone he gave me in my other hand. "What's with the stone?"

He gazes nostalgically at my fisted hand. I wonder if onyx means a lot to him, given that he has so many.

"It's onyx. Rumored to banish grief. You'll have to let me know if it works for you—I didn't get much use out of it."

The stone warms in my palm with the meaning he gives it. I have no clue if that's true or not, it's a fucking rock for all I know, but the mind is a powerful thing. The hope that it *could* banish grief is more than I've had in a while.

"Do you think...it can cure me?"

He tilts his head and his eyes darken as he murmurs, "No—"

"What the *hell* are you doing in here?"

James stands furiously in the doorway.

Liam flinches and a nervous grin forms on his beautiful face. He winks at me before shoving his hands into his hoodie pocket and heading toward James and the exit. "Was just leaving, man. See you later, Wynn." He raises his hand in a wave and his ebony rings glint back at me. I try to remember every little thing about him, because I'm not sure fate will ever bring us together again.

I look back down at the stone he gave me and a smile tugs my lips. *Liar—those rings are all onyx.* He's still holding onto the hope they'll banish his grief too.

Chapter 3

Wynn

James pulls up to the pick-up bay of the hospital in his blacked-out Escalade. He's worked really hard to get where he is, which makes me uncomfortable because I don't know how much this institution is costing him, not to mention my hospital bills that he also demanded to shoulder from me.

It's pouring rain today. The crisp scent of the world entering its slumber and the pitter-patter on the pavement soothe my anxiety. I stand under the awning with one of the medical assistants as the SUV pulls around the loop.

James gets out and thanks the staff member as I slip inside the passenger-side door. He has country music playing; I scowl at the sound of it, scrolling the sound all the way down before he gets back in the car. He throws my small duffel bag in the back seat and shuts the door a little too hard, tipping me off that he's in a hurry.

"Long morning?" I ask after he clicks his seatbelt. I rub the sleeves of my oversized gray sweater between my thumb and forefinger, a nervous tic I need to shake.

He runs his hand through his brown hair, slicking it back with droplets of rain, and scoffs. "That's an understatement. It's been a fucking shit show trying to get all my appointments moved around today. I'll have to hop into a meeting when we get to Harlow but it shouldn't be more than thirty minutes. Then we'll get all the paperwork wrapped up quickly so I can catch my flight back home."

"I'm not a fucking dog that you're dropping off at a pound...I can handle the paperwork. You don't need to stay if you're busy." I try to keep the disappointment out of my voice, but it's hard. He's like Mom before she died, pretending like work is more important than anything else in life—like he'll never die.

His eyes dart over to me, shock and a bit of hope brimming in them. "Really? That would help out a lot, actually."

"Yeah, it's my own ordeal anyway. I'm thankful that you came to begin with. You didn't need to...but I appreciate it." I sink in my seat a bit, just able to see the fields and city grow further in the distance.

Harlow Sanctum stands tall and lonely in vast, darkened fields beneath a dreadful stormy sky. Montana is a good place to be sick. The weather sucks, the winters are long, and the mountains beckon to you. *Mountain sickness* is what I've frequently heard it termed, where the higher altitudes fuck with your brain and make you depressed.

Part of Harlow's marketing is that they are located in the northwestern part of the state, in the lowest elevation.

Great, out in the middle of nowhere.

I check my phone and am not surprised that there's no service out here. It's okay, it's not like anyone has messaged me anyway. I'm looking forward to unplugging from the socials for a while. I don't have any friends that will miss me.

The rain has hardly let up since we left the hospital over an hour ago. The closest town is Bakersville, which has a cute Main Street that we drove through to get here. They already have decorations for an end-of-summer Brewfest strung along the lampposts and some flyers for their Fall Festival the weekend of Halloween.

I stare expressionlessly at the gray stone walls of the sanctum. This place looks like the castles I once saw in Ireland with James. Vines cling to the bricks. The stones are wet, drenched with relentless rain. Fancy black planter boxes filled with orange and yellow marigolds line the massive entrance, four on each side. A large, modern chandelier hangs from the center of the portico. James pulls up beneath it and I take in the large windows framing the front doors.

It's straight out of a storybook.

Once James parks his car, we don't waste any time grabbing my single bag from the back seat and rushing to the enormous front doors. They are black and modern, an obvious addition to the original structure, but they tie in perfectly.

"Hurry, I'm running late." James checks his watch obsessively as I open one of the huge doors.

Musky air invades my senses as we step through the threshold and into the three-story foyer. Black marbled tiles make up the floors that stretch to many hallways on each side of the institute. Weathered wood pillars that could use another stain frame the massive room. Large chandeliers hang from the ceilings.

The lobby is quiet. A small elderly woman sits at the front desk. Her thick-framed glasses hardly manage to stay on her face; they cling to the very end of her button nose. Her gray hair is curly and short. She reminds me of my old piano teacher—except the wrinkles on this lady's face are clearly from smiling, not scowling, like the witch of my past.

I frown as the dread of this place starts sinking into me. It looks a lot like a fancy hotel, except this place is depressing. Gray walls, black floors, gray everything else. It could just be in my head since I know it's not some cool vacation spot. I know the people that dwell in here are sick.

We are the ghosts here.

One would think these places should be a little bit more cheerful. Maybe hang a smiley-face poster behind the clerk or *something* other than the white, black, and shades of gray.

I nudge James with my elbow. "I was picturing more of a bulletproof-glass-walls, everyone-in-restraining-jackets type of thing."

My brother scowls at me and sets my bag at my feet. "No, of course not. You're not criminally insane. This is a rehabilitation center, and an expensive one too."

I raise a brow at him. "We couldn't afford anything better?" I jest.

James laughs sarcastically, making me flinch as he pats my back like I've just told the best joke ever. "I've got to get going. I'll call you this weekend, okay? If you need anything, text me. Your motorcycle is already here and I've had the rest of your things put in a storage unit in Bakersville." He hugs me tightly. "I love you—you're going to beat this."

I smile grimly into his shoulder, not bothering to even ask how he got all my shit sorted in such a short amount of time, including me. He's efficient in that way, at packing people and their things away like crumbs under a rug. It's what he did with Mom, it's what he's doing with me. I know in my heart he means well, he's trying to make everything be simpler and easier for me, but I can't help but wonder if I'd feel less disposable if he let it be more of a mess. "Yeah—I'll try."

He says his final goodbyes and I watch as the ridiculously big door closes ominously behind him, leaving me utterly alone and stranded in this unfamiliar place. I tap my phone again and there's still no service. I'm guessing this is a Wi-Fi-connection-service type of living situation.

Groaning, I shove my phone back in my pocket and take a deep breath.

I can do this.

My nerves are on high alert and I'd rather be literally anywhere but here right now. I swallow the lump in my throat and glance back at the check-in desk. The little old lady is watching me through her abhorrently dirty glasses and it takes more than I'm willing to admit to not hand her a cloth and tell her to clean them.

I try to straighten my features into anything but a grimace. "Um, hello." My lips forcefully pull upward in an awkward smile. I lean down and grab my bag before approaching her.

She's even more petite up close. She smells like mildew and cats, and that's about as unpleasant as it sounds. My brows pull together the longer I stand here with my stupid fake smile. Didn't she hear me?

"I'm here to check in," I mumble, rubbing the back of my head and glancing back at the door. Maybe it's not too late to fucking bolt out of here.

The sound of paper sliding across the counter brings my eyes back to her. She slowly sets a pen on top of the small stack and taps on a line at the bottom.

I don't bother reading the paperwork. I sign my name and nudge the pile back to her. I trust James to have already scoured this thing. I'm still not entirely sure what his job entails, but I'm pretty sure it revolves around contracts and finding potential issues within them. Nothing gets by James.

The clerk simply nods at me and taps a button on her desk a few times before spinning around in her chair and filing my papers in the cabinet behind her. Her nameplate reads *Mrs. Abett.*

My smile drops the second her chair swivels and I let out a long sigh. This place already sucks. If everyone here is as *lovely* as Mrs. Abett, then I'm not sure I'll make it through the week.

"Hello, Miss Coldfox. It's nice to meet you."

I look up and find a pair of green eyes staring back at me.

"My name is Jericho Melvich. I am your program counselor." The man extends his hand to mine and I shake it stiffly.

"Nice to meet you," I mumble. He has a lot of hope in his eyes, too bright for my liking. He looks maybe two years my senior, the kind of guy who's sexier with glasses rather than contacts. His jaw is sharp but not as defined as Liam's. I glance down at my bag, where the onyx stone and ring he gave me are tucked away.

Jericho grabs my duffel bag for me and leads the way down the large hall to the left side of the foyer. Old photos of people who look entirely too happy to have been clinically depressed line the walls.

"Dr. Prestin gave me your file so I could get a good feel for your case. Of course, I can't get everything from paper though, so tell me about yourself. What do you enjoy? I'd like to integrate anything you like into your weekly treatment." He looks back at me thoughtfully before adding: "I didn't expect you to have pink hair. That's a surprise."

I roll my eyes behind Jericho's back when we resume walking, though a grin pulls at my lips as I think of something I do actually enjoy. "I like sex."

He stops and glances back at me with knitted brows. "I've worked here since I graduated college, Miss Coldfox. I assure you it's not the first time I've heard that heinous answer." His cold green eyes inspect me like he's searching for something.

I can't help but wonder if he'll find it.

"Well, you asked what I enjoy." I shrug and cross my arms. "Do you want me to lie to you and say I enjoy cooking or something stupid like that? Because I don't fucking cook."

Jericho's gaze narrows. His ears are turning bright red. "Right. Well, not to let you down, but I won't be adding *sex* to your treatment plan. I'll be sure to not have them set you up with cooking either." He jots something down on his clipboard before we continue down the dark hallway.

The sound of people talking flutters through the air as we come up to a gathering room. It's filled with nice leather furniture, fancy coffee bars and counters, and a few black oak tables. Floor-to-ceiling windows stretch the length of the room.

Men and women in normal street clothes lounge on the couches or lean over the railing that lines the porch outside, smoking cigarettes and breathing in the cold fall air. Everyone seems...happy. Or at least content enough to not have that blank stare or dark circles beneath their eyes.

My eyes widen at the gorgeous baby-grand piano facing the windows, against a background of sage-colored fields and a lush, dark green forest mixed with orange maple trees. Clouds mist the pale blue mountains in the distance.

My heart aches a bit at the nostalgic songs flowing through my soul just from looking at the beautiful black and white keys.

"You play?"

I flinch, having completely forgotten that Jericho was standing next to me. The room transported me to a place I hadn't visited for a while. Somewhere filled with both resentment and deep, unsettling pain. The music there is somber and distant. Cold.

"Yeah...I did," I mumble, fisting my trembling hands at my sides. "I don't play anymore though."

"I'd like to include it in your treatment plan if that's okay. Even if it's just sitting at the instrument." Jericho brings out his clipboard again, jotting some notes down as I nod, eyes still locked on the piano. I wouldn't mind staying in this room for a while and just existing for a tiny, insignificant moment.

We walk further down the hall, my eyes lingering on the gathering room until it's no longer in sight. The west wing turns into a section of dorm rooms. The walls are painted a lovely shade of gray, reminding me of impasto-style paint that has big clumps of texture smoothed in. Jericho stops at an intersection in the hall and waves at a few staff members who are carrying some blankets to what looks like a storage room. Besides Mrs. Abett, the staff seem pretty friendly, unlike the workers at the hospital. I wonder if it's out of pity or whether they truly care about people like us. They don't carry the disconcerting look that dealing with people like me is a burden, and that makes my heart lighten considerably.

"My brother said that my bike was here. Are we allowed to leave the grounds?"

"Bike?" Jericho says. "Oh, you mean your crotch rocket? Yes, it's parked in the garage. We have several lovely roads you can drive in the area. We find that driving can be very therapeutic for our patients and encourage getting outside and looking at the scenery here," he states proudly. It sounds rehearsed.

I nod. "So those gates we passed through a few miles back, I'm guessing we can't actually leave?"

He shrugs and continues down the hallway. "Of course you can. This isn't a prison. Many of the patients go to Bakersville on the weekends to go shopping or to the bars. I think you will really enjoy it here, Coldfox."

I hate when people address others by their last name. It feels like a distancing tactic.

"That's not what I expected," I mutter as I look at the framed photos down the next hallway.

"Yes, well, this institute is very much unorthodox."

I eye him with my brows pulled together tightly. *Unorthodox?*

We stop once we reach what I'm assuming is my room. The door is black, as is the one across the hall. The rest of the doors in the hall are brown.

Jericho knocks twice before he starts fumbling with his key ring to locate the right one. "The communal bathroom is just down the hall. For obvious reasons, we can't permit you private ones," he mumbles as he pulls out a black key and shoves it into the door.

"You're worried about bathrooms but not about people offing themselves in their own rooms?"

He glances back at me and smirks. "Which is precisely why we assign you roommates based on your treatment plans." I raise a brow as he pushes the door open. Light dapples across the wooden floor, and white curtains sway on a soft breeze that flows in from the open window.

"But I didn't agree—"

"Yes, you agreed to it when you signed. Your brother didn't tell you?"

My shoulders slump. *No, of course he didn't.* I'll have to send him a very long, wordy text later. I hate not having my own personal space to escape to.

A lone figure stands by the window, a man with dark hair and blood dripping from his forefinger.

He's hurt.

Jericho doesn't seem concerned as he walks across the room and wraps the man's finger in a handkerchief. "I knocked twice, why didn't you open the door?" he says with an annoyed tone. The bleeding man looks over at Jericho and my heart stills in my chest as those blue eyes slowly shift, connecting with mine.

"*Liam?*" His name leaves my lips on a breath.

Liam's eyes widen before they flick back to Jericho. "*She's* my new roommate?" He doesn't sound upset, more surprised than anything.

Jericho smiles and nods, but before he can respond, I cut him off.

"What kind of rehab is this? I can't share a room with a *man.*"

Jericho narrows his eyes at me but waves me off. "You signed off on it, Coldfox. We pair you up with a room-mate ideal for your treatment plan. I know this seems odd, but our rehab has among the highest recovery rates. Like I mentioned before, we're unorthodox. And didn't you say you enjoyed sex earlier? Well, here you go. Liam Waters," he says sarcastically.

My fists instinctively clench at my sides.

I can do this.

As weird as this entire place is, I owe it to James to try. Sneaky as he may be, I have to admit, this is all sort of... exciting. I hesitantly look at Liam again; he appears so calm and disconnected. He's every bit the mysterious man from the first night we met.

I should've known.

He's sick too.

Chapter 4
Wynn

Jericho doesn't need to introduce us since we've already met. He sets my bag on top of the bed closest to the door, smiles, and tells us lunch is at noon, then leaves as if this is completely normal.

Liam and I stare at each other for a few uncomfortable moments before I turn to my bed and unpack. Every nerve in my body is sensitive because I know he's watching me. How did we end up in this situation? It's fucking insane, right? I thought I'd never see him again and he was going to be the mysterious guy—you know, the *one that got away.*

Sometimes I think encounters are best left that way. Always wondering what happened to that person and where they could be out in the big world.

I unzip my bag and take out my makeup, phone charger, and Kindle. How am I going to sleep tonight? Does he snore? Is he a psychopath? Clearly, he's a psychopath. He fucking hooked an IV to me when he wasn't even a nurse... Isn't that like... illegal?

"So you aren't a nurse."

He moves to his bed and lies on his side so he's facing me, his head propped up with his hand. His cold blue eyes watch me carefully. "Obviously," he mutters with indifference.

It takes all my willpower to not flinch beneath his cruel tone. I make a mental note to tell Jericho about the hospital incident. Maybe then I can get a different roommate.

I eye the handkerchief that's wrapped around his finger. His blood is already soaking through the fabric.

"What happened to your finger?" I return my gaze to my bag as I put my clothes in piles on the bed, setting aside my nightshirt so I don't lose it.

"I cut it."

I freeze. The blood chills in my veins and goosebumps crawl up my arms. I'm reluctant to look at him, but my need to see his expression prevails.

Liam unravels the handkerchief from his finger. The wet, red rag sends false waves of pain through the wounds on my wrists. Sweat beads down the back of my neck and my mouth opens a bit with horror.

I *hate* pain. Seeing someone hurt, being hurt, any sort of pain—I can't stand it. I want it to stop. The gash in his flesh is deep and his blood pools quickly, flooding over and spilling down his hand once more.

I instinctively rush to his side and I clasp his hand gently to see how badly he hurt himself. The cut is deep, but it's not anything life-threatening and won't affect the functionality of his hand.

"Why did you do this?" I shake my head. I can't understand why he'd... My gaze trails down his hand and arm. Scars of all sorts and sizes mark his beautiful olive skin. They're hard to see because of his tattoos, but they are there. Some old, most new. "You—"

He brings his hand up to my cheek and presses his palm against my skin softly, running his bloody finger across my flesh as his lips form a wicked smile. My chest grows heavy and the air becomes harder to breathe in. Anxiety and stress make the effects of my heart condition worsen, but I can't calm the chaos in my mind right now.

I can't room with someone like him.

"I'm a masochist, Wynn. I crave the endless ebb and flow of pain to feel alive. It's really grounding for me." His blue eyes flicker with amusement at my repulsion.

"I . . . I can't be your r-roommate," I stammer as my heart rate increases and I move toward the door. I'm going to be fucking sick. How could Jericho think this is a good fit? I'm fucking leaving. Right now.

Liam's hand wraps around my wrist and pain flares up my still-healing wound. I yelp and turn on him but he doesn't let go. His eyes are an icy inferno and his smile twists as I wince.

"Let go!" I scream at him and viciously claw at his hand. He loosens up enough so the pain stops but doesn't completely let go of me.

"Don't you see?" he mutters quietly, so calmly that I stop and stare bewilderedly at him. His oaky scent consumes me as he leans in close, his nose touching mine. My heart pounds erratically inside my chest and my cheeks heat. "We're the perfect elixir. I want to feel alive so fucking desperately—I'll chase the high forever if I have to. Nothing's worked for me yet."

He lets go of my wrist and something warm and wet runs down my hand, dripping down my fingers and tapping on the black tiles.

I open my mouth to say something, *anything,* but nothing comes out.

There's so much blood.

Fear stings my mind and my voice gets stuck in my throat. My vision blurs. I can't breathe.

"You want to die. I hate that so much, Wynn. The thought of you wanting to leave this world hurts me, but...for the first time, it's a pain that I really don't like. It's disgusting to me that you don't want to live. You don't like seeing pain or enduring it, right? You'd rather run away and not feel anything."

Tears pool in my eyes and my stomach twists. This interaction is traumatizing. I want to leave. I want to scream.

He's saying that someone as cruel as him could be my—

"*Remedium meum*," he murmurs, a breath away from my lips, smiling as he gently runs his fingers up my arms. I take a deep breath of his crisp scent and quirk a brow. I don't speak Latin, but I've watched enough horror movies to know that anyone who does is either a hardcore Catholic or into occult stuff. Neither option is great for me. "Remember our promise?"

I hesitantly nod. *I have to wait...* But what about him? I didn't know he was as unwell as I am. "What did you say just then?"

His blue eyes darken and he leans in close, his lips cresting the shell of my ear. "*My cure.*" His voice is a mere whisper but it sinks into my bones. "I'll stop you in your darkest hours. Do you promise to do the same for me?" Liam pulls back and his lips brush against mine. Heat pools in my core with every single sensation this man pulls from me. The fear he instills dances alongside it.

Instinct tells me he's dangerous—but I cannot pull away from him. He's gravity itself. I was caught in his orbit the moment I laid eyes on him at the hospital.

I consider him for a moment. He's bold, crazy, everything I'm not. But he's right. I run away from emotions and I'm here to face my demons, aren't I? Maybe he's insane, but I don't think there's a chance I'll survive without a little insanity.

I told James I'd try my best.

After thinking for a minute, I look up at him, clenching my fists.

"Yes, I will."

He leans forward, his soft lips pressing against mine. I don't know if it's the tension that burns the air around us right now, if it's the pulsing pain in my wrist, or if it's just...simply *him*. But the spark that ignites between us burrows deep into my heart.

Liam pulls back and smiles. "Till death do us part, sunshine."

He kissed me. Not out of love or longing—it is a pact. A horribly toxic pact for two broken souls that have hit rock bottom.

But it is our pact, our promise.

And just like that, I think I've found something as compelling as death.

Resenting my new roommate, Liam Waters.

"I hate you," I say, wiping my lips with my sleeve.

"Hate takes a lot of effort. I don't think you hate me." He traces my jawline with his finger.

I regain some composure and set my palm on his chest to push him back. His black hoodie is soft, but his body beneath it is taut. "You're vile and cruel. Do you kiss all your roommates? You're sick."

"*Clinically.*" He smirks with amusement. "And you didn't seem opposed to it."

I furrow my brows as I examine my stinging wrist. The stitches are irritated but the bleeding has stopped—thanks to my sweater, which is now ruined. "You surprised me. I don't think we should do that again," I say venomously.

I fold the sleeves of my sweater to hide the blood in case Jericho comes back in.

"*Shit*, sorry about that. I didn't think I grabbed you that hard," Liam mutters with the first bit of concern I've heard from him.

Asshole.

He walks over to his nightstand and pulls open the drawer, bringing out some medical gauze and tape. Like hell I'll let him touch me again.

I shoot him a vicious glare. "Of course, the *masochist* has medical supplies in his nightstand."

"You'll hurt my feelings, Wynn," he fires back with a sharp, sarcastic tone, but the mischief in his eyes is flirtatious. Good God, is this how everyone's first day goes here? He's practically an angel in the flesh with the mind of a demon. "Give me your arm." He sits on the edge of his bed and looks at me expectantly.

I glare at him. "No."

"Excuse me?" His face hardens.

I will myself to steel my expressions just as well as he does. "I. Said. No."

He looks at me for several moments before he holds out his hand and softens his expression. "I'm sorry, Wynn. Okay? Please let me tend to your cut." His eyes lower to the floor and guilt pulls down at his frown.

I hesitate.

Do it for James. Give it at least a week. Do it for James.

I repeat the words in my head as I slowly get up and sit next to him. Our beds are so close we might as well push them together and have a fucking California king.

I let him take my arm. His touch is surprisingly gentle— his fingers are ice cold though.

"Do you ever actually smile?" He slowly unravels my bandages. I don't want to watch so I avert my eyes to the window.

"I smile all the time."

He sets the old bloody bandage to his side and dabs my stitches with some gauze. I wince at the pressure of his fingers as he says, "That fake-ass smile doesn't count. It looks like you have bad gas or something."

My cheeks heat. "*Excuse me*? No, it doesn't." I glare at him as he wraps new medical tape around my wrist.

His playful eyes find mine again. His grin is intoxicating. "Sure, you keep telling yourself that, sunshine. Your dead eyes give you away."

My dead eyes...I've never really figured out how to smile with my eyes. How do you hide your weary soul? The fake one works on most people.

"All done." He pats my forearm softly. I pull my sleeve back down and stand, moving to unpack the rest of my things without another word.

The timer on his cell phone dings, making me flinch. Liam stands up, pulls off his hoodie, and tosses it on the bed. His white undershirt is pulled up a bit, and his taut muscles make my cheeks warm. I avert my gaze and trail my fingers along the bandage he gave me. It's perfect, as if he's done this a thousand times on himself.

Liam heads toward the door and stops before he turns the handle. "Aren't you coming? It's time for lunch."

I shake my head and gesture to my bag and clothes. "I'm not hungry. I'd rather unpack and get adjusted." I don't bother with a fake smile since, apparently, he can see right through it.

He shrugs and leaves. Once the door clicks shut, I take a deep breath. I need the silence. I'm already worn out and it's only noon.

I sit on the edge of the bed and take out my blood-pressure device. It's battery-operated and small enough that most people won't even know what it is. I slip it over my left arm and line up the artery marker to the right spot, tightening the cuff before pushing start and waiting as the air pumps into the cuff. After a few moments, it deflates and the screen shows 160/120.

I'm literally a walking heart attack.

I let out a long sigh and fold up the machine, sticking it back in its small bag before hiding it at the bottom of my nightstand drawer. It's been hard trying to keep my heart condition in control. My anxiety and stress don't help either. The medications don't work as well as they should. If I hear another doctor say, *"Oh no, but you're so young. It's so tragic,"* and give me that pitiful fucking frown...

I take a deep breath and try to relax. Even thinking about it stresses me out, and my heart is still racing from my encounter with Liam. I brush my lips where he kissed me and jolt when I hear vibrating.

Liam's phone buzzes on his bed and draws my attention to his side of the room. I don't approve of snooping, but he's been horrible and God knows what he put in the IV the other night.

These aren't normal circumstances. So snooping is indeed on the table.

I shift off my bed and hover over his nightstand. *Am I really going to do this?*

His phone dings again and a message icon pops up. *Mom.* Well, at least he talks to his mother. It's more than I can say. My mother is dead and I don't speak with my father, so he might as well be dead too.

Deciding to bite the bullet, I reach for his drawer and pull it open. It's filled with medical supplies: tape, ointment, gauze, and Band-Aids. All immaculately organized like the psychopath planned out everything he'd need for his own torture. Other than the supplies, it's pretty empty. There's a phone charger, Chapstick, and a notebook.

I grab the notebook and open it. It doesn't look like a journal, with all the loose pages stuffed in it. The cover is black and worn. Half of the writing is in a different language.

The portions that are in English are research notes on plants and insects, while other sections are drawings of human anatomy and bones. It makes absolutely no sense, yet I'm convinced it's not nothing. It's eerie. Liam has spent an extensive amount of time collecting cryptic information on odd things.

This just solidifies my theory about him being into the occult.

I hop back on my bed and dig through my bag until I find the onyx stone. Why did he give it to me? As I'm flipping through the pages of his notebook, I notice a few pages on stones and symbolism. According to his notes, onyx is a symbol of protection against evil. A talisman of sorts. Does he really believe in that sort of stuff?

I spend the better part of an hour reading through his notebook, and by the time I reach the end, I'm more confused than I was when I started. Tucked in are articles on missing people from a decade ago, black and white and odd. It says that they all checked out of Harlow Sanctum before going missing.

The only thing I've learned when I shut the book is that Liam might be a dangerous person. Well, more dangerous than I already thought.

I set his notebook back in the drawer as I found it.

Rain patters against the window and draws my attention. Stepping over to the window, I notice a woman in a blue dress dancing in the downpour. My heart thumps at the magic she seems to feel. She doesn't appear to carry the chains of the world that I feel weighing me down.

I want that freedom.

The window opens easily. I pop the screen out and carefully climb over the frame. I'm sure there's an easy way down the hall to get out to the courtyard, but I don't want to waste time trying to find it. I want to experience what she's feeling—that weightlessness that I've been chasing for so long.

My bare feet press into the wet grass and a chill runs through my veins. Icy rain pelts against my skin, kissing my flesh. I approach her and watch as she dances, twirling with her arms wide, her white shirt completely soaked and hugging her breasts.

"Are you going to join me or just stand there?"

I flinch and stagger back. I didn't realize she was aware of my presence. "Um, I was just admiring how happy you seem." She stops twirling and smiles at me manically. Her eyes are unusually wide and crazed. Jesus, she just went from majestic to creepy real quick.

"I'm performing the rain curse ritual!" Her green eyes glint and her smile grows. I take a step back. I don't know what the fuck to do—I clearly misread what she was doing.

"Oh...okay. I'm just going to head inside now. Sorry for interrupting." I turn on my heel and start back toward my window when she runs in front of me and puts her hands out.

"Hold on, I'm not crazy. I'm just having some fun, you

know. I think you should join in too. Might help lift your spirits like you were hoping it would."

I consider her for a moment. "What's your name?"

She laughs and smacks her forehead. "Oh *duh*, you're probably so weirded out by me. I'm Yelina." She extends her hand to me and I reluctantly shake it. "Now come! We dance while the storm is strong." She tugs my hand and starts dancing in a circle again, this time with me in tow.

Yelina's blonde hair is completely drenched and stuck to her head and neck. My pink hair starts to cling to my skin too and my breaths curl in the brisk air. She throws her head back and time slows as the rain greets her face. Her smile turns blissful as she gets lost in the moment once more.

I want that feeling.

Letting my arms loosen up, I open them wide and twirl alongside her, tilting my face to the sky and shutting my eyelids against the cold drops as the dark clouds whisk me away into a dream-like state.

Yelina laughs. "Now you're finding it!"

Chapter 5

Liam

Lanston leans over the table and grabs a piece of fried chicken from my plate. "You sure you don't want it?" He raises a brow, pulling the fried batter off and popping it in his mouth.

"Yeah, I'm not very hungry today." I look down at my finger. The cut is already scabbing over and the itch to slice another finger is eating away at me. "The hospital food made my stomach upset."

"Shit." Lanston frowns at me. His brown hair is hardly visible beneath his baseball cap but his hazel eyes pin me with worry. "You weren't trying to hurt yourself that badly, were you?"

That's a hard question to answer.

Yes? No.

My hand unconsciously glides to my side, where my ribs got cut a little too deep. Jericho freaked out when he found me in the greenhouse. I was leaning over the drain in the storage room and trying to stop the bleeding. Chills crawl up my spine at the memory of that night, and my hands tremble beneath the table.

"Of course not," I say in a low voice.

Lanston stares at me like he doesn't buy it, but nods anyway. It's good that he doesn't like to talk about that night. No one does.

"I heard you had a little excursion. Jericho said he reported you missing just to find you in your bed the next morning." Lanston laughs and looks over his shoulder to see if our counselor is in the cafeteria or not.

I smile too. Unlike my new little muse, I know how to make it reach my eyes. "Yeah, I couldn't stay cooped up in that fucking room for another night. I was only stretching my legs. You know Jericho, he's wound up *way* too tight." I glance out the window and watch the rain fall like it'll never stop.

I don't tell Lanston that I found something I hadn't been looking for and that she's here too, somehow.

Fate can be funny like that—if you believe in those kinds of things.

My eyes widen as I see two women dancing in the courtyard, their clothes fully drenched and feet bare in the grass like it isn't fucking freezing out there.

"Who's that?" Lanston says slowly, as if he's in a trance. He stands from his chair, walking over to the window and pressing his hand against the pane, staring at Wynn.

I get up and stand next to him, watching my lovely, sad roommate with pale-pink hair dance in the rain like the storm calls to her soul. Her sweater clings to her flesh and reveals just how thin she is. It hurts deep in the chambers of my heart, that a creature so woeful and enchanting as her wants to die.

It hurts.

It makes me despise her more than anything, yet crave her all the same.

I need to find out why.

"She's my new roommate," I mutter indifferently as I slide my hands into my pockets, watching Wynn dance with Yelina like a lost fool.

Lanston snaps his head to look at me. "You're kidding."

I keep my eyes on her body. She's moving like a siren, beckoning me to go to her. I shake my head. "I'm not kidding."

I want to touch her, to feel her. To bite her and tell her how much her mind repulses me.

I want her to live.

"Fuck—I guess I'll be sleeping over in your room in a few nights then," Lanston teases, but I glare at him. He doesn't even flinch. Instead, a curious light flickers in his eyes. "She's a heartstopper."

"Not her," I warn him.

Lanston's condition is just as bad as Wynn's. Two people who want to die, sleeping in the same bed—no. I won't allow it. He's so close to getting better.

I look over at him and watch as his thumb traces over the old scars on his wrists. We all have scars here, some deeper than the rest. My eyes linger around his neck, and a cold shudder shoots down my spine. The night I found his body limp in the showers resurfaces in my mind and my chest grows heavy.

I'll never forget the way his eyes lost their glimmer for a moment. He'll never feel that low again, not if I can help it.

He wraps his arm around my shoulder and laughs. "Well, at least tell me her name."

"Coldfox! Bergmot!" Jericho shouts as he struts across the courtyard, startling the two of them. They take off running, Yelina guiding Wynn to the west wing's entrance.

My bones yearn to follow her, but I remain standing still.

"Coldfox?" Lanston smiles as her last name leaves his lips.

"Her name is Wynn," I mumble as my thumb caresses the fresh scab on my forefinger, sending small thrills of pain through my nerves. "And she's mine."

Chapter 6

Wynn

Yelina and I run into the west wing, my heart beating faster with each step we take into the dim hallway. Light fixtures crafted to look like lampposts jut out every ten feet with a warm glow that isn't quite bright enough to feel welcoming.

She lets out a laugh that rings through me and pulls us into a small closet, pushing her finger to her lips as Jericho runs by the door.

My clothes are soaked and the chill is starting to set in now that I'm not dancing like a lunatic in the rain. I wrap my arms around myself to retain any heat I have left. "Why are we hiding?"

Yelina winks at me. "Because Jericho is fun to fuck with." She laughs and cracks the door to peek out. "Okay, I think we shook him. Run to your room—"

The door pulls open, revealing Jericho with his arms crossed. His cheeks are red from chasing us, and his brows are pulled low with rage. "All right, *out*, both of you."

Yelina sighs and rolls her eyes as she slides past him and exits. I move to follow her, but Jericho catches my shoulder and stops me. My eyes meet his and he scowls at me. "Day one, Coldfox. You found trouble on day one." He emphasizes *trouble* like he's talking about Yelina.

I can see how she'd be one to cause havoc. She's beautiful and completely crazy. I'm tempted to ask Jericho why he considers her trouble, but think better of it.

I give him my most innocent smile. "We were just dancing in the rain. I wouldn't consider that *trouble*."

He doesn't seem impressed and his brows remain firmly pinched as he guides me back to my room. "Who do you think gets reprimanded when the patients get sick from *dancing* in the freezing cold rain?" My shoulders droop. The moment I start to feel any fleeting emotion that makes me feel alive, it gets thwarted. "I want you showered and dressed before your afternoon group session." I nod and don't bother saying anything until we reach my room.

I let out a long sigh of relief when I find our room empty. I forgo the shower and just dry my hair; I hate community bathrooms. If I'd known, I would've had James stop somewhere so I could grab flip-flops and a swimsuit, since adult men will be in there as well.

My cold, wet sweater clings to my skin. It's heavy and difficult to pull off. I leave my clothes in a pile in the corner. I'll have to have Liam show me where we do our laundry later. I grab my black pullover hoodie and tug it on. It falls a few inches above my knees, so I pair it with long black socks and fuzzy slippers.

The door clicks open and Liam peeks his head in. "Hey, sorry, wasn't sure if you were dressed or not," he mumbles as he steps in and opens his nightstand, pulling out a Band-Aid and wrapping it around his index finger.

"Well, most people just knock."

He shrugs and gives me that damning smile of his. His blue eyes twinkle; his sharp features are to die for. "This is my room too, I don't have to knock." His eyes trail down my legs and then back up. "Nice outfit. Did depressed gnomes raid your closet or something?"

My cheeks heat. "I *like* wearing comfortable clothes."

Liam puckers his lips like he's trying not to laugh. "Yeah, I can see that. Anything besides black? What were you doing out there in the rain anyway?" He picks up the screen that I popped out of the window earlier and puts it back in place.

"Yelina said we were performing a rain curse or something."

He lets out a deep chuckle and quirks his brows. "Did it help?" He's looking at me with interested eyes like he's genuinely curious about all the little things I have to say. Does he actually care?

Does it matter?

I shrug. "It was nice. Yelina is pretty friendly too."

"Yelina is one of the crazier patients here. She might be friendly today, but we'll see about tomorrow."

That's good to know. I grab my notepad from the nightstand and write down her name and the word *unstable* next to it. How else will I remember anyone here?

Liam's eyes catch on my wet clothes in the corner and he shakes his head as he sighs. "Oh come on, you're one of *those* roommates?" He picks up my drenched sweater.

I snatch the sweater from him. His scent sweeps over me as I do. "I was going to ask you where the laundry room was after our group session."

He wraps an arm around my shoulder and butterflies flutter through my chest at the connection. "Let's go now, then." He guides me to the door and we step out into the hallway.

I shrink in his hold as we walk down to the bathrooms. Steam spills out as he opens the door and I'm instantly struck

47

by the sight of naked men and women, all of them around my age, some older, some younger. A few moans rise from the last stall and my wide eyes flick up to Liam's with horror.

A big smirk forms on his lips and whispers in my ear, "Just part of the therapy here, sunshine. Don't be such a prude." His voice drips with sarcasm. Heat pools in my stomach with the pleasure-filled sounds and Liam's deep voice settling deep in my mind.

"Who says I'm a prude?" I throw back at him.

His eyes narrow at me and his smirk grows uncomfortably dark. "You think you can play on our level?" His hand clamps down on the nape of my neck; his fingers are cold and instantly make goosebumps rise across my arms.

Don't let him intimidate you.

I reach down and cup his privates. His sweatpants leave him completely vulnerable, and based on his shocked expression, he didn't think I'd grab his dick so freely. "Can you play on *mine*?"

A low groan rolls through his throat as he composes himself and leans into me further. My cheeks heat but I stand my ground.

"Wynn, I didn't know you were so eager," he says with a horrifying look on his face. His lips brush against my neck as he yanks my hand away from his dick. "Unless you want to get bruised in the showers though, I recommend we wait until tonight. I promise I'll have your hips unaligned by morning." He shoves me toward the laundry area.

My heart pounds wildly in my chest and I shoot him a glare over my shoulder. "You're disgusting."

"You started it." He shrugs, looking down at me with callous eyes.

I'm writing James the angriest text after my group session.

48

We continue across the white tiles of the bathroom until we reach a small room in the back. A row of laundry machines stretches across the wall and on the opposite side are baskets with patient names taped on their rims.

Liam and Crosby.

I furrow my brow at the other name. "Who's Crosby?"

"Nobody," Liam mumbles as he grabs a Sharpie and crosses out the name, penning in *Sunshine* over it.

"Really?" I cross my arms but Liam ignores me.

Obviously, they were someone...In a place like this, surely they left because they got better, right? Why is death the first thing that comes to my mind when I see their name crossed out like that? Didn't they matter?

"Crosby was your old roommate?"

Liam's eyes turn cold and empty, sending a shudder of dread through me. "Drop it, Wynn. I won't ask nicely again." Irritation pulls at his features.

I guess I'll have to ask someone else.

"All right, everyone, we have someone new with us today, so I want you to say your name and something you enjoy doing to introduce yourselves to Wynn." Jericho leans back in his chair and points his pen at the woman to his right to start.

She's a beautiful woman with brown hair, tan skin, long legs, and perfect boobs. "Hi, Wynn, my name is Poppie. I like reading books when I'm not dying inside." My jaw drops and Jericho snaps up in his chair.

"No negatives, please." He writes something down on his chart and glares at Poppie before pointing to the next person.

He's a handsome man with light-brown hair and a baseball cap. His eyes lock with mine. His grin is soft, so unlike Liam's. I quickly avert my eyes; I've never been good at holding eye contact.

"Lanston Nevers. I like coffee and taking long naps, and I want to die."

My eyes flick back up.

He's still looking at me. My chest churns. Someone as beautiful as him wants to die? I want to know why. Does he have the same pit of dread within him that I do?

Jericho taps his feet angrily against the floor. "What did I just say? Do any of you have even a shred of respect for me?"

Lanston just smiles and shoots me a wink. My cheeks warm. Maybe I *can* make friends here.

I listen as everyone in the circle says their name followed by something they like. Everyone ignores Jericho's rules, apparently finding his fury amusing. The vein in his forehead protrudes the entire ten minutes and I'm half certain he'll stroke out if I join in on their fun.

I realize it's silent for a few moments and look from side to side. Everyone stares at me with expectant eyes.

"Oh, uh, I'm Wynn Coldfox. I like . . ." I pause. That's how it always goes, isn't it? You're sitting there thinking the entire time about what you're going to say and then it's your turn and you have no clue what you're actually going to spew out. "I like drying flowers."

At my side, Liam huffs with annoyance like my answer is stupid.

"I'm Liam Waters, your roommate." He glares at me and a few others laugh. Jericho's brows are still pulled together firmly. "I like pain. So don't be afraid to bite my dick while you're sucking it tonight."

My head turns and our eyes meet. At first I think he's joking, but there's a silent promise in his dark eyes.

"Waters—*very* inappropriate." Jericho marks his chart, but everyone in the circle laughs. I mean, I heard people fucking in the shower earlier, so I'm not taking him too seriously either.

Liam shrugs and crosses his arms, leaning back in his chair.

"Why don't we start with you today then, Waters? Since you seem so eager to talk." Jericho taps on his clipboard with the end of his pen as he eyes Liam. They have to be close to the same age. What a hard job to perform, treating people your own age like children. Especially when it's obvious no one here respects this man at all.

Liam puts his hands behind his head and looks at the ceiling. "I don't have anything really to share today. I still like to hurt myself—still chasing the high of feeling alive. Nothing's changed."

Jericho watches him carefully. "And why do you think you relentlessly crave this feeling, Waters?"

Liam's blue eyes flicker with pain. "Because it's better than feeling nothing."

I clench my hands in my hoodie pocket. It's hard to hear others talk about their darkness. It hurts. But more than anything, I resonate with it.

The counselor nods and probes for more. "Do you find yourself using it as a form of self-punishment? When you feel you let others down?"

A weak, somber smile spreads across Liam's lips and he looks back at Jericho with resolve flashing across his blue eyes. "Yeah. I do."

"Then you aren't trying to feel something, you're trying to relieve your guilt by punishing yourself. You know this. Great job today, Liam." Jericho flips the page in his notepad, his eyes locking with mine next. "Wynn, care to give it a try?"

I swallow hard. It's really not something I like talking about. Not just the judgment that I've always faced, but there's something about saying out loud the things that have only ever existed in my head. Almost as if once I actually speak it...it will become real.

Out in the world for everyone to see.

I shake my head and keep my eyes on the floor. The rain outside patters rhythmically against the windowpanes.

"That's okay. Remington, go ahead." He moves onto the girl to my left.

My breaths feel heavy. I tune out everything around me.

I've never been to a therapy circle before and the only people I've spoken to about all the shit inside my head are myself, my brother, and individual therapists. There are at least twenty people here...all of them listening and waiting for me to spill my soul out. The anxiety is too overwhelming.

The session lasts a little over an hour. Everyone talks about their sickness, and the more I listen, the easier it seems to just...let it out. They all speak briefly and oddly enough, after each one, I can see the weight lift from their eyes a bit. Like talking in a safe space helps them. I want to try again tomorrow.

"All right, head to dinner, everyone. Good progress today." Jericho stands and everyone follows suit, heading for the hall that leads to the cafeteria, I'm guessing. "Coldfox, can you hang back for a second?"

I hate that he keeps using my last name; it reminds me of my old gym teacher who did that with everyone. Liam stands next to me silently. I'm assuming he's just going to wait for me even though I wish he wouldn't.

"You did good today," Jericho says. "Most patients don't talk their first day, so don't let it get to you. We'll have a full session tomorrow, so get some food and rest up tonight." He pats me on the back and I try to give him a genuine smile.

Liam starts laughing and while I'm thinking it's because of my *dead eyes*, Jericho seems completely shocked by his outburst.

"What's so funny?"

Liam shakes his head, covering his mouth to hide his smile. "Nothing."

"See you both tomorrow. Waters, behave and make sure Coldfox has everything she needs tonight." He tucks his clipboard in his bag and heads out different doors than everyone else did.

I reluctantly follow Liam as he guides me to the cafeteria. "You're eating dinner since you skipped lunch."

I raise a brow at his demand. "*Okay*, anything else you're going to force me to do besides eat?"

He glances at me from over his shoulder. "Sure, I've got plenty of things I can recommend, since you're asking, sunshine."

Chapter 7
Liam

Wynn eats a small roll at dinner.

It's not my business what she eats or how much, nor do I care...but she didn't have lunch. She might not feel hungry because she's still deep in her mental fog after everything. Today's been a hectic day for her, I'm sure. I snag a few granola bars from the snack counter before I leave. Just in case.

She looks so damn tired by the time the door shuts behind us tonight that I don't even bother trying to joke around with her. I sit on my bed and pull my sweater off, tossing it on my desk chair and grabbing the journal from the nightstand.

Wynn's eyes flicker at me with curiosity for a moment before she returns to her task of putting clothes away and getting what few items she has set up on her side.

I try to give her privacy, I really do, but it's sort of hard when she's such a lovely woman. Her mind may piss me off, but she's beautiful. Her oversized hoodie reaches perfectly down to her knees and her long socks tuck into fluffy slippers. Long, pink hair keeps falling over her forehead and begging for my hand to sweep it to the side.

A frown tugs on my lips as I watch her somberly tuck a few pairs of jeans in her dresser. Her eyes carry a weight not unknown to me. In fact, it's too similar to my own. The dark circles under her light-brown eyes burden my chest with desire. I want to know her completely, so much so that we'll never be able to untwine our vines.

She's the image of heartache—and I want the pain she instills inside my heart forever.

"What?"

My head snaps up and I refocus my eyes on hers. "Huh?" I say like a complete idiot.

Her brows furrow and she scowls at me like I'm some brute. "Why are you staring at me like that?"

Shit—my gaze lowers and I find her nightshirt fisted in her hand. She's getting undressed. God help me, she wears a nightshirt to bed? Please tell me she's putting shorts on too. The thought of nothing but her underwear beneath that silk shirt sends a pulse of blood to my cock, making my sweatpants uncomfortably tight.

"Oh, sorry, I was...I don't know, thinking." Her scowl deepens and I feel like a complete asshole. "Right—sorry." I roll over to face the window, pulling up my journal even though I have absolutely zero interest in reading now.

"Why did you leave that ring in my hospital room?" she asks as I hear her hoodie hit the floor.

My boner is tenting my sweats at this point. I'm regretting wearing gray—at least black would've sort of hidden it. "What ring?" I ask. Obviously, I know what she's talking about, though I didn't think she'd assume I put it there. Guess I'm not as sneaky as I thought.

She's quiet for a moment and I instinctively turn to look at her without even thinking twice about it as Wynn is pulling the black silk nightshirt over her head. Her breasts are bare to me and, *surprise*, no underwear either. My mouth immediately drops open and my dick throbs painfully as new blood pulses there, begging.

Wynn pulls the collar down over her head and eyes me like the cold vixen she is. There's a fire burning in her eyes. She doesn't pull her shirt down right away—she slowly guides her fingers along the hem of her shirt as she pulls it down over her plump breasts and stops for a moment just over her pussy.

My expression darkens, a hunger as fucking carnal and raw as it gets settling over me. I don't like being teased if I can't have the prize.

"You better cover that pussy up if you don't want me to fuck your brains out tonight, Wynn."

Fear flickers across her eyes but she stiffens her hold on the hem of her shirt. I'm not sure what she's doing. I already warned her, and if she wants to play games, then I will happily amuse her.

I roll to the edge of my bed and set my feet on the floor, my dick making itself known. Her eyes lower to it and the hunger that consumes my every thought crosses her gaze too.

She pulls the shirt down and narrows her eyes at me cruelly. "You looked on purpose, so I wanted you to see what you *won't* be having." Her nipples are hard and the nightshirt does nothing to hide them.

"You sure about that?" I murmur in a low, dangerous tone.

She stares at me like she doesn't know what to say, looking down at my swollen dick more than once before she rolls her eyes and crawls into her bed. "How old are you anyway?" she quips, facing her closet doors instead of me.

I lie back down and smirk. It's actually sort of fun having her here. "I'm twenty-nine, and you?"

"Twenty-six."

"Tragic," I whisper, not intending for it to come out as a snipe, but it does.

She doesn't respond. I turn my lamp off after a few minutes of silence. It's already past midnight and I'm fucking exhausted. The wound on my ribs that I had treated at the hospital is still sore, but the dull throb of it doesn't really bother me now. My eyes start to shut when I hear her voice.

"Liam?"

"Yeah?"

"If I'm tragic, what does that make you?"

I think about that for a second.

"Cruel."

She huffs, not in an annoyed way, but more like a breath of relief, the kind that you know someone is smiling after.

We don't speak again. I fall asleep watching her body softly move with each breath she takes.

Chapter 8

Wynn

My sleep is as restless as my waking moments are. I'm so fucking tired...Even my dreams bring me no peace, no ease from my long, dreary days. If anything, they make things worse. Sometimes I dream so vividly that I'm more exhausted when I wake up than I was when I fell asleep.

Tonight is one of those nights.

The shitty part is that the dreams aren't even exciting. I'll be sitting at a desk working, or grocery shopping, sometimes even just going for a walk. All I know is that I am so, so tired.

The ceiling of my room is covered with ugly coats of beige paint, well past due a renovation. I wonder if that's where the mildewy smell is coming from.

Old painted ceilings are all that keeps me sane in the wee hours of the night. How depressing.

I shift to my side and pull the covers up to my mouth as I watch Liam take steady breaths. His dark lashes kiss his cheeks in the dim light. At least he doesn't seem to be in pain anymore. He woke me a few hours ago with low whimpers from what I'm assuming were nightmares.

My gaze shifts to the window. The rain stopped thirty minutes ago, but the moisture is still heavy in the air. I like that about rainy days. The weight makes me feel like

THE FABRIC OF OUR SOULS

it's okay to be down. No one judges you if you're sad on a rainy day.

Hushed little chirps draw my attention to Liam's nightstand. His phone lights up and he stirs awake, tapping on the screen to silence the alert. I close my eyes enough so if he looks over at me, he'll think I'm sleeping.

Liam quietly gets up, pulls a hoodie over his head, and slips on his sneakers. I lift my head slowly as he steps out of the room and shuts the door.

Where the fuck is he going at four a.m.?

I walk toward the door and peek out into the hall. It's already empty and quiet—Liam's nowhere in sight. My brows knit together. Maybe he's just going to the bathroom or something.

I wait for him to get back, staring at the ceiling and thinking of what sessions I'll have today. After thirty minutes have passed, I unplug my phone from the charger and start typing out all my complaints to James.

> Wynn: How could you leave me here without telling me it's unorthodox? Did you know my roommate is a MAN.

> James: Jesus, it's four a.m., should I have them add sleeping medication to your prescriptions as well? :)

> Wynn: Fuck you...yeah that would actually be nice lol.

James: Love you. Sorry
about the roommate, is he
your type? Maybe it's not
such a bad thing.

Wynn: He's something.
Love you too.

I can't help but smile. James never keeps his phone on
sound, so maybe he was expecting me to text him and
complain. It's been a long time since I've done that...and
somehow it makes me feel better.

As the minutes tick by I find myself thinking about
Liam's old roommate. Who was he? Did he ever notice
Liam getting up in the middle of the night, or was he a
heavy sleeper? Crosby. I want to know more about him.
I make a mental note to ask around tomorrow when Liam
isn't nearby.

The door creaks open and Liam walks back in. He shuts
the door behind him and leans his body against it like he's
tired, breathing heavily.

Where did he go? Why at this hour?

I sit up in bed and his head tilts in my direction.

"What?" he grumbles. He sounds either drunk or in
pain.

I fist the sheets. He's so insufferable. "Where did you
go at this hour?"

His figure is dark in the dim room and I can't see his
facial features, but the tone of his voice is sharp as he says,
"It's none of your business. Go back to sleep."

He's acting odd enough for me to tap on the bedside
lamp. It illuminates the room and my stomach curls at the
sight of Liam.

His clothes are wet, mud coats his shoes, and…and blood drips down from his knuckles. His expression is hard like stone, looking at me with rage.

"Oh my God." I stumble from my bed and approach him carefully. "What happened?" I reach for his arm but he pulls away and gives me a death glare.

"I said go back to bed, Wynn."

My legs tremble but I refuse to move. "I asked what happened."

We stand face-to-face, each glaring daggers at the other. Finally his stony expression softens and he takes off his shoes and sweatshirt. He sighs when I stand firm, waiting for a response.

"I just went for a walk."

"And hurt yourself?"

He eyes me with annoyance before muttering, "Yeah."

"You said we were to stop each other. I'm confronting you on it." I steady my breathing and try to reach for his arm again. This time he doesn't pull away. He lets me grab his arm and his eyes meet mine wearily.

I push his sleeve up and find a long cut running down his forearm—not over his artery, but along the side. His blood is hot and sticky, dripping to the floor and infusing the air with a metallic scent.

"*Liam*," I mutter in disbelief. How could he do this to himself on purpose…He woke up in the middle of the night to do this? Why?

"I'm fine," he growls, pulling his arm back.

"That's not fine," I protest and head toward his night-stand, opening it and grabbing the gauze and tape. I snag him fresh clothes while I'm at it. "We have to get you cleaned up." He's not himself. He's sick and he's lost a lot of blood already.

Liam stares blankly up at me. I take it as compliance as I lead him back into the hall and into the bathrooms.

It's pitch-black outside. Rain begins to *tick* against the windows again and wind rattles the panes. I flip the shower lights on and a section of the bathroom lights up. Liam just watches me and follows obediently. Thank God. But it's so unlike the person I've known for only a day now.

The shower warms up quickly and I motion for him to head in. His arm is still bleeding but at least it looks like it's clotted enough to slow a bit. "Keep your arm out of the water until the end."

He nods, takes off his clothes with no worry or regard for my leering eyes, and steps beneath the steaming water. I try to keep my attention on anything except his body, so I focus on the blood on my hands.

It looks so much like the night I tried to die. Red. Every shade of red. Bright at first and then thick crimson and rose, dulling to maroon.

I walk over to the sinks and rinse off my hands three times for good measure, keeping my mind on anything but that night. My heart hammers in my chest, making me focus more on my breathing.

The shower turns off and Liam sits down on a bench next to the pile of clean clothes I brought with us. I grab a towel from the rack and hand it to him, keeping my eyes elevated and away from him.

"I knew you were a prude."

My cheeks flare. "Liam, can we not right now?"

He chuckles and wraps the towel around his waist. Once he's covered, I dry his wound and dab ointment on it. He probably doesn't need stitches, but still, it's deep. I gently place gauze over the ointment and then wrap his arm.

"There." I tuck the end so it doesn't lift and sit back on my haunches before looking at him.

Liam's eyes are dark, sunken, and dreadful. He doesn't even have his usual ire. His hair is wet since he didn't bother drying it.

I grab another towel and drop it on his head.

"I'll be in the room. Please don't do anything else tonight, I'm tired and don't particularly feel like having to do this again." I wait for a minute and when he doesn't respond I leave.

I feel like I work here.

The hall is dark and silent, and the reprieve of our room is welcoming. I feel as though I could sleep for days. Liam's muddy shoes will have to wait until tomorrow morning.

I strip out of my clothes and pull on a baggy shirt, then fall into my bed.

The door opens a few minutes later.

Liam's steps stop at my bedside and I hesitate before opening my eyes. He looks down at me, hair dry and a distinctive flicker of anger in his eyes.

The *audacity*.

"You're welcome," I grumble and roll in my bed, pulling the covers over my head and wishing he'd just let me be.

The bed sinks and my heart jumps in my chest as his weight pushes down on me. He pulls the covers back until he can see my eyes.

"Why did you do it?" he asks, not unkindly, but his voice is low and empty of warmth.

"Because you were hurt and I—"

"Not that," he snipes. "Who...Who hurt you so bad that you wanted to die?" His eyes hold firm on mine.

He's leaning over me and has me pinned. I don't think he intends on letting me sleep without an answer.

"Well, it wasn't just one person."

He looks at me expectantly.

"Why do you want to know? I thought I repulsed you." I try to wriggle from the blanket but he tightens his hold.

"You do." I fight the pain the insult threads through my chest. "But it only makes you all the more a wonder. So again, who could possibly plant such dark, sinister seeds into a heart like yours?" His eyes soften.

Was that supposed to be a compliment?

My chest feels heavy and it's hard to breathe. A dizzy spell falls over me and Liam takes notice, quirking a brow.

"I need my medication," I rasp. How could I forget to take it? Day one and it's a complete shit show.

His brows draw together with concern and he grabs a few bottles off my nightstand, handing them to me and watching patiently as I pop open all of them and take one from each bottle.

"What's wrong with you?" he asks once I gulp down a few swigs of water.

I side-eye him. "I have a heart condition. So if you could refrain from pinning me in my bed that'd be great. Stress and anxiety make the side effects worse."

His face visibly pales and guilt shadows his eyes. "I didn't know... I'm sorry."

"Can we just go to sleep now?" I set the pills down and lie back. Liam remains sitting on my bed a few moments longer before he returns to his own.

Chapter 9

Wynn

It's already ten by the time I'm showered and dressed, hurrying to my first session of the day.

Skipping breakfast is fine. I found some granola bars on my desk and snagged one for the walk to the workout room. Exercise is crucial to mental health, according to Jericho, and we always begin our mornings with an hour-long workout.

I wolf down the granola bar and steel myself to meet more unfamiliar faces today. The shower this morning was pretty vacant besides a few other women, thankfully.

The workout room is on the second floor and over-looks the rear of the manor. I enter the room hesitantly and Jericho stands.

"Good morning Coldfox. You look like you slept like shit," he mumbles as he checks off my name on his clipboard.

I feign a smile. "Yeah, first-night jitters, I guess," I lie.

Liam was already out of the room when I woke up and I have no clue what his schedule looks like. I'm relieved I don't see his name on Jericho's list though.

"Yeah, that should pass soon. As well, your brother contacted us this morning requesting some sleeping medication for you, so I'll have that to you by tonight." He looks over my head as a few more patients step in and head toward some treadmills in the back.

"Thanks," I mutter and take a look around the room.

Everyone seems to be in their own zone. Most people have their headphones in or are buddied up with someone. The options are treadmills, cardio cycles, ellipticals, or weights.

I settle for a treadmill in the front of the room so I can at least look at the forest and the low clouds, heavy with rain.

Someone takes the treadmill to my right. I don't bother looking up as I press a low setting on the machine. The belt starts moving and I walk in a steady stride.

A few of the other patients behind me are chatting in low voices. I can't help but eavesdrop.

"Did you see the updates in the hallway?" one woman asks the other.

"No, why?"

"The lobby now has surveillance, and if you leave Harlow for good, you must check out or they'll report you missing."

The other girl is quiet for a moment. "Do you think it's about those missing people?"

"From like ten years ago? I don't think they're actually missing. I think they're dead and buried in the basement."

Wait, missing people? Like the articles in Liam's journal?

"Sidney says that if you don't push your shoes up against the door at night that they'll whisper underneath it," another girl says with a fearful tone.

I couldn't be walking quieter if I tried as I desperately listen to each word they say. Fear drips through my body. How did I not hear about this? Then again, this is Montana, where nothing is ever a big deal except the bison at Yellowstone.

"So, what's with the pink hair?"

I physically jump and a small squeal escapes my throat. I glance over at the man to my right. He's easy to recognize because of his handsome features. One of the only people I remember from yesterday.

He laughs as he turns on his treadmill. "Fuck, sorry about that. Didn't mean to scare you."

I take a few grounding breaths. "Lanston, right?"

He grins and nods. "Yeah, I'm surprised you remember. And I meant my question in a good way. I like your hair. I was curious, why pink?" Lanston sounds nervous and his cheeks are already bright red.

His black Under Armour shirt is tight against his sculpted chest. His gray sweatpants don't leave much for the imagination either.

"Pink is my favorite color. I dyed it after I quit my corporate job, you know, just in defiance of it all." I quirk a small smile at him.

Lanston laughs. The low rumble of it comforts me. He's one of those people who radiates warmth. His smile makes you want to smile.

I wish I could be like that. I wish I could have that warmth.

"Well it looks really good on you."

"Thanks," I say as I return my eyes to the window overlooking the forest. The conversation behind us has ended but their words are heavy in my mind. What happened at Harlow Sanctum?

We walk in silence for several minutes before he starts up again. "Are you getting along with your roommate?"

I sigh and my brows pull together with frustration at the mere mention of Liam. "Not particularly, no."

Lanston chuckles under his breath. "You know, I'm not surprised. Liam hated my guts when we first met too."

I look at him with curiosity. Are they friends or something? I'm shocked, given how cold Liam is. Lanston is his stark opposite. "Are you a masochist too?" I ask. I can't recall if he mentioned his illness in session yesterday.

"No, I used to be suicidal. I'd like to think I'm better now, but I still fall into that pit some days. You know?" His smile falters, vulnerability flickering across his eyes.

"Yeah, I do." Lanston, he's like me. A small light in this dark, lonely place.

I hesitate before deciding to open up a bit. Why is it that strangers are so easy to talk to? The lack of history, I suppose.

"Right now, I feel sane. I know that deep down, I don't really want to die. I like looking outside at the clouds touching the trees. I like the crisp air in my lungs. I am content being here. But tonight, that could change. Tomorrow, it could change. There's no telling what will trigger me. What will make me throw in the towel? I *know* I'm sick. But in those dark moments...I can't seem to think rationally. Not sane."

He frowns and his hazel eyes watch me with deep sympathy. He murmurs, "I'm not sane either, Wynn. You're not alone in this castle of tragedy."

We look at each other for a few seconds.

"So Liam hated you?" I ask, not sure how Liam could get past Lanston's illness. It seems to be the sole reason why he dislikes me so much.

"Yeah, that asshole would let me have it. He'd go on tangents on why I should cherish my life. How lucky I am to be able to feel emotions so entirely that I'm overcome with them." He pauses when my expression turns to horror, and laughs, his perfect teeth showing and tugging on my heartstrings. "I know, a fucking monster, right? Well, I thought so too at first. But then I had a really bad mental slump." His smile dims and his eyes grow distant with memory. "I tried to kill myself in the bathrooms. It was really early in the morning, so I didn't think anyone would find me until after dawn. But the second my feet left the stool, Liam was already holding my legs, keeping the weight of my foolish act from killing me."

Liam saved him...I wonder if it was by chance—if Liam was on one of his weird early-morning walks and just happened across him.

"And after that incident, we sort of became inseparable. We'd sit next to each other at meals and spend time hanging out. We even got matching tattoos." Lanston pulls up his sleeve and reveals his tattoo, a Roman numeral II.

"So you're saying he's not a total dick?" I deadpan.

"Yeah, he has a hard exterior but he's all mush on the inside. Don't let his initial scary phase spook you."

Jericho flicks the lights to get our attention and announces that the morning workout is over.

Lanston groans as he turns his machine off. "We hardly get enough time for the morning workout. Where are you heading next?" he asks before taking a swig of his water.

I grab my phone and check the schedule. "One on one with Dr. Prestin."

"Yikes."

"Yeah."

He pats my back as I step down from the treadmill and heads toward the door. "You'll be fine. Just don't expect a ton of chitchat. Prestin is like a gargoyle."

My lips pull up into a smile. "What a weird comparison."

He shrugs and nudges me. "See you at lunch?"

I nod as we part ways in the hall. I watch Lanston until he vanishes down the stairs. Did I just make my first friend here?

The first friend I've had in a long time.

Dr. Prestin's office is in the corner of the second floor, facing the front of the mansion. It's bright with multiple windows lining both sides of the room. His desk is fancy, made of dark, glossy oak. His doctorate degree hangs behind him, along with many trophies he's apparently won for his research in mental health.

"How are you acclimating, Miss Coldfox?" Dr. Prestin looks at me through his thick-framed glasses. He certainly looks just as tired and impassive as he did when I met him at the hospital.

"Good," I state plainly.

He writes down a few sentences in the file before shifting back in his seat and threading his fingers together in thought.

"Do you find your roommate suitable? Waters is your partner, correct?"

"He's...fine. That's correct."

God, he talks about us like we're lab rats. I suppose we probably are rats to him, the people he steps on to get those blood trophies he's so proud of, hanging from insignificant nails on his gray walls.

"Fine? Waters is probably our most deviant patient and the hardest yet to cure. Surely, given your personality charts, you've already quarreled?" Dr. Prestin presses me.

My fists clench at my sides and I can't keep the disdain from my voice as I say, "Yes, he's been *fine*. We've disagreed on a few things, but it's manageable."

Do it for James. Do it to get better, I scold myself.

Dr. Prestin watches me for several moments before nodding. "I see. Very good."

He spends the rest of the session talking about new medications he would like to try and boring psychological stuff that I don't understand the majority of. Then he sends me off with a stiff nod and a "See you next week."

I grab an apple and a wrapped Italian sandwich at the buffet. There are tons of available tables but I venture out into the courtyard for some fresh air. The three-foot stone wall lining the garden bed is dry, so I take a seat and wipe the apple off with my shirt before taking a bite.

The marigolds and mums are bright yellow and orange, a nice contrast to the dark, gloomy weather we've been having. I enjoy sitting in solitude. Some people hate it, feel vulnerable even, but there's nothing more peaceful than embracing your own silence. Only you exist, no one else.

"Hey, I was looking for you in there." Lanston's cheerful voice draws my attention away from the garden flowers and I see Yelina and Liam in tow behind him.

So much for solitude.

"It's a nice afternoon so I thought I'd get some fresh air." I smile the best I can. Lanston and Yelina beam back at me and eagerly sit down while Liam just gives me a dirty, sarcastic smile that says he knows mine is fake.

I hate this man.

My eyes linger over his arm where I bandaged him up this morning. His hoodie hides it well and I'm sure no one suspects a thing.

Yelina eyes Liam as he sits next to me, so close that we're touching shoulders.

"You can sit next to me," Yelina chirps to him. Liam snags the apple from my hand and takes a bite. I take a deep breath and ignore him. Yelina's brows pull together. "Do you know Wynn already?" Her green eyes lift to Liam.

He takes another bite of the apple and grins. "Yep."

"They're roommates, Yelina," Lanston mutters as he unwraps his sandwich.

Her cheeks flush red and her eyes flash at me. I still, squeezing my sandwich harder than I intend to.

"That's not fair." She stands abruptly and storms back inside.

I raise a brow and glance at Lanston. He looks tired. I wonder if he took a nap since our workout this morning. "What's her deal?"

"Yelina is prone to outbursts. It doesn't help that she's in love with Liam either."

Oh, well that makes sense.

"Why did you ignore her then? That was rude."

Liam shrugs. "She's annoying. I've never been nice to her, so it's not my fault she's into me."

Lanston laughs but stops when I shoot him a warning look too.

The three of us are silent for a second before I crack a smile. Lanston elbows me playfully.

"I think that's your first."

"My first what?"

Liam leans to look at my face. A glimmer spreads through his eyes as he murmurs, "Your first genuine smile."

Chapter 10

Wynn

Lanston invited me and Liam to hang out in his room tonight.

He's one of the only people here who gets his own room. Apparently, he used to share with Yelina, but due to her bipolar behavior and his improvement, he was rewarded with the best room in the manor.

I can't help but wonder if Jericho or the staff ever knew about Liam finding him that morning he tried to kill himself. Obviously not, I guess. *Unorthodox* is a very loose term for what this place is.

Very, *very* loose.

Liam's phone *dings* and he checks it immediately.

"Tell Yelina to stop trying to bone you," Lanston jests.

"It's not Yelina, it's my mom," Liam says like he's not particularly happy about it. He shoves his phone back into the pocket of his black hoodie without responding to her.

"Popcorn?" Lanston holds out five different bags of flavored popcorn. I grin and point to the kettle corn. "No way, that's my favorite too!" He throws a bag of kernels into the microwave and leans against the table, staring down eagerly at the board game he's laid out for us tonight.

Liam rolls his eyes as he arranges the board. We're playing a version of Clue that revolves around Harlow

Sanctum. Good lord, who on earth thought this was a good design? It stirs up my irrational fear that this place is haunted. Why would anyone make a mystery game based around this place? Did something worthy of a slasher film happen within these walls? My mind runs rampant with everything that may have happened here.

"You don't like popcorn?" I raise a brow at Liam. He's been quiet since the music session this morning.

He shoots me a scowl. "Of course I like popcorn. Lanston just gets too excited when you like the same things he does." I don't miss his annoyed tone and the subtle way he tries to hide it by taking a gulp from his glass of water.

Lanston smirks easily at him, bringing the bowl of freshly popped kettle corn over. "Do you blame me? I'm *obsessed* with her." He winks and presses a kiss to my cheek as he sits down beside me.

My cheeks warm with his kiss and the rosé I've been sipping on. He has his own secret stash of alcohol, such a rebel. Lanston's affection comes so naturally, it feels like I've known him forever. His smile is weightless and conversation never feels forced with him. He's so kind and attentive, a man your parents would welcome home with open arms and hope for news of an engagement.

Liam's expression is perfectly schooled into a blank stare, but rooming with him for a few days has taught me many things about that blank look. He's seething beneath. Thinking better of stirring the pot, I change the subject.

"So why this creepy game?" I swirl my glass of rosé and try to catch a few pomegranate seeds with my next sip.

Lanston looks at the board like it's beyond fascinating. "The positions of the rooms are accurate to this building. It's rumored that the murder weapons and playable characters in the game are all based on unsolved events that happened here."

I set my glass down and lean forward with a horrified expression. "*No.*" This is what those girls were talking about earlier. I did notice that poster they were talking about too, with the updated rules on checking out and staying in groups when leaving the grounds.

Liam's eyes flicker and a beautiful grin pulls at his lips. "Yeah, I've heard it's true too." He holds up a card and shows it to me. The name on the bottom says *Monica*. The image is of a beautiful young woman. Her hair is curly and dark and she wears a sweater up to her chin. "No one knows exactly which stories are true. They all interconnect, you see, but no one knows what ever became of them."

My eyes couldn't grow wider if I tried and my hands are noticeably clammy. I look at Liam expectantly. "Do you know the stories?" I pry.

Lanston laughs and throws some popcorn in his mouth. "Looks like we have a fellow horror enthusiast on our hands, Liam."

"Well?" I look between them.

Liam nods at Lanston, who smirks, stands up, and turns off the lights. We're plunged into darkness and my heart skitters with fear.

Lanston shuffles back to his seat in the dark and sits close so we're touching shoulders. Liam's lighter sparks and he lights the candle on the center of the table. *Oh, old school storytelling, huh?*

"Do you guys do this often or something?" I whisper to Lanston but he shushes me. He grabs my hands and I can't help but chuckle at the spectacle they're making of this.

This is something dramatic and dark, like out of a slasher film. I let them play it out though. It's fun to get sucked into something so cheesy. A year ago, in my corporate life, I'd scoff and call them childish—but now, I can appreciate the raw fun of it.

Why dull life with the bleary lines that the adult world draws for us? I want to be childish. I want to run free with all the dark things in the night.

I soak it all in as Liam clears his throat. I'm entirely holding my breath for old ghost stories. His sharp features are even more defined in the dim, flickering light. The light draws shadows in a waving motion over his jaw and cheekbones. His eyes are focused solely on me, and the hunger in them stirs up desire in my chest.

"Ten years ago, Monica was a businesswoman. Simple. Quaint. In her early thirties. When she had a family tragedy and found herself mentally unwell, she fell prey to Harlow Sanctum."

It is the same rumor I heard others talking about—the one from Liam's articles about those people going missing a decade ago? Lanston scoots in closer to me as Liam goes on.

"She made friends here: Charlie, Bev, and Ned. She also made enemies: Brooke and Vincent. Those five were all sick. All committed to Harlow just as Monica was. But one by one, they each disappeared. In each story, the order changes; no one can say for certain who went missing first. But one fact remains the same: someone got away. Someone finished what they started at Harlow."

I open my mouth to interrupt but Lanston shushes me again, wrapping his arms around me tightly and chuckling.

"They say that their blood is still beneath layers of paint here. That their bones are buried in the basement under the cement. But no one ever found the six of them. It's rumored that sometimes you can see them in the recreation room at night, in the reflection of the windows, looking out into the rain and crying. Some say they're still alive and went on with their lives. But no one, not even the staff, knows for sure."

Liam stops and blows out the candle. Lanston gets up and turns the lights back on. They both look at me, expecting to see fear twinkling in my eyes or something, but they only find my very unsatisfied expression.

"What the hell was that?" I cross my arms.

Lanston's smile fades. "That didn't scare you?"

"No, it made no sense at all."

Liam shakes his head. "That's why they made a Clue version of it. It works for the game, doesn't it? Full of holes and mystery. Multiple endings and whatnot."

I scowl at him. "I guess so, but how could the staff not know what happened to them? They have files on all of us, don't they?" I realize I'm anxiously picking at the hem of my sweater and quickly fist my hands at my sides to stop the nervous tic.

"Sure, but this is also a voluntary institute. Many people over the years just decided to up and leave. What do you think happened to Cros—" Lanston catches himself and bites back his words quickly.

Liam shoots him a warning look and his jaw flexes. "People leave constantly without warning. That's the crux of it."

I know I shouldn't push, but I do anyway. Maybe it's the wine talking but I want to know so badly. Crosby was Liam's roommate before me. What happened to him? Did he go missing too?

"And who was Crosby?" I demand, pinning Lanston with a look.

"Gone," Liam bites out and Lanston looks absently down at the board game. "Let's play already."

I need to ask Lanston alone or I'll never get an answer.

I grab a card and Lanston does too. We go through the rules, brush up on the motions, and start playing a round.

What an odd story to spin. I wonder if they were real people. Harlow is certainly real, and the rooms seem to be as well. After hearing the girls talk about the people and seeing the posters for checkout and safety, I figure it has to be loosely real, at least. The board itself is strange, with images of insects and bones spread throughout the rooms like decorations. I've seen these images before...

Liam's journal.

Why would he have notes on this game? His journal was packed with research, some of which was in Latin.

He believes too.

I need to take another look at his journal.

We finish out the game and laugh over a few more drinks before Liam and I head back to our room. It's well past midnight and he keeps checking his phone with a grimace.

I ask him what's wrong twice but he doesn't answer either time, so I drop it.

I'll ask him tomorrow.

Chapter 11
Wynn

The first week hasn't been so bad.

James texts me regularly, making sure I'm taking my meds and keeping up with all the therapy and recommendations from the counselors. I've been telling him everything is fine. Routine, yes, but fine.

Manageable, I remind myself.

The sleep medication has been helping a great deal. I stay asleep all night and wake up well-rested in the morning. Liam hasn't woken me up again since the first night. From the small glimpses I get of him getting dressed in the mornings, he doesn't have any new cuts, so hopefully that means he isn't still sneaking out.

Avoiding the men's showering schedules has been another story.

I am not ashamed of my body. No. In fact, I think I look pretty good. But I hate people looking at me.

Early morning is the only time I can get the bathroom to myself (and a few other early-bird women). I woke up late on Wednesday and had to shower at nine.

Never. Again.

The men had something new to look at and every stall was full. Some people were fucking, others were singing nonchalantly and enjoying their shower, while I was like a deer in the headlights trying to get in and out as fast as I could.

Thank God Liam wasn't in there.

On the way out, I bumped into Lanston, and the deep red of his cheeks told me he'd probably seen every inch of me.

Manageable.

The sessions are already getting easier to sit through. I have the same schedule every day, except Tuesdays, when I meet with Dr. Prestin after the morning workout. I still haven't played the piano during the music session. Neither has Liam, who I was surprised to see in there with me. We just take turns sitting at the piano as Jericho calls us up.

It's surprisingly easy to fall in line and go with the flow. Without external forces like a social life, work, family, and pressure from myself to do better, I'm finding that life here isn't so bad.

The few people that I call my friends are as sick as I am, and I've never felt like I've belonged somewhere more.

"What are your plans this weekend?" Yelina grabs the pink polish and spreads a fresh coat on her fingernails. I settle for a nude beige. My room already stinks of nail-polish fumes and I even cracked the window before we started. Liam's going to throw a fit—I just know it.

"I don't have any plans."

She sets down the bottle and gives me a once-over. "Really? You're not doing something with Liam?" She seems more annoyed on my behalf than jealous. It's been hard for her to accept that I'm his roommate, but I've assured her that we don't get along.

"Are you really surprised? He hardly talks to me, and when we do talk, we're either arguing or talking about how much we dislike each other." I sigh, finishing the coat on my thumb before blowing on it so it dries faster.

Yelina looks down and deflates a bit. "Well, at least he talks to you. He won't even look at me." She pouts, drawing skulls on her nails with white paint now.

Liam's always looking at me, watching me constantly when we're in the same room. I can't seem to escape his icy gaze.

"So, what do you do on the weekends?" I change the subject.

She tilts her head so her blonde hair falls over her shoulder as she tries to get a better angle in the light. "I visited the town last weekend but there wasn't much to do. There's like one bar and a tattoo parlor."

Bakersville is pretty small. I'm shocked there's even a tattoo shop.

"Well, want to meet in the lobby in the morning and make plans together?" I say casually. I suck at asking people to hang out and I'm not afraid to admit it.

She tuts and side-eyes me. "Sorry, Wynn. I'm booked all weekend. I'm sure Lanston has time for you though. He's always sulking around. You two are good for each other in that way."

"You don't have to be a bitch about it. Just say you're busy." I glare at her. Damn, these new meds make me a hard-ass. I kinda like it.

She snatches the polishes she brought with her and stands up furiously. She doesn't say anything, but she slams the door behind her.

Manageable.

Liam comes back into the room later than usual.

I don't bother looking up at him. I'm reading a thriller and just got to the part where the heroine falls in love with the murderer. He chases her into an abandoned factory and then switches his identity before going to her. I flip the page. She finds blood on his collar and screams—

"That good?"

I jolt and grip my book so hard it bends the spine.

"Fuck, Wynn. What are you reading?" I don't have time to protest before Liam's invading my space and lying beside me on the bed. I scoot over a bit so we're not smashed together in the center.

"Jesus, invite yourself over, why don't you," I grumble, narrowing my eyes at him. His blue eyes are intent on the book and a boyish grin pulls at his lips. "Are you drunk?"

"I had a few drinks with Lanston. That doesn't mean I'm drunk." He rolls his eyes and taps the pages carelessly, crinkling a few of them. "Come on, what were you reading?"

I pull the book away from him hastily and shoot him a glare. "Stop that. It's a thriller romance."

He laughs and rolls to his back. "So it's a porno?"

My cheeks warm. "*Oh my God.* Go back to your bed, Liam." I set the book on my nightstand and watch him. He's just staring at the ceiling, breathing deeply with a stupid grin on his lips.

"Can we play a game?" he asks, lifting his head to meet my eyes. His dark hair is disheveled, making him all the more beautiful. His icy stare digs deep into my soul.

"What game?" I raise a suspicious brow.

He sits up and leans closer. "Truth or dare."

I hold my ground and stiffen my resolve. "That's childish."

"Ask me first, come on." His expression is cold and curious.

Am I really going to play this game with him? Then again, why not? It's Friday night, I have nothing better to do, and at least we're talking. That's progress, I guess.

"Fine, truth or dare?"

"Dare." His eyes trail down my chest before flicking back up.

"I dare you to paint your nails." I grab the black polish from my makeup bag and toss it to him.

His lips curl and a dark, unsettling look falls over his features. "All right. Truth or dare, sunshine?" He unscrews the top and starts painting his toenails.

I think for a moment. If I choose truth, he might ask me things I'm really not in the mood to dig up right now. "Dare."

He chuckles and narrows his eyes at me. "Kiss me."

"Are you sure you're not drunk?"

Liam laughs again and shakes his head. "I'm not. Are you going to do it or not?" He stares at me with a burning fire in his eyes.

My heart thrums unsteadily. His blue eyes pierce me with need and his sharp jaw begs to be touched. He finishes his last toe and tosses the bottle of nail polish on the bed. "Well?"

It's just a kiss. He already kissed you before, so it's not a big deal.

I lean forward and give him a quick peck on the lips. His oak scent burns my senses and heat coils in my stomach just being so close to him.

"What was *that*?" He barks out a laugh. "You call that a kiss?"

Oh my God, this man. He infuriates me to no end.

Fine. Fuck it.

I look at him from beneath hooded eyes and crawl into his lap. His chest is taut and warm against mine, his arms open like he doesn't know what to do, taken by surprise with my boldness. I wrap one hand around his head and fist his hair while the other splays across his tight jaw. I can feel the gulp he takes as my lips draw close to his. Liam's eyes widen with lust and desire. His length is already hardening beneath me and I haven't even kissed him yet.

"Here's your kiss, *masochist*."

I press my lips against his. It's like sailing right into a storm you know you'll never come back out of. The second his hands trail up my hips and lower back, I know I've landed in his trap. My heart pounds and I can't help but let him deepen the kiss. His tongue coaxes my lips until I open for him and our tongues explore each other.

My legs relax on either side of him as the ecstasy of this moment starts to take me. Our breaths grow harder as we kiss viciously—every pull of my lip and bite of his has us moaning louder and squeezing each other's flesh harder. His hands are burning into my waist and the more my body jerks to rub on his cock, the shorter his breaths become.

Why'd he have to be so fucking beautiful? I hate this man. I hate him.

His hand slips under my sweater and quickly finds my breast. I inhale sharply and he smiles, pulling away just enough to look into my eyes.

"This is what you get for teasing me before." He gently pulls on my nipple. I try to cry out but his lips are already crushing back on mine, so it's muffled into a groan. He kneads my breast and holds me tightly against him with his other hand, pumping his hips so his dick rubs against me feverishly.

"I remember you promising to *unalign my hips by morning* days ago," I say with venom against his lips.

His eyes are icy as he whispers, "Are you calling me a liar?" His voice is so low it stirs fear in my veins. That delicious, dark tone of his that skates on my nerves like fire on ice.

"Maybe," I say breathlessly. "As long as you don't get the wrong idea."

"And what idea would that be?" He pulls down my tank top to expose my breast, taking my nipple in his mouth eagerly. He swirls my nipple with his tongue, urging my hips to grind into his boner.

"Don't think for a second that I like you. You're just a guy with a dick, it happens to be Friday night, and I'm horny."

He bites my breast and I cry out. Did he seriously just bite me? Oh, the things I want to do to Liam, how I want to hurt him and punish him.

"I fucking hate you, Wynn. You repulse me." His eyes lift to mine with fire within them, but they widen when he sees a tear rolling down my cheek. I can't say if it's from the sting of his bite or his words, but it's a bodily response only. My cold heart doesn't bat an eye at his attempt to hurt me. I've got that shit steeled and reinforced.

He doesn't say anything, and neither do I. But I don't miss the way his ire lightens as he traces every angle of my face. I find myself doing the same to him. It's not so hard when you're staring at someone as painfully and irrefutably beautiful as him. His dark lashes are so long and thick they highlight his entire face, making his ocean eyes all the more irresistible. How many women have lost their hearts to eyes like his?

Liam lifts his hand and drags his forefinger down the side of my face. I fight the urge to lean into it because I'm positive that it is anything but comforting. He presses his tongue against my cheek, licking the tear from my face like an animal.

"Even your tears repulse me."

I hate him so fucking much.

I drop my head to his shoulder and sink my teeth into his flesh to let my anger out. My breast stings from where he bit me, and I hope this fucking hurts him just as bad.

Liam grips my ass hard and lets out a groan so deep that it rumbles in my chest. "*Fuuuck*, you know I love pain, baby." His hand slides up to my throat and tightens, then slides down to my sternum, pushing me back so I fall on the bed.

My veins fill with adrenaline as his eyes darken and he yanks my silk shorts off with one swift pull.

"Safe word is *pancakes*," he says indifferently, bending down and nipping the inside of my thigh. I hold my breath and watch as his beautiful face dips down again, closer to my pussy. His dark hair tousled from the way I fisted it. "Did you hear me?"

I nod like a furious, sex-drunk idiot.

His feverish grin sends chills up my spine. "Good, because unless you say it, I'm not stopping."

His tongue teases my clit and I'm instantly fisting the sheets. He slides a finger inside my pussy, groaning when he finds how wet I am already. I let my head fall back as the pleasure rolls through me. He licks me slowly, in agonizing strokes that have me rolling my eyes and clenching my jaw to keep the pleasured moans I know he wants to hear in my throat. He pumps his fingers into me hard, with a rhythm that has me coasting close to my climax.

Liam's other hand is planted on my thigh, squeezing my flesh so tightly I know there will be bruises in the morning.

I hate you. I fucking hate you.

He takes me closer and closer to the edge until I'm coming undone. My thighs fight to close around his head but he holds them firmly in place as he devours me. My pussy is so sensitive, but he is relentless, licking and stroking me until he's satisfied, leaving my legs trembling.

I hardly get a moment to breathe before his hand wraps around my throat. My eyes widen and fear trickles through my veins. He dips his face to mine, licking up my jaw until his lips are against the shell of my ear.

"Are you scared of me?" he whispers in a low, raspy tone.

My heart thrums and my breaths are labored. His grip on my throat isn't tight; it makes me wildly uncomfortable but also…excited? My brain tells me it's wrong on so many moral levels, but my traitorous flesh screams something entirely different. I like it—I really, really fucking like it.

"*Yes.*"

He chuckles and leans back, pulling his sweatpants down and freeing his dick. I swallow several times, trying to make sense of how we got to this point—me staring at his unnaturally large penis and him rubbing the tip of it along my stomach. My core hurts with how much need pulses there.

"Your skin is so soft, Wynn. Your hair is perfect. Your eyes are damning. There's nothing more I'd like than to have you choking on my dick." His eyes hold contempt for me, but my focus is on his swollen cock pressing into my flesh and drawing lines on my stomach.

Would he fuck me with as much rage as his eyes betray? Would it make him stop being so spiteful? I've never been hate-fucked. I'm sure it's not passionate or adoring, but you only live once, right?

It's Friday night.

This is *manageable*.

"Just fuck me and get it over with, jackass," I sneer at him.

Liam stares at me with his jaw flexed. A smooth, too-calm smile spreads over his lips and manic light flickers across his eyes.

"Bareback then," he growls, flipping me over ruthlessly and lining his dick up with my pussy.

"You have to wear a condom!" I try to crawl away but his grip is bruising on my hips.

"Do I? After you said such a nasty thing?"

My blood chills, and I panic as I feel his length sliding up and down my slit. The skin of his tip is so soft and sensual it makes my knees weak. "*Pancakes! Pancakes!*" I scream.

He instantly releases his hold on me and I huddle up against the headboard, pulling the blanket up to cover myself from his lingering cold eyes.

"Jesus, Wynn, I thought you could play on my level, remember?" he says casually, like he knew exactly what he was doing this whole time. He stands and pulls his sweatpants back up, not even sparing me a second glance. I truly disgust him, don't I?

"God knows what a *degenerate* like yourself has," I snarl at him. "Do you even know what a fucking condom is?"

He turns fast, looking over his shoulder at me with new fire flickering in his gaze. "You know we have to all be clean to be admitted here, right? It's part of the requirements, since obviously people fuck like rabbits here. Did your rich big brother mention that to you, or did he just send your tests without your knowledge?"

I stare at him dumbfounded.

James. I hope you're prepared for another wordy text.

I feel like a complete idiot—I should've read the fucking contract.

"That's what I thought. Poor, dead-eyed Wynn. Can't even get her rocks off because she's so belligerently boorish."

That sets off something so feral inside me that I don't even realize I'm moving until I'm already committed to it. I tackle him to his bed and pound on his chest furiously, screaming that I hate him over and over until his surprised expression breaks into a cruel laugh.

My eyes widen and I freeze, palm still fisted over his chest and trembling with rage. Did I just attack someone like a fucking wild animal? Oh my God.

"Same safe word?" He glares at me as he secures my body against his chest and pulls his dick out again. We eye one another with gnashing teeth and hate brimming past any healthy point.

"A worm like you can't make a woman like me come." I level my eyes with him and give him a daring, spiteful grin.

"I'll take that bet."

"You're disgusting." I spit in his face and he groans, pretending to like it.

"And you're cheap." He laughs, shoving his dick inside me so hard I cry out with the pressure of his length filling me to the brim. He doesn't give me a second of reprieve before he's pumping into me savagely, every inch of him buried so deep inside me and it feels so *fucking good*.

I hate him.

But as his dick pumps into me and sends heat and pleasure through my core unlike any I've ever felt, as I press my breasts against his wide chest and my head falls into the crook of his neck, I don't think it's hate.

And that thought scares me.

More than God. More than dying and rotting in the ground.

Liam breathes sharply and holds me close, fingers digging into my back and ass. His hard, violent thrusts slow to a rhythmic pump. This close, I can hear his heartbeat quicken.

I moan as he pulls all the way out to his tip and teases my entrance with his head before pushing in again, all the way to the hilt, and grinding hard into me like we'll never part.

I look up at his face, with curiosity or desire, I'm not sure which. To see if he still has that look on his stupid, beautiful face from when he called me *boorish*.

His brows are pulled together in anguish and his eyes drip with lust and pleasure. He stops moving for a moment, his dick fully inside me. Liam reaches up for my jaw and pulls me in for a desperate kiss.

It's so much more than a kiss. My heart pounds like a war drum in my chest and butterflies flap their wings inside my stomach.

Our tongues quickly find one another and he starts to thrust into me again.

It's too tender and warm, especially after our heinous words. "I might get the wrong idea if you fuck me softly like this, Liam. Don't be afraid to be your brutish self," I say with venom.

"You just can't stop egging me on, can you?" he snarls against my lips.

He pulls out of me and shoves my chest into the bed, pulling my ass to the edge of the mattress where he stands and slaps my pussy with his dick. I fist the sheets and scream into the blankets as he pounds into my heat once more. Ruthlessly, the way a man like him knows how.

He fucks me so hard it hurts. I scream with each thrust. His dick hurts, his hands hurt, his words hurt.

Everything about Liam hurts.

He ceases and groans low as his dick pulses inside me. I can feel the throbbing of his release as my pussy clenches, desperate for his come.

Asshole.

He holds himself there for a few moments before withdrawing and rolling me over so my back is on his sheets and I'm facing him. His forehead is sweaty, his black hair clinging to the side of his face.

He's beautiful. A fallen angel—a devil.

"I hope you're on birth control," he says indifferently, fire burning in his eyes.

I smile innocently. "No, I'm not, actually. I'm on my fertile cycle too." His eyes shift to horror and he looks down at my pussy, dripping with his come. "I'm joking. Of course I'm on birth control, you fucking psychopath."

He audibly sighs and I don't miss the smile he covers with his hand. "Okay, I'll admit that was too far, but I was waiting for you to say *pancakes* again...and well, you didn't."

"After you called me boorish and cheap?"

His expression softens. "I was pissed...I shouldn't have said those things. You're not cheap. Boorish *sometimes*." He grins playfully at me. Something has lightened between us. "I'm sorry."

"Sorry for saying you're just a guy with a dick and that you're a degenerate...and disgusting."

He laughs and helps me up, his fingers lingering on my wrist as I move by him. I wrap myself in my bathrobe and spare him a glance before I reach the door.

"Coming? Or do you not shower after hate-fucking your roommate?"

Chapter 12
Liam

My eyes linger on Wynn as she scrubs her chest with her champagne-and-rose-scented body wash.

I intended to have fun with her tonight, but I didn't think it'd spiral out of control and we'd... What did she call it, *hate-fucking*? She glances over at me and I quickly avert my eyes.

Why can't I stop thinking about her? Why can't we just get along?

I want her... more than I care to admit. *I want her.*

That brief moment when we were pressed so close, her chest against mine... I want to comfort her, hold her while she sleeps. But she won't let me. Not while she's awake at least.

I run my hair beneath the water one last time before shutting it off and wrapping a towel around my waist.

Her new meds keep her asleep at night but don't stop her from dreaming. Her whimpers were quiet at first, but as the nights have passed, they've gradually become too much to ignore.

Wynn finishes up with her shower and doesn't look at me as she slips by. She tries so hard to not look at me. I grin; I like this game we're playing.

We get dressed and spend the rest of the evening

reading and don't talk much at all, especially not about the hate-fucking.

Do we hate each other? I don't think that's accurate.

She falls asleep around eleven and I don't bother putting my book down until her soft whimpers start up. I glance over at her.

Her lips are still puffy from our brutal kisses. Dark lashes kiss her cheeks. Her face is somber, dreams bleak.

She's beautiful. If I let her, she'll break my heart a million times until she can no longer find a weak spot in my armor. We hurt each other. That's what I've learned so far. We're each other's pain.

But do we have to be?

I watch her whimper for a few more minutes before setting my book on the nightstand and shutting off my lamp.

Her hair is still wet. It smells so sweet—she loves the expensive, floral-scented shampoo brands that claim to keep the color in your hair brighter. I gently move her hair up a little so it's on her pillow and can dry out more, and then I slowly crawl in behind her.

Her body is warm but she unconsciously moves closer to me for my heat. I grin and she rolls to face me, nuzzling into my chest and breathing easier than she was a moment ago.

She's like this every night. I don't know why, and I'm not sure if she'll ever tell me what plagues her dreams, but I don't mind holding her like this. It makes the itch in the back of my mind fade. The need to feel pain is almost completely gone when I'm with her.

I tuck my head in closer to her and press a kiss to her forehead.

"*Remedium meum.*"

Chapter 13

Wynn

Passion—that's this week's theme.

Find your passion.

Well, that's certainly easier said than done, isn't it? How many times have I tried to find my calling? What makes me uniquely me? I'm not special. I'm not unique.

Though, once upon a time, I did have a passion. A true gift from the universe that I thought was only for me.

I stare at the piano with empty eyes. Jericho has been trying to get me to play the damn thing since I got here. He knew the moment I arrived that my heart yearned for the music behind these cold white and black keys.

But another soul had already stolen the joy from me. The music of my heart is buried alongside my old self.

I glance up at the group. Liam sits in the back with his arms crossed, but his eyes are on me. I look back down at the keys again. He's been weird since this weekend. Maybe all we needed to get along better was to have aggressive, angry sex and degrade one another.

That can't be healthy.

But now I have a hard time looking at him without blushing and he's been significantly less sarcastic and cruel.

"Well? You think you could play me something today, Coldfox?" Jericho's legs are crossed as he waits patiently, always tapping his pen on the clipboard. Lanston and Poppie are among the others in this class. I don't recall the others' names.

I've heard the girl with long black hair play beautifully, structurally, like she was raised to only read the notes as they are on the page. Never to dally or create anything from the heart.

Funny, that's how I was taught as well.

I wonder why she can play so easily while I remain at a standstill.

Must be the unbalanced chemicals in my brain. I wonder if Dr. Prestin has pills to erase bad memories too. We already have quite the supplemental diet of manufactured little pellets that are supposed to cure us, so let's add one more to the mix.

My horrendous music teacher's face looms in my mind. Her frown always hung lower than anyone else I'd ever known. How could someone who teaches something so beautiful and rhythmic be so dead inside? Her and my mother. My mother's tall, cold figure looms in my mind. I can still feel the chill rolling off her frosted heart.

I'm convinced they are the ones who stole my happiness, my love for the music of my heart. I heard notes echoing from my soul, begging to be played. But they stomped the spark out before I could kindle a flame.

A warm hand presses down on my shoulder. I turn and find Liam standing at my back. A sad smile pulls on his lips as if he understands why I hesitate.

He's been careful with me since we collided. I've been careful with him too.

"Can I try?" he murmurs. "I hope it reaches you." I quirk a brow but nod and scoot out from the piano bench, walk back to the group, and plop down in the chair next to Lanston in the back. What did he mean by that?

Liam sits there momentarily, staring down at the keys like they're old friends he's dearly missed. He's done so every day.

"Does he play?" I whisper to Lanston.

He scratches his light-brown hair beneath his cap and shrugs. "He never has before."

Why did he seem so reassuring then?

Liam's posture straightens and one of his feet takes position over the three pedals at the foot of the baby-grand piano. His fingers glide soundlessly over the keys until they settle on their destined locations.

I watch as a sea of blue, as bright and sunny as a day at the beach, takes over his normally grim eyes.

His fingers expertly press the keys with speed and elegance. My bones pacify. The chill sends goosebumps up my arms and my heart clenches.

I know this song, yes, just from one verse.

"London Calling" by Michael Giacchino.

It's a difficult one to master due to the fast rhythm, but he plays as though he's channeling the melancholic demons he locks inside himself. He's neither looking at any notes nor worried whether he's playing the right keys.

He plays from his heart.

Tears brim in my eyes, but I'm not sure why. I try to blink them away but they stay, wishing to be freed from the cage I've locked my emotions away in for so long.

His eyes aren't even on his hands. He's looking through the bay windows and out at the gorgeous fall gardens as the drizzling rain falls rhythmically with his song. Moss grows on the dark, drenched stones, and deep orange and yellow mums line the garden's edges. A flock of birds take to the sky and coast beneath the low clouds before disappearing through them.

As my tears roll down my cheeks, I realize something I've not dared think about for years.

I'm still hurting from the frowning, cruel piano teacher who stole music from me. Hurting from the pain of my mother forcing me as a child to play exactly as I was instructed, to be the prodigy she so desperately wished me to be. I'm still holding a grudge as dark and sinister as the clouds outside for the both of them. Because I was never enough, I was never going to be the golden ticket into a life they craved.

That's when I first realized how cruel life could be. How easy it is to lose the love of my soul's keepers.

How easy I am to discard as useless.

Liam finishes his song and spins on the bench to face the rest of the group. He avoids my eyes as he stands, taking an exaggerated bow as we all clap for him. Lanston nudges me with his elbow and murmurs, "Fucking drama king." His voice trails off when he looks at me.

Tears still spill over my cheeks and there's no stopping them. I haven't cried in years...Liam playing from the heart so freely was like a bullet to the chest. No chains kept his music away from the world.

It reached me.

And I'm...sad.

It's a feeling that's as painful as it is freeing. When I'm emotionally detached, everything is easier, because nothing matters. Even if I were to die, it would not matter. But the second sorrow is able to burrow its way into my bones, I'm more melancholic about the defining moments in my life than I ever thought possible.

Liam lifts his head and his eyes land on me. His brows pull together with concern as he walks up to me, clutching my chin with his hand and lifting it so I look at him. The soft pad of his thumb brushes the tears off my cheek as he mutters, "Did I reach you?"

He touches me delicately. It's the first ray of warmth he's shown me.

And that makes me really fucking sad too.

"Yes, you did."

Chapter 14

Wynn

Yelina and Poppie are boobs-deep in the hot tub.

I didn't even know Harlow had one, to be honest. It's nice though, not a free-standing one like people have in their back-yards. It's built into the floor and is the size of a small pool.

The two women eye me carefully as I sink into the water across from them. I let out a long, relieved sigh and rest my head against the wall.

I try not to dwell on what others think of me, but it can be hard sometimes. Obviously, Yelina is into Liam and he and I are...hate-fucking now, apparently.

My innermost conscience is still screaming at me for entertaining him. But you know what? I don't need morals about sex in a place like this. If anything, I'll just think of it as another form of therapy.

I mean, it sort of is. I think? Sex therapy? I make a mental note to Google that later.

It's quiet for the most part in here, but I overhear something that catches my attention.

"We should probably wrap up our soak soon. I don't want to be out too late. I hear sometimes there's a man standing out in the field, watching. Leigh said that it's the ghost of one of the people that went missing all those years ago," Poppie says, fear making her voice tremble.

"I saw him once, so he's no ghost," Yelina tuts back and moves her blonde hair to one side as she sinks further into the hot water.

"Seriously?" Poppie's eyes grow wide.

I can't help but tilt my head toward them more. My eyes dart to the large windows. I wonder if someone is actually out there.

Yelina nods. "Yeah, it was dark, and I was so scared I left as fast as I could, but I saw his figure. He looked young." They both rub their arms uncomfortably before Yelina notices me staring at them.

Shit. I quickly turn away and feign ignorance. How else would I hear all the rumors if I didn't eavesdrop?

The doors swing open and someone walks in, catching both Poppie and Yelina's attention. I can't see who it is, but by the way they gawk, I can guess.

Please, God, not him.

The lights in here are already dim as it is. During the day, the skylights let in plenty of light. But evenings like tonight, when even the moon isn't out, it's like movie-sex-scene lighting. A few couples are already making out in the far end of the pool.

Please, not him.

Liam plops into the water next to me and shoots me a tight grin. He looks indifferent again. That short moment in the recreation room when he was actually kind now seems so distant.

I take a deep breath. "What?"

He raises his brow at me. "I can't come hang out with my roommate?" His eyes dip down to my submerged breasts.

We shower naked—we sit in the hot tub naked. At

least this room steams up really well so there's less visibility than the showers.

Those are the unofficial rules. Like I said, sex therapy.

"Since when did you get the idea that I'd like to *hang out* with you?" I ask incredulously. His dark hair is already sticking to his head with sweat. His blue eyes are sexy when he glares at me. I don't know if I've thought that before about his eyes, but I sure as hell do now. I try to shake the thoughts from my mind.

"Don't act like you don't crave my tongue on your pussy again."

I bat my lashes at him and say with a counterfeit smile, "Go lick Yelina's pussy; she's right over there."

His cheeks turn red and he closes in on me, pinning his arms on each side of my head and staring into my soul. Yelina and Poppie are watching us with shocked expressions. A few others on the deeper end of the pool notice as well.

"Tell me to go lick Yelina's pussy one more time, Wynn," he says in a dangerously low voice.

My breath catches in my throat. His oak scent invades my senses, bringing me back to the other night. Why does his smell, his face, *everything* about him draw me in?

Liam's eyes are cold as he waits for me to speak.

"Go. Lick. Someone. Else's. Pussy." I brush my finger gently down his bottom lip, leaving a drop of water behind. A cruel smile curls along his lips as I pull myself out of the pool, tits and all out for the world to see. I don't give a shit.

I turn to head back to the changing room. I hear him get out of the water and my pulse rises.

This is kind of fun.

I shouldn't be entertaining his attention, but I can't help it. Liam's rage is the kind that simmers your flesh until you can no longer stand it. His gaze so filled with lust that it reduces your sanity to nothing more than desire.

He chases me into the changing room. There are several stalls to choose from and no one else is in here. *Shit. Shit. Shit.*

I close a few of the other doors and lock myself in the last one, stepping up on the bench to hide my feet. I have to cover my mouth to stop myself from laughing.

Liam's footsteps come in a second later. He's silent and still, trying to decide if I left the room or am hiding in one of the stalls.

He opens a few to my left, and I'm holding my mouth tight and trying not to breathe. I'm having one of those silent laughing fits you get in the worst of situations, where you're not sure whether you'll snort or not if you take a breath.

He heads toward the exit. The second he's out the door I let out my breath and laugh silently. I haven't been this giddy in a long time.

I should be relieved that he didn't find me. So why do I have disappointment brewing inside my chest?

My mind is clearly not functioning right today. Or ever.

I wait a few more minutes before deciding to head back to the pool. I didn't get the full soak I wanted, thanks to him.

The pool is empty when I hop back in. It's pretty late and I'm happy for the peace of being alone, finally. I swim to the center, enjoying the space to myself. The hot water eases my muscles. Everything is quiet around me, leaving me with my thoughts.

Normally this would be bad, but I can only think of one thing.

Liam.

No matter how many times I scold myself or try to think about other things, one way or another, it comes back to him.

It's better than thinking about death.

"There you are."

I gasp as Liam jumps in and swims toward me.

I make it to the edge before he has me pinned again, his chest against my back.

"Oh my God, can you just leave me alone for two seconds?" I frown, not that he can see it, and that pisses me off even more.

"I thought we were having fun?" he asks, lips against my ear. His chest is taut against my back, and I try hard not to think about everything else I feel.

My legs are pulled tightly together with need.

I don't want to admit that I am having fun...I don't want to admit that I like his attention.

"Tell me to stop then, Wynn. Tell me you don't want to suck my dick and get fucked out of your mind. *Say it.*"

He reaches forward and grabs my breast, kneading it softly with his fingers and pulling gently on my nipple. I lean my head back against his shoulder and moan.

"Say it," he whispers, pressing kisses along my neck.

He's already completely melted any resolve I had. "I want it." I reach back and grip his hard dick.

"You want what, sunshine?" He moves his hips so his shaft fucks my hand while his tip pushes against my ass.

"I want to suck your dick."

"Not get fucked out of your mind?"

I stay quiet, wiggling my ass and hoping he won't make me say it. "I want it so bad," I whisper, ashamed to speak aloud.

Liam groans at the desperation in my voice and hops out of the pool. He sits on the edge, his dick lined up perfectly with my mouth. He watches me as I lick his shaft bottom to top before giving extra attention to the tip of it. I swirl his crown with my tongue in gentle strokes and he throws his head back, groaning and clutching the side of the pool like he's trying his best not to fuck my mouth.

I take him in deeply, hollowing my cheeks and sucking him hard. I stroke the tender flesh under his dick with my tongue and start dip my head to take him deeper and deeper until my eyes start to water.

"Oh, *fuck*, Wynn. That feels so fucking good." Liam bucks his hips in small thrusts and fists my hair. "You like sucking dick, don't you? You're such a dirty girl." His deep, raspy voice and filthy words make me moan on his cock.

He stops my bobbing head and pulls me out of the pool.

The look in his eyes is pure lust. He glances down at my breasts and dripping pussy, then back to my eyes.

"How do you want it, Wynn?" He advances on me and I back up until I'm pressed against the freezing windows. I hiss at the assault of icy glass on my skin.

"I want it from behind." I turn, giving him my ass and pressing my hands against the glass. I can't look at him while he fucks me; it's too intimate that way. There is no window covering. It's completely dark outside, nothing but an empty field out there, but anyone could be watching if they happened to be out there.

And I don't fucking care.

"Filthy. You like being rammed from behind and fucked until you can't stand, don't you?" His words are like beautiful poison dripping from his soft lips.

"Yes," I moan as his tip circles my swollen clit. He teases my entrance a few times before pushing inside me.

He pushes all the way in until his hips are against my ass and I cry out. I'm so full and it feels so fucking good. He starts pulling in and out slowly. We're both panting heavily. Each thrust feels like he's going to push even further into me.

"Oh, God, Liam, fuck me harder," I moan, barely keeping myself standing as he ruts into me over and over.

"I want you coming undone and falling to your knees by the time I'm done fucking you," he grunts and fucks me harder like I asked.

I cry out again and my mouth instinctively falls open, eyes rolling back as he takes me closer and closer to the edge. His thrusts become longer and harder and I know he's about to come too. Our eyes connect in the reflection of the window and my heart skips a beat. His eyes are hooded and filled with pleasure, his mouth barely open as he pants and works himself into me.

He groans so loud it sounds like he's dying, but the pleasure leaving his lips sends me over and I'm coming with him. Liam pumps into me a few more times, hips shaking and dick throbbing inside me until we start to spill from where we're connected.

"That was the hottest thing I've ever done," I say on a breathy laugh.

Liam pulls out of me slowly and turns me around. His cheeks are so red I'd think he had a fever, but his eyes are full of emotion, like he has a million things he wants to say.

He looks at me and opens his mouth, thinks better of it, and leaves without a word.

That wasn't hate-fucking.

I think we both realize it.

And we know we're in deep trouble.

Chapter 15

Wynn

Mornings start slow. I'm an early bird, so I'm usually up by seven a.m. and looking for things to do. Liam is the opposite. He sleeps in each morning and only rises from his grave fifteen minutes before breakfast, saying he gets too hungry otherwise. *Men.*

We've silently agreed to not speak about what we did in the spa, though I'd be lying if I said I didn't think about it often.

Researching the missing people from the game has kept me entertained in the mornings, while Liam's soft snores create a calm atmosphere in our room. The warm light from my lamp doesn't seem to bother him at all.

The newspaper articles are far more disturbing than Liam and Lanston's horror show. Liam doesn't mind me snooping through his journal, so now I keep it on my desk and study it each morning. The six of them all went missing without a trace. No one ever found evidence that they'd died, but they also couldn't prove they ever left the walls of Harlow Sanctum. Police searched, but without families reaching out and pressing their disappearances, the case went cold.

I tap my finger on the bundle of papers I brought with me to breakfast.

Liam leans in closer to my tablet and points at three of the people huddled together in a group photo. The patients stand on the steps of the rehab. I recognize them from the game photos: Charlie, Monica, and Beverly. Their faces are mischievous and a few of the orderlies are looking over at them with furrowed brows.

Lanston shuffles through the stack of paper and starts reading an article titled "Six Missing from Local Mental Hospital."

I've asked myself why and how the three of us have become some hodgepodge, mentally ill trio of detectives, but you know what? What the fuck else are we going to do in a sanctum where a mystery lies unsolved? Toss pills into each other's mouths?

Yep. Exactly.

"That's them. Their names are on the bottom of the page," Liam murmurs. The cafeteria is loud, so we're not worried about anyone overhearing us at our isolated table.

"And you've never thought to search the grounds yourself?" I sigh as I grab one of the cherries from my plate.

Liam pops one in his mouth too and mumbles between bites, "No—of course not. This was like a decade ago, Wynn. I'm not a cold-case detective or anything, but I think it's cute that you pretend to be." He smiles at me. My cheeks heat, but I manage to keep a straight face. Lanston laughs and nods his agreement.

Okay, I guess I was the only one who thought the three of us were of the same mind on the detective hodgepodge thing.

"I'm not pretending to be anything." I glare at them both before clicking the button on my tablet and the screen shuts off.

Liam raises a brow but quickly smooths his features again and sets his hand on my thigh. "Have you looked into *us* yet, Miss Detective?" His eyes are dark and serious, searching mine to see if I'll lie.

"Of course not. Should I?" I click my tablet back on and pull up the search engine. He leans in close, his chest brushing against my shoulder and his lips warm on my neck. Chills course through my veins as he weaves my hair through his fingers and whispers:

"You won't like what you find."

I pause, instinctively tilting my head to the side as he presses a kiss to my neck.

"Why's that?" I murmur, half desperately wishing to know and half not daring to imagine his past. My past isn't anything I want him to look into. He'd only find a broken family and a washed-up woman who's been through the wringer.

Broken. Like he is.

He taps on the search bar and types in his name.

Liam Waters

Lanston shifts his hat in discomfort and looks from me to Liam. "I don't think this is a good idea, Liam."

Liam ignores Lanston and hits *Go*. "Because my story is a sad one."

The search pulls up many articles with Liam's picture in them. He's young, possibly seventeen or younger at the time. In the photos, his eyes are empty. Distant and hollow. The headline of one article reads:

Car Accident Kills Teen Driver, Passengers in Hospital

My breath catches in my lungs. I want to say something, anything, but I remain silent. Lanston looks away, his lips pressed in a thin line. *He already knows.*

"My brother Neil was taking a turn when I tried to show him something stupid on my phone. I don't even remember what it was—it was so stupid." Liam's voice cracks. He sits back in his chair and looks at me with dull eyes. "You remind me of him. He had the same cancerous sadness that you carry in your eyes."

I put my hand on his lap and squeeze, hoping that this small motion can communicate the words I cannot find. Even though we've been callous to one another, I hope he feels my sentiment at this moment.

"You blame yourself."

He nods.

"Is that when you started to hurt yourself?" I murmur.

His dark blue eyes find mine, hesitation and grief flickering through them. He nods once more. A somber, nostalgic smile tugs at his lips. This was the beginning of Liam's curse.

Lanston pulls him in for a tight hug and pats him on the shoulder before getting up to leave. Lanston has a harder time with tragic topics—even in group sessions, he excuses himself frequently.

We sit silently for a moment before I tap on the search bar and type in my name. Before I can hit search, Liam grabs my wrist and stops me.

"I don't want to know," he says plainly.

"Why not?"

"I don't want to know what made you want to die, Wynn."

He stands. The same distant look that was on his face in the photos consumes his expression now. Liam pushes his chair in and walks out of the cafeteria, leaving me confused, with hurt spreading through my chest.

Liam didn't talk to me for the rest of the day.

Sometimes he dissociates and seems like a different person altogether. It's easy to deal with because I do it too.

We sit in silence with his bedside lamp on the dimmest setting, the pattern of rain crashing against the bricks of Harlow being the only sound.

I move toward the open window and breathe in the crisp scent of rain. My sweater isn't enough to prevent the chill that falls over my bones. I can feel his eyes on me; my skin is uncomfortable beneath his gaze. He hasn't touched me since yesterday. The memory of his lips on my neck still stirs something carnal deep inside me.

The fabric of our souls is thin—we've been wandering this world just to unite in this small corner of the universe. Our connection is frightening and enchanting all at once. A shudder crawls down my spine as I recall the look I saw in his eyes through the window in the spa. Fire and ice—we are impossible together.

I want to know what it means. I want to know why we've crossed paths.

His breaths become heavy and slow, telling me he's already found rest. Who knows if he has another alarm set or not. He's quirky like that. Sometimes he gets up and leaves Harlow late at night. Other times he sleeps soundly for hours.

My bed creaks as I nestle in. I leave his lamp alone. A voice in the back of my mind tells me he occasionally leaves it on for a reason. We're all afraid of the dark at some point in our lives, but with Liam, it's when his mom texts him. When he spends the evenings staring off at the walls, deep in thought.

I stare at the ceiling for a few hours. Once my eyes start to shut, he groans as if he's in pain. My gaze shifts over to him. His brows are pulled in tight with torture, teeth bared in agony.

The thought of waking him crosses my mind, but I've had many bad experiences waking people from their nightmares. So I sit on the edge of his bed, gently brushing hair from his forehead, and listen as his whimpers slowly fade. Peace replaces his anguished expression and I fall a little deeper into the pit in my heart.

I memorize the raven-black locks of hair that fall over his pillow, the long lashes that kiss his cheeks, and his sculpted jawline. His tattoos are harder to look at now that I know how much they hide beneath their ink, but even those I find beautiful.

After a few minutes tick by, I move to head back to my own bed, but his hand finds my thigh. Liam's brows pinch ever so slightly and he squeezes me gently.

"Don't go."

"I didn't mean to wake you," I murmur, surprising myself with the softness in my voice. We don't do soft with each other.

I debate getting up anyway.

He shakes his head, keeping his eyes closed. "Please, stay."

I hesitate before sliding to lie down next to him. He wraps his arm around me and pulls me in tightly. His warmth and heavy oak scent instantly surround me and everything else in the world fades away.

It's just me and him.

Nothing else matters tonight.

"What were you dreaming about?" I ask, my lips brushing against his collarbone.

He pulls me closer, holding me like I've always wished someone would.

"Nothing."

Chapter 16
Liam

Guilt tugs in my chest all afternoon.

Wynn cried again this morning during the music session, and while that's good from a therapy standpoint, it still hurts to see. I thought if she heard me play again, it'd make her happy—I thought it would inspire her to play too.

Maybe I should stop playing. It's not like I even enjoy it anymore. It's just a cold reminder of the life I used to have. Of before.

I hardly remember what it was like on the outside of these walls. It's been, what...two years now? Time jumbles together here. All I know is I'm far more content in the walls of Harlow than I ever was on the outside.

My time in the army haunts me. I watched all my short-term friends die until I learned to stop connecting with others. It's easier that way. It always has been. The pain I felt watching them bleed and cry, begging for their mothers and for me to help them, is a feeling I've lost over the years.

The punishment I self-inflict has remained the same, if not worsened.

If I could go back in time, I'd tell my seventeen-year-old self that the car accident with my brothers was just the first tragic scene of my unfortunate play. I'd tell him that it gets much worse before he ends up in an institution.

Before he finds *her*.

I look at Wynn.

Lanston laughs at something she says but I only hear their muffled sounds. I glance down at my hands.

That itch pulls beneath my skin, the desire to feel pain, to hurt myself. I want to hurt as much as she and Lanston do; I want to feel the pain they experience. I want to punish myself for not being a better man...for not being good enough.

For being so mean to her...My thoughts muddle as the warmth in my chest ignites like it did when she crawled into my bed and let me hold her.

I know it's wrong. I know they worry. But it makes the weight in my chest evaporate every time.

It's euphoric.

My thumb brushes over the edge of my room key. Dull things take longer to break skin, but the wounds they leave last longer. They fester worse and keep the edge away.

The last remnants of the garden are dying, the orange and yellow mums bend in the breeze, and the green vines that climb the stones of Harlow curl with slumber. I shut my eyes and take a deep breath of the fresh air, telling myself I don't need to do this.

I don't need to hurt myself.

That's why I'm here; I *have* to get better.

The key lifts from my hand and warmth replaces it. My eyes open in surprise as I look down at Wynn. Her beautiful pale-pink hair shifts with the wind's grace and her honey-brown eyes scorch me. Her lips turn up as she grasps my hand tighter; the smile fills her soul completely and...I think my heart stops.

She doesn't want to die—I can see the tendrils of hope in her eyes.

When did they appear?

It's only been a few weeks and she's already healing. What's wrong with me? She and Lanston are pulling ahead and leaving me in their wake.

"I have a session with Dr. Prestin. See you guys later." Lanston heads back inside, leaving me and Wynn sitting silently.

"Do you get upset when I play?" I ask.

"What?"

"When I play the piano. Does it upset you?"

Wynn raises a brow as she grins. "No...It's actually really nice to listen to." Her tone is genuine and her eyes glint with curiosity. "Is that why you've been gloomy all afternoon?"

I shrug. "I didn't mean to make you sad earlier—you cry every single time I play."

Her eyes widen and before I can say anything else, she pulls me into a tight hug, my face pressed into her soft sweater as she wraps her arms around me.

It robs all the breath from my lungs. She's embracing me so delicately, and for the first time, I feel as broken as I perceived her to be.

No one's ever hugged me so desperately with their entire heart.

"You didn't make me sad, Liam...You opened up old wounds. I felt the music coming from your soul, and I felt the pain and sorrow that I've locked away for such a long time. I'm happy that I cried—and that it was you who broke my walls down enough to do so."

My arms instinctively coil around her small body. I try to ignore the trembling in my hands, but I'm sure she feels it.

"I'd like to hear you play someday," I murmur as I inhale her intoxicating lilac scent.

She pulls away and a somber smile crosses her lips. "I'd like that too."

We stare at one another in silence for a moment. The damp fall air makes me want to wrap her up in a blanket and read all day. Or research the missing people she's so interested in.

"Coldfox, Waters—get inside. Forecast says heavy rain soon." Jericho holds the garden door open as we walk past him. He inspects us with a little too much interest. "Happy to see you two are getting along so well."

I rub my onyx forefinger ring with my thumb, a nervous tic I have. "Well, yeah, we're roommates." I try to guide the conversation in a different direction. "Are we still going to the Fall Festival next weekend?"

"Yes, I actually finished up the paperwork this morning. I'll have the schedule soon with the odd jobs they need help with." Jericho waves dismissively as he continues on without us to his office down the hall. His dark suit is pressed and professional. I wonder if a guy like him ever cuts loose.

We stop by our room on our way to the common area; Wynn grabs her blue fluffy blanket and her notebook. The common area is much like a hotel lobby, filled with furniture and tables, a little coffee bar for the addicts. And what great foyer doesn't have an outrageously large fireplace? The stones are tan and cream, the fire roaring all hours of the day and night.

Keeping ghosts out, maybe.

We say hi to Mrs. Abett, the front desk lady, and she nods at us. Cold old woman, that one. She's the one staff member who rubs me the wrong way. Maybe she could use some therapy too.

The fire warms my cold skin. Wynn settles on the couch closest to the mantel, cozying up in her blanket as I sit next to her. I'm one hundred percent certain the air between us has changed. The way she stares longingly at me—it's undeniable. I think about last night and how she came to my bedside to calm me from my nightmares. How we fucked in the spa room, so much more than hate-fucking. The fear in her eyes told me everything I needed to know about her feelings toward me.

My thoughts drift to our *personal sessions*. Her breasts were so warm and soft. The taste of her soaking wet pussy still sweetens my dreams at night.

I open my arms, my black hoodie pulling up and showing my stomach a bit. I don't miss her eyes dipping down and heat filling her gaze.

"Come here, Wynn."

She watches me for a moment. I'm about to lean up and snatch her when she smiles and crawls over. Her lilac aroma fills the space around me. I'm in my own heaven with her this close. She snuggles up to me like she did last night.

Just me and her. It's not often we get time away from Lanston. I wonder if she's told him about what we do after dark. We've been keeping things strictly business and pleasure, but I'm curious if she wants more like I do.

Wynn pulls the blanket around us and I wrap my arms around her, our bodies instantly warming and that comfort I've yearned for all day consumes me. Her breaths are as short and uneven as my own.

The blood flows to my dick and it's a feat in itself that she doesn't make any sort of comment because there's no way she doesn't feel the press of my swollen cock along her lower back.

She opens her notebook and flips to the section on the missing patients. I dip my head forward and press my lips to her neck, brushing a kiss on her perfect olive skin. It's surprising that someone like me could find a familiar soul, one that I am finding it harder by the day to exist without. I've kissed her body countless times and I'll do it countless more. The way she tilts her neck so I can nuzzle in closer makes my dick throb uncomfortably in my sweatpants.

"What was Charlie doing in the basement?" she asks.

How on God's green earth does she expect me to know? I've read the same articles that she has. There's no answer to why that patient was in the basement as often as he was. The reporter thoroughly interviewed many of the staff; one woman in particular mentioned that she always found him down there, acting odd and afraid.

"No clue. I thought it was weird too though."

She shifts in my hold and smiles. "We should go look. What if he was hiding something down there? Or maybe the killer was?"

Sure, she has a point, but this was ten years ago. Is she suggesting that *we* investigate this? I school my amused expression. "Detective Coldfox, I don't think it's for us to find. Can't we simply enjoy this rainy day for what it is?"

She slumps back into my embrace and laughs a few times. "For a little bit, then promise you'll help me check out the basement?"

An uneasy sensation prickles at the back of my neck, thinking of the basement. But my answer is steady and sure.

"How could I ever resist helping you?"

★

All right, I made a promise, so here I am.

But what I did not agree to was inspecting the basement at fucking two a.m. Lanston was really on the fence about coming down here too, but I've watched enough horror films to know that three people are less likely to get ax murdered or possessed by ghosts than two.

Wynn is basically coming out of her skin with excitement, not an ounce of fear in those damning eyes of hers.

Goosebumps crawl up my arms as I look down the cold cement stairs that lead beneath the earth. Who doesn't hate basements? I firmly believe that my fear is rational. Lanston's might be irrational, based on how he's begging Wynn not to go down there.

She laughs, the sound of it tugging at my heartstrings as she walks down the steps easily. She waits for us at the bottom with her brow raised. "Don't tell me you two are *scared*."

I can't even pretend to be tough, and Lanston's way past pretending.

"Look, everyone's afraid of *something*." I steel my spine and start walking down toward her. "I'm like everyone else in the world who knows better than to do this at night. Haven't you watched horror films? This is how the movie starts—we're the dumbasses who die in the intro scene. We literally wouldn't even be the main characters, that's how stupid this is." I give the old wooden door a once-over and frown.

Lanston nods. "Yeah, this is giving me really bad vibes, Wynn. Maybe we should head back up."

The wood has water damage and an odd dusty smell. Stale air emanates from it. I'm about to grab her arm and force her back to our room, but she takes out a key ring and smirks slyly at me.

Little minx.

"Snatched these from Jericho earlier," she mutters, trying a few before one *clicks* and the door opens.

"Noted, you're a thief too," I grumble as the three of us step through the doorway.

Chapter 17
Wynn

Men.

They sure act tough, but the second they catch a cold or have to investigate a sinister dark basement for missing people, the charade is over—the cards are on the table.

Liam's brows couldn't be pulled closer together if he tried and Lanston looks like he's about to have a fucking heart attack. Fear dances in their eyes and I find it more amusing than I should. They look like they are in physical pain from being down here.

"Do you even know what we're looking for?" Lanston rubs his arms as the chill from the cement walls ebbs into us.

I pull out the note I made today.

What was Charlie doing in the basement? He acted weird for a few days before the three friends disappeared. Staff caught him sneaking out of his room one night.

"Honestly, we don't have much to go on. I just want to make sure there's nothing down here." I know the police searched down here a decade ago, but if I know one thing from murder TV shows, it's that the predator always returns to the site. I stuff the note back in my pocket and use my phone's flashlight to look around. Liam steps closer to me, his chest pressing against my back and sending heat through me.

Our cuddle session on the couch earlier still lives rent-free in my mind.

"Well, let's hurry up and get back so Jericho doesn't notice we're gone again," Liam murmurs, lifting his own phone flashlight toward the closest corner of the basement. "It's huge down here."

I was expecting to find a cellar or something, but it's enormous and oddly empty down here. Unlike my mom's basement, which was stuffed with all our memories, this is just a cold and unused space.

"Where's all the stuff?" Lanston grabs my hand reassuringly—I think more for himself, but I still grin.

Liam shudders. "I think it's worse that there isn't anything down here. Let's hurry up." He nudges me forward. His eyes flick down to Lanston's hand secured around mine and he grimaces.

We walk the length of the basement and turn a few corners where the walls follow the structure of the main building above. When we round the last corner, our flash-lights hit a damp cardboard structure. My blood chills at the sight. It looks like an old fort of some sort.

Lanston gasps and pulls back on my hand. "Okay, we're leaving right fucking now." He turns and tries to pull me with him.

I tug my arm back and shake my head. "I'll be quick," I say as I firm my trembling hands at my sides. His eyes widen, but he stiffens his posture and comes with me anyway.

Liam curses under his breath and follows. "Wynn, I think we need to call it. Let's head back up."

I ignore him as I inspect the boxes.

As best I can without touching anything, I dip my head and phone into the fort. A nest of blankets and pillows is inside, dust long covering it, but this definitely used to be someone's home. Was Charlie sneaking down here to meet whoever this was? Or is this Charlie's fort? It doesn't look ten years old...it's fresher than that.

"Well, what do you see?" Liam tugs on my sleeve.

"It looks like someone was living here not long ago." Before I back out, my eyes catch on something beneath the corner of the blanket. It's the only thing in here without a layer of dust over it. I carefully pluck it out of the fort to inspect it beneath Liam's flashlight beam.

"What's that?" Lanston asks as the three of us huddle over it.

"A photo, I think." It's crumpled and fragile, so I'm careful when I unfold the edges. It's a photo of four people. I flip it over and find names written lousily on the back.

Monica, Beverly, Charlie, Crosby.

Crosby.

The name on Liam's laundry hamper, the roommate he refuses to talk about.

I flip it back to the faces, all smiling and aloof, Harlow Sanctum at their backs in the distance.

"*Crosby*?" I mumble as my attention shifts up to Liam. Lanston does the same, his mouth parted slightly like he's stopping himself from saying something.

Liam's eyes are wide, filled with horror and undiluted fear.

"Are you okay?" Goosebumps crawl up my arms at his tangible distress.

He seems to be in a trance of sorts for a few moments before he snaps back to reality, ripping the photo from my hand and throwing it back into the fort. His cold hand grips my wrist and then he's pulling me out of the basement in a hurry. Lanston silently takes up the rear, frequently glancing behind us like someone may be watching.

"What's wrong?" I ask breathlessly, panic already making my heart race. My stomach is in knots and my mind whirls with infinite questions, but one in particular. "Who the fuck is Crosby?"

I stare, worry tugging at my brows as Liam pokes his hash-browns with his plastic fork. They don't allow us metal ones here for obvious reasons. It's fair enough.

He didn't say a word for the rest of the night. My gut says Crosby is someone so malevolent that even Liam fears him. Whoever he is, he has Lanston scared too. He slept in our room last night. Liam wasn't opposed to sharing his bed with our friend; he seemed more comforted by it than anything.

The absolute terror in his eyes last night made me sick. He left his lamp on and crawled into my bed at some point in the night. I woke with him trembling around me and sweat beading his forehead.

Crosby knew the missing people. He came back eventually, obviously—he was Liam's roommate before me. So who the fuck is he? What aren't they telling me?

I hardly slept last night, wondering, thinking, dreading the thought of the monster that slept in my bed just a month ago.

If Liam won't tell me who Crosby is, Lanston will, even if I have to force it out of him. I scoop a bite of waffles drizzled in syrup into my mouth as I eye Lanston from across the table. He notices and takes a hesitant gulp of his coffee.

He knows we can't just ignore what we found there.

We have morning yoga in the courtyard together today, so I'll have to corner him and wring the information out of him.

Lanston waits for me to finish up my breakfast so we can walk to our session together. Things have been weird between the three of us this morning. No one wants to break the silence.

Even so, Lanston gives me a warm smile. It's nice to have the friendly smile of someone as depressed as I am.

Unlike Liam, Lanston is the mirror image of me. We like all the same things and we both want to die. I wish he was around when I was in high school; we would've been best friends. Possibly even more. He's handsome and thoughtful, someone I could talk to for hours and never feel out of place with.

"Please don't tell me you're going to interrogate me." Lanston wraps his arm around me. He's tall enough that it rests perfectly across my shoulders. His pale-blue baseball cap is tipped up a bit and his soft brown hair kisses his forehead. The real killers are those beautiful hazel eyes of his.

I smile and shrug. "You know *something*."

"How can you be so sure?" He pulls me in tighter and I can't help but blush. His chest is warm and my hands instinctively wrap around him too. I can't tell if he's flirting with me or just being friendly, but I'm not sure it matters.

Liam stares blankly at us from across the cafeteria and stands, walking back toward the dorm wing. When my eyes meet Lanston's, I know he saw his friend's empty eyes too. Pain and worry twist his lips with secrets he hasn't told me.

We walk through the main foyer and out the back exit to the courtyard. The stones are dreary with age. Thankfully it's dry since the rain finally stopped this morning. We have to use extra yoga mats to keep from getting wet. It's not a huge inconvenience laying them out, but picking them up afterward is another story.

We each grab two mats and find a spot in the back of the class. The instructor is pretty chill. He knows we're all a little *off,* so he never cares if we chat or even sleep during the sessions. "The point is to find your peace," he says every single morning as if we'll forget overnight.

If only I could find my peace.

Lanston sits down on his mat and stretches out on his back. I start by reaching for my toes and leaning forward until I feel the pressure in my thighs.

"Are you going to tell me?"

He raises a brow but keeps his eyes closed as the sun warms his gorgeous tan cheeks. "Tell you what?"

My jaw clenches. Why is he dancing around this, avoiding it like the plague? I can only assume that Liam's made him swear not to tell. But they can't keep me in the dark like this.

"Well... Liam refuses to talk about it." I shift to lie on my stomach. Lanston opens an eye with interest as he waits for me to get to the point. "Who is Crosby?"

"Not here, Wynn." His hazel eyes are stern. I open my mouth to protest, but he cuts me off. "I said not here," he snaps, his tone sharp and deep.

My heart thumps erratically in my chest and my breath catches in my throat. "W-why?" *What the fuck did this Crosby guy do?*

Lanston's forehead beads with sweat. His discomfort is contagious.

I harden my expression and lean in to whisper, "I need to know... You guys are scaring me."

He glances around us to make sure no one's looking our way. "Meet me in the greenhouse after dinner tomorrow night. We'll talk about it then...and *don't* tell Liam." He seems upset and after staring at me like I'm some tragedy, he stands and picks up his yoga mats.

I watch Lanston walk up to Mr. Bartley, telling him something and handing in his mats before walking back to the manor.

The instructor raises a brow at me like I have answers, so I shrug and lie back on my foam mat, trying to salvage what's left of my morning class.

I can't shake the thought that Crosby is a dangerous person, someone that people here don't want to speak about. I wonder if Yelina knows him too. She certainly seems to know about the missing people from a decade ago.

One thing is certain—I won't be finding any peace this morning.

Chapter 18
Wynn

A soft chime wakes me—Liam's phone alarm.

He presses it quietly before sitting up in his bed. I squint my eyes so he won't notice I'm awake.

He runs his hand down his face, looking so fucking tired. I'm tempted to ask what he's doing but he stands and pulls a hoodie on, then his shoes, before he steps out of the room.

It's just like my first night here.

The grotesque image of him walking in with mud and blood coating his shoes resurfaces in my mind and sends a shudder down my spine.

I'm not letting him hurt himself again.

I slip out of my bed and pull my hoodie on. There's no time to find my tennis shoes, so I settle for my slippers.

The door creaks a little as I crack it open to peek out. The hall is dark and eerie. The exit sign at the end glows a sinister red.

I quietly slip out of our room and prop the door open with one of Liam's shower flip-flops I find lying near the entrance. I take off down the hall in a hurry. I have to admit, I'm still surprised that they don't lock us in our rooms at night.

I know James said this isn't a psychiatric hospital and it's *unorthodox,* but still, what kind of rehab just lets people do what they want at all hours of the night?

I suppose the same one that lets the patients fuck in the showers and spa room.

As I turn the corner, I catch a glimpse of Liam's sweatshirt as the exterior door shuts behind him. He went through the side door, probably because a night guard stands at the main entrance, though I can't imagine him stopping anyone from doing as they please.

The cold night air drifts over my exposed ankles as I push the door open. Everything in my being says that I should turn around and return to bed, but I know that I won't be able to sleep knowing he could be hurting himself again.

He walks casually through the back fields and onward to the forest of maples behind the manor. Once he's out of sight, I slink through the field after him. The grass is wet from all the rain we got today, but at least it's not drizzling anymore. The air is crisp and bites at my skin. Leaves crunch beneath my feet.

I stop at the edge of the forest and glance back at the manor. The moon brims over some dark clouds, illuminating the building in pale, iridescent light. The red hue of the vines that climb the walls makes it look like a haunted mansion, sleeping in the dead of night and waiting for some fool to wander in.

A branch snaps and my head swings back toward the forest.

Liam's standing in front of me with his arms crossed and a sleepy grin on his face. His dark hair is tousled, a few strands falling beautifully over his forehead. The dark circles beneath his eyes give away his restlessness, and the thought of him being as tortured inside as me breaks my heart.

"You're trouble. You know that?"

My brows pull together in apology. "Well, I wasn't planning on getting caught."

He chuckles and a sense of calm falls over me. The corner of my lips pulls up with his alluring voice.

Liam extends his hand to me and jerks his head toward the forest. "Let's go then."

My eyes round as the moonlight illuminates his warm gaze. He's like a perfect fairytale character. The kind of man that doesn't exist—yet here he is, in a rehab for his mental illness. Stuck with me as his roommate.

I take his hand, the warmth quickly banishing the cold night air.

This is unlike him. He's been unrelentingly kind lately.

"Where are we going?" I ask on a breath.

He tugs my hand and we walk into the forest of maples and pines, the last drops of rain dripping sporadically around us. A few tap on my head and I become conscious of how wet my slippers are. They're destroyed at this point. I may as well have gone barefoot.

"You'll see," Liam mumbles. It's darker under the canopy of the trees, but I can hear the smile in his tone. Is he happy that I followed him out here?

We walk in silence until we reach a clearing. I'm not sure how he knows where he's going in the woods at night, but here we are. Dark grass sways in the evening breeze. The moon is covered by clouds, but one look tells me that the wind will soon push them out of the way. The scent of wet, fallen leaves and fresh rain envelops me.

"It's just a field," I murmur with confusion. Why come here at four a.m.?

Liam bends down and points as he says with a somber voice, "Look again, sunshine."

That name rolls off his tongue so perfectly I can't even pretend to be annoyed about it. My eyes return to the field, and just as they do, the moonlight showers down as if the pale light is liquid. A thousand little white blooms illuminate at once, returning the light back to the sky and the world around them.

My heart stills in my chest, a quiet, somber little thing in these wee hours of the night, desperately clinging to hope that the daylight steals away from me.

"Moonflowers," Liam says with admiration. They mean something to him, and as much as he seems happy to gaze down on them, there's melancholy imbued in his eyes.

"You didn't need to show me this." I feel bad. It really seems like something private. "I'm sorry for following you out here. I didn't want to see you hurt again."

Liam shrugs. A breeze shifts his hair to the left, and sorrow gleams in his eyes as he stares at the flowers. "It was never my own to share. Those before us...they made this place."

Those before us.

"What happened to them?" I murmur, unsure if I should be asking. "Those before...did they get better and leave? Did they find the remedy for their minds?" I bend down and let my fingers trail the edge of the beautiful moonlit petals. They're soft and still hold drops of blissful water from the rain.

"I hope they found their cures—I'd like to think that they got better," he says as he moves to stand beside me. "Anyway, I stumbled across this place a few months ago. No one was taking care of it, so I figured those who did have long since moved on from Harlow Sanctum. Their absence from this place haunts me, yet at the same time gives me hope. Their rings are a symbol of perseverance."

He turns and looks at me with weary eyes. I feel that soul-draining ebb, that exhausting pull, the never-ending search we seem to share for that silly little thing called hope.

To find our *cure*.

"Their rings?" I mumble in a daze.

Liam nods and plucks one of the moonflowers, placing it in my hand. "You asked me about the ring I left you at the hospital," he mutters sincerely. I figured he didn't hear me at the time because he was staring at my breasts and never replied.

I nod.

"I found three of them. I kept one, Lanston has the other, and then I decided you should have the last."

My chest tightens at his admission, the moonflower warming in my palm as my heart beats faster.

"Why *me*?"

His eyes narrow with longing as he guides his forefinger up my wrist. A small wave of pain spreads across my forearm and he winces at the way I flinch. "You have this air about you. It calls to me like a beacon. The nurses spoke of how much pity they felt for the patient in room forty-seven, being so young and beautiful, but cursed with a horribly unwell mind."

I clench my teeth. Everyone pities me, everyone except—

"I knew then I had to see you for myself. To see if you were indeed pitiful, though I had a feeling you wouldn't be." His blue eyes caress my face as if I'm a lost treasure he's been searching the ends of the earth for. "No—I knew the moment I saw you. *You* were not to be pitied. Your mind is a beautiful and dangerous thing, Wynn, sick as it may be. But your soul illuminates the world around you, setting all else ablaze with your inevitable anguish."

My clenched fist smothers the moonflower. My heart is both sinking and racing at the same time.

"I saw a young woman. A confused little flower trying to bloom in the daylight when you were always meant to thrive beneath the stars, unlike those around you. You've wilted enough for the world. Don't you think?" Liam's smile and question fill every part of my weary soul. "It's time to let go of the things that hurt."

He extends his hand to me once more. I slip the flower I inadvertently crushed into my pocket before taking his hand. He warms my cold skin as he guides me to the center of the flowering field.

"Will you dance with me, Wynn?"

In my drenched, cold slippers, my oversized hoodie, and messy bed hair, I smile at him—really, *truly* smile at him.

"Promise you're not a vampire or werewolf?" I say as he pulls me closer to his chest.

His grin pulls up sarcastically. "And if I am?" He chuckles. Then his eyes turn serious. "I've been searching for that lost smile."

I laugh as he wraps an arm around my waist and starts to twirl us through the field. It doesn't take long to lose one of my slippers, but I don't care. I don't stop.

"Liam, thank you for being so weird."

He laughs. "Is that a compli—"

"Coldfox! Waters!"

We come to an abrupt stop, our feet inches from one another as our heads snap toward the staff member calling our names. It's too far to distinguish if it's Jericho or not, but their flashlight tells us exactly where they are.

Liam takes my hand. "Run!" He laughs as we take to the darkness of the forest again. Nothing but the sounds of our feet crushing leaves and our heavy breaths fill the air.

"Where's your slipper?" Liam's eyes are trained on my one shoeless foot, laughing wildly at the way I'm running without it.

Fresh air and boisterous energy wash through me. "I lost a slipper during our dance." I laugh between breaths. My cheeks hurt from the inability to lower my smile.

He shakes his head but keeps his grin, stopping us in the field that circles Harlow Sanctum and scooping me up into his arms like I'm weightless.

"What am I to do with you?" He wraps his arms around me tightly. I inhale his scent and hold on for dear life as he jogs the rest of the way to Harlow with me in his arms.

Jericho doesn't look happy—not at all.

His frown is long and tired; he looks like he's been up chasing two ghosts all night.

"Liam, you know better than anyone we *highly* advise against nightly excursions. Especially on weekdays." The counselor taps his finger on the table.

"We were in the bathroom. I don't know what *excursions* you're talking about." Liam shrugs, that damning smirk playing on his lips.

Jericho narrows his eyes as they shift from me to Liam and back to me. "I don't believe that for a second."

Liam nudges me with his foot and I straighten in my chair and add: "We had the same fruit at dinner. It made us sick all night." I wince as if my stomach is still hurting.

The counselor is silent as he considers us. Each minute is as painfully awkward as the last.

"Fine—you're both lucky this is an expensive self-check-in facility."

Liam crosses his arms, seeming a bit annoyed about all the fuss. "How'd you even know we weren't in our room? It's not like you check on us, and we aren't on lockdown, so what's the deal?"

My eyes widen—*shit,* the flip-flop I stuck in the door so I could go back in. I want to drop my head to the table but I remain sitting straight, biting my lower lip as I wait for Jericho to say it.

His green eyes flick over to me passively and he seems to catch on to my worry. "Just happened to see two people sneaking out and figured it was you. Your nightly outings aren't uncommon, but that doesn't mean you need to start dragging Miss Coldfox along with you."

I silently exhale and thank Jericho with my eyes. He's a good person. He probably already knows about the moonflower field and how patients sneak out to go there. I wonder how long he's worked here...Maybe he knew them.

Those before us.

Chapter 19
Wynn

Liam doesn't play the piano as softly today. His timing is off and he presses the keys with too much emotion. It drowns out the light notes and emphasizes the more aggressive ones.

My heart sinks.

I shouldn't have made him come with me in the basement. What we found really fucked with him. It's been two days now and he still seems far away, somewhere distant in his mind. We shouldn't be looking into the past. Maybe it'd be better for all of us if I just let it go and forget about it.

Jericho taps his clipboard like he notices the shift in Liam today too, but he ignores it as he calls my name next. "Coldfox, you're up."

I stand and pass Liam. He doesn't look at me. His eyes are sunken and dark, as if he didn't sleep a wink after we got back to our room.

Sitting on the wooden bench, I take a deep breath, feeling a song I thought I'd long forgotten the tune to rising in my soul.

He played for me when I was at my lowest. I'm unsure if this will pull him from the darkness he's found himself in, but I have to try.

I straighten my posture and lift my fingers to the cold white keys.

"For the Damaged Coda" by Blonde Redhead.

This is a piece I know by heart. I close my eyes and let my hands play with the memories of my horrible past. Pain is what inevitably brings this song to life...because no great piece of art is made without a little suffering backing it.

Will I reach him?

I dare a glance over and he's staring at me with surprise. I wonder if he knows this song too. Or perhaps he's just stunned that I'm actually playing after sitting here and refusing to for the last three weeks.

The melody comes easy to my muscle memory, even though it's been years since I've played. My hands remember and my heart knows the keys.

When I shut my eyes once more, I'm met with my mother's angry face, her undiluted hatred for me glaring right into my soul. The scowl she wears wrinkles her nose in disgust and bores deep into my bones, instilling fear in my veins. The bruises she left on me never heal in my mind. Never.

Not good enough.

Never good enough.

I stop playing mid-song, dropping my hands into my lap and standing abruptly, dismissing the rest because I don't feel like reliving some of the worst segments of my life.

It hurts too much. It's easier to leave the bones in the grave undisturbed.

Jericho calls up the next person without meeting my eyes. As I step past him, he mutters, "Good job today, Coldfox. This is great progress."

I manage a small smile at him before plopping into my seat. Liam looks over at me. The distant fear in his eyes has faded and in its place is awe.

"That was beautiful, Wynn."

My shoulders slump. It *was* beautiful, but not on the inside. The music is lovely, but the havoc of playing corrupts my mind like poison snaking into what's left of my shell.

I shrug.

He grips my chin and forces me to meet his gaze, and reluctantly, I do.

"Can you teach me to play that song?"

I raise a brow but I'm desperate to know: "Why?"

His blue eyes sear into me like the coldest rain. "Because it looked so painful, and I want to take that pain from you. We can make better memories for you to play to, don't you think?"

A smile curls my lips and I nod. "I'd really like that."

"It's a date then." He wraps his arm around my chair, and as he does, I see red bandages beneath his shirt.

The sight of his blood makes me nauseous. When did he do this? He was doing better...At least, I thought he was.

But I guess he probably wonders why I want to die, and I bet it makes him sad too.

Maybe we *can* cure one another.

Wouldn't that be something . . .

Liam smiles sadly at me as he whispers, "It's just a small cut, Wynn. Don't look so upset. I tried not to...but I—"

I grin cruelly back at him because how dare he say something so dismissive about his illness to me. "I just want to *die*, Liam. Don't look so glum."

He barks out a laugh—maybe because it isn't funny at all.

"That's fair. But if you don't exist, who will cure me?" His brow raises with interest. His dark eyes on me make my skin feel tight. He's so beautiful it hurts, so broken it's disastrous.

I want him to always look at me this way. With warmth and need—like I truly am his cure.

Jericho shoots us a disapproving glance and shushes us as the next person in our session takes a seat at the piano.

I cross my arms, rubbing the onyx ring between my fingers as I try to avoid looking at Liam. I close my eyes, trying to mentally prepare to meet Lanston tonight.

The onyx rings tie us together. Liam, Lanston, and me. I can't help but wonder who they belonged to prior. Was one Monica's? Why did they leave them out there in the field? Which ring do I have?

I'm not sure we'll ever know. Sometimes it's fun to wonder.

As our session ends, Jericho taps on his clipboard to get our attention before we all disperse. It feels like I'm in college all over again, and as nostalgic as it is, I don't miss it at all. This place is much, much better. I'm not stressing myself into a heart attack over some stupid exam.

"All right, everyone, please remember that we're heading to town on Friday next week for the Fall Festival. A little festive fun can be enlightening and inspiring. It's going to be cold, so dress warm, and I know we're all adults here, but we insist you buddy up because...well—"

"Because we're not of sound mind," Poppie remarks with a snide grin.

Jericho scowls at her but nods. "Yes...For your overall safety, anyway. Have a nice weekend, everyone. I'll see you Monday morning, bright and early."

Liam rolls his eyes at the counselor, and then his attention finds me. "Be my *buddy*?"

I shrug and walk past him so he won't see the excitement blooming across my cheeks. "Who else would be?" I laugh. He follows after me and slows down once he catches up to my side. "Please tell me we have something planned for the weekend other than scary stories in Lanston's room."

Liam grins for the first time today and I'm glad to see it, though he frequently glances warily over his shoulders as if he'll see Crosby looming in the hallway.

"Lanston wants to get tattoos this weekend. Care to join us?"

I raise a brow. "Really? What's he getting? I'm surprised he didn't mention it to me." I guess there are still things we don't share between the three of us.

"It's a surprise." He nudges me. "Just join us, you'll see."

"Okay. It will be nice to get out of this place for a bit." I look out the windows as we walk down the hall. It's only been three weeks, yet I feel like I no longer belong in the real world. I don't want to go back.

I think of James, how much he must be paying for me to stay in a place like this. I hope I'm not wasting his time and money. The only thing I want to do is get better, and with Lanston and Liam, I think I have.

I need to text James back; we message each other frequently, but I haven't gotten back to him today since his morning text.

Which reminds me: "How much does this program cost?"

Liam's eyes widen and he looks down at me like I'm pulling his leg. "You seriously don't know?"

I stare at him blankly.

"Shit. Well, per month, it's around six thousand dollars, depending on the severity of the patient's condition."

My legs stop working and I come to a halt in front of our door. I stare at Liam and he stares right back at me like he's unsure what he's supposed to say. "I'm sorry, I thought you said *six thousand*." I shake my head and laugh.

His frown grows and so does mine as reality comes bearing down on me.

"I did."

No fucking way.

Nope, I'm packing right now.

How could James afford this? Why would he think I'd let him pay for this? Guilt swarms me and panic sets in. I need to pack my things and check out—three weeks, it's been three goddamn weeks and that's already over five thousand dollars.

"*Wynn*, what are you doing?"

"I can't stay. My brother is paying for all this and I can't do that to him," I mutter absent-mindedly as I empty my nightstand drawer into my bag. "He's all I have left and I'm such a fucking burden to him. I didn't know it was that much...I should've asked him." Tears blur my vision as I thrust open the closet doors and start grabbing sweaters off the hangers.

Liam grabs my arm and when I try to tug away from him, he firms his grip.

"Let me go!" I scream, inches from his face, over-whelming emotions rampaging through me. My blood is on fire and my breaths are labored. I sob and jerk my arm repeatedly to get away from him. "Liam, let me go!"

He grits his teeth and pulls me close, securing my thrashing arms and holding me so tight I can hardly breathe.

"Wynn...you need to calm down. Please," he says in a soothing voice. But my inner demons are waging war, my heart beating too rapidly for me to hear reason.

I sink my teeth into his bicep but he still refuses to let me go.

"That hurts." He chuckles darkly as he lowers himself to the floor with me still wrapped in his arms. "That fucking hurts so much, sunshine. You know I love pain, but I don't think you'll like what you leave behind." His voice is hauntingly low and raspy.

My jaw trembles as my tears wet his sweater. A metallic sting touches my taste buds and I instantly release him, pulling my head back and looking up at his face with utter horror at what I've just done.

Liam's eyes are a sea of calm and understanding, reeling me back in from my mania and instilling a new fear within me.

I'm afraid of what I can do when I'm not myself, in the brief moments when too many horrible thoughts run through my mind. This is why I hate myself. Because I do awful things to people I care about.

My eyes shift to his arm, where I sank my teeth into his flesh. Blood seeps through his sweater and dizziness falls over me.

"It's *okay,* Wynn. Are you okay?" He lifts his hand and brushes my cheek softly, but I'm too focused on his arm. Why isn't he mad at me? I try to lift his sweater to see the wound; he needs to be treated immediately, he needs—

"Hey." Liam guides me to face him once more, my eyes meeting his. The look he gives me is both bewitching and heart-wrenching. "Are you okay?"

He stares into my soul, waiting for an answer. My eyes fill with fresh tears and I shake my head.

"No."

He cups both of my cheeks and pulls me in. His soft lips press against mine and with every beat of his heart, mine crumbles. His oak scent consumes me, and for a blissful moment, I'm not me anymore. I'm not the character I've hated my entire life.

I'm just a woman kissing a man.

Wynn kissing Liam.

Is it as simple as that?

Can it be?

Warm tears meet my lips and my eyes flutter open.

Liam's crying.

I pull back and try wiping his tears away, yet they still trickle down his cheeks. "Liam, are you—"

"I'm not okay either," he whispers, his voice trembling. "I've never been okay. But when I watch you fall apart, it hurts too much for me to bear. Please don't go to those dark places, Wynn. Please stay here in the dim light with me. You're my last hope—my cure." He lets his arms hang heavily at his sides as he sobs, his forehead resting on my shoulder. "Let me try to help you, *please.*"

I wind my arms around him and hug him like it will be my last.

"I'm so sorry. I never meant to hurt you...but I did." My fingers twine in his soft, dark hair. "I feel like such a burden on everyone. Even you—look what I did." My shoulders tremble as I sob with him.

A knock comes at the door and before either of us can move, it clicks open. Lanston steps in, his eyes landing on me immediately. "What's going on in here? I heard screaming." He pauses when he sees blood and both of our faces covered in tears.

A few other heads peer in through the doorway but Lanston kicks the door shut and locks it before kneeling beside us.

"Did he hurt you?" Lanston's hazel eyes search mine worriedly. Liam manages to glare at him but doesn't respond.

Why would he think that?

I shake my head. "No. I...I hurt him." My hands still tremble with the adrenaline rushing through my veins.

Liam stands, the air between us suddenly colder than it's been in weeks. "Everything's fine. Get out." He scowls at Lanston, holding his arm to cover the red that's spreading through the fabric.

Lanston looks at me once more and only stands to leave after I nod at him. "I'll see you later, okay?" I utter, remembering we're to meet tonight at the greenhouse.

"Yeah...See you later." His eyes are filled with worry, but he reluctantly leaves.

I lock the door to make sure no one else bursts in on us and sit next to Liam on his bed. He doesn't look at me—his eyes are weary and distant again. Instead of trying to talk, I open his drawer and grab his medical supplies.

He doesn't fight me when I carefully pull his shirt off. The bite isn't too deep, but it still broke his skin. Liam watches me in silence as I dab the wound with ointment and clean it before wrapping it with gauze and medical tape. Tears fall from my eyes as I work.

How could I do this? I'm just as awful as everyone says I am. Just as heartless and cold as I was raised to be. All I do is hurt people, no matter how hard I try not to. I can't exist on neutral ground. No one sees me as the person I sometimes dream I am.

THE FABRIC OF OUR SOULS

A nice girl.

A person worthy of love.

A soul that didn't crawl up from hell.

If I wasn't here anymore, it would all stop. The pain. The dread. All the things that hurt my stupid conscience...If I die, maybe I'll wake up somewhere better.

Or I'll just be dead.

And I'm okay with that too.

"Does that feel better?" I can't keep the guilt from my shaky voice.

He meets my eyes and nods.

I move to get up but he grabs my wrist. I don't turn to look at him. I remain facing my bed and looking at the mess I've made. I feel hollower inside than I've felt for weeks—since *that* night. That's how fast I can make the decision. That's how irrational and stupid I am.

I don't want to be here anymore. I don't want to be *me*.

"You're not going to leave, are you?"

My jaw tightens before I mutter, "What if I do?"

He slowly releases my wrist and I stand in place for a few minutes, neither of us saying a word, before picking my bag and sweaters off the floor.

Does he hate me again?

I know I do.

Chapter 20

Liam

Wynn texted her brother back before we left for dinner.

Something's wrong.

Once her eyes finally dried, a darker resolve settled in place of the tendrils of hope I saw days ago.

She stared blankly at her phone until he messaged her back. Whatever he responded with made her feel less guilty about the money. She doesn't have that fight-or-flight look in her eyes anymore, which makes me feel a little more at ease.

But the darkness, the hurt, *that* worries me.

Lanston and Yelina sit with us at dinner. I'm sure he's told her everything already by the way her eyes keep flicking over to my arm with worry.

I know Yelina is into me—she has been since the day I arrived—but I've never been one for romance, not until Wynn.

Our eyes meet and I try to give Wynn a reassuring grin, but it must fall short because her brows knit and sorrow ebbs into my soul from those beautiful brown eyes.

Lanston clears his throat and mutters, "So, Yelina is going to town tonight, Liam. You should go with her."

That gets my attention.

"I don't really want to go out tonight." I shift uneasily in my seat. Fucking asshole, he knows I try to avoid Yelina like the plague.

Yelina's smile falters, but she straightens back up. "Well, it's not like Wynn will be able to hang out with you tonight. She's spending the evening with him." Her thumb juts into Lanston's chest and he flinches.

My cheeks heat with jealousy.

Wynn looks at Yelina indifferently. "She's right, you should have fun." Her raspy voice hurts to hear.

The bite wound burns on my arm, reminding me that she hurt me before wrapping me up tenderly. I want to hold her. I want to tell her it's okay. I want to make her forget everything that happened today.

"*Fine*, I'll go with you, Yelina." I rest my elbow on the table and lean my chin on my palm. Wynn avoids meeting my eyes and Lanston frowns, worry pulling his brows low.

I can't believe he thought I'd hurt her...I'd never.

Yelina clasps her hands together and giggles, clearly unable to read the depressive mood of the table. "I'll go get ready now! Pick me up out front in twenty." Her blonde hair waves behind her as she hurries away toward the dorm wing of the manor.

I guess I should get dressed too so I don't look like a bum.

"I'll see you tonight," I say over my shoulder. I don't miss the dull ache I see in Wynn's eyes. *Lanston, make her smile, make her not want to die.* I grit my teeth and force myself to leave.

I zip up my black leather coat and wear my least distressed dark-blue jeans. My mind won't stop swarming with what Wynn and Lanston are going to do tonight. How is she feeling? Is she really okay? I don't know if he can help her the way I can.

She was made for *me*—not him.

I take the side stairwell to the underground garage and remotely start my car. It's been a while since I've taken a drive. Maybe this won't be so bad. Yelina isn't completely insufferable.

My white Camaro is spotless, still basically new and hardly used. A frown pulls the side of my lips as I get in and set my hands on the steering wheel. I used to tear out of back roads and race through highways late at night.

Back when I had friends.

Before I took to hurting myself.

Before my brother died.

Chills crawl up my spine and I have to suppress the urge to run back inside.

Yelina stands beneath the front canopy in a tight, marigold-yellow dress. Shit. I should've asked why she wanted to go to town because she's not dressed for grocery shopping or a bar.

Her green eyes warm on me as she slips inside and fastens her seatbelt. She smells like grandma perfume and dead things. *Ugh.*

"You look nice," she says smoothly.

"Thanks. You too. So, where are we going?" I say tightly, returning my eyes to the road.

Yelina slides a hand across my thigh and goosebumps crawl up my arms. "I was planning on going to that steakhouse they have at the edge of town."

My brows pull together. "Don't you need a reservation for that place?"

Her lips curl. "Yep."

"What if I didn't want to go with you tonight?"

She shrugs. "I would've found someone else to come with me. It's not like I can't find someone interested in

148

me. I have half the men in Harlow wrapped around my finger." She's like a fucking snake.

I give her a pointed look. "Yeah, because that's something to brag about," I snap. She scowls at me, returning her hand to her own lap, and remains silent as we drive down the long road leading away from the mansion.

The trees are going to lose all their leaves in the coming days. Halloween is right around the corner and the Fall Festival is next weekend. I wonder if Wynn likes things like pumpkins and hot chocolate, cozy blankets, and midnight moonlit dances. *Of course she does. She's an autumn soul.*

"Did Wynn really bite you?"

Pulled from my daydreams, I sigh. "Did Lanston tell you that?" Yelina nods and eyes my arm like she wants me to show her the wound. "Yeah, she did."

She glares out the window and crosses her arms. "You should've told on her. We can't have deranged people like her in our program... not after last time."

I clench my jaw and snap my head toward her. "Shut the fuck up, Yelina. I don't want to talk about it."

Her lip pouts out and she tries to move closer to me, touching my arm as if attempting to calm me down. I shake my arm but she only clings tighter.

"You have to talk about it, Liam. You haven't been the same since coming back from the hospital." She threads her arm through mine. Everything in my body is in overdrive. My heart's racing with the traumatic memories she won't leave in the grave and the car's going too fast.

My eyes dart down to the speedometer. *100 mph.* Fuck.

I slam the brakes and the tires screech as the vehicle comes to an abrupt stop. Yelina screams and grabs onto the door handle like she'll go flying through the windshield if she doesn't.

"What the fuck are you doing?!" she screams and unbuckles her seatbelt. She steps outside and slams the door so hard it startles me.

My hands are trembling on the steering wheel. I hit the gas. I need to get the fuck away from her. I need pain, to feel, and to think of anything else except *him*. Anything except that dull, dark look in Wynn's eyes that tells me she wants to die.

I peel away and gravel pelts Yelina. I watch in the rearview mirror as she stomps and throws her purse on the ground.

I don't fucking care. She can throw as big of a fit as she wants. I don't care.

Not about her.

The sun is setting and distant wildfires scorch the autumn sky with a bright-red fury. I want to be that angry. At anything. I want to be as alive as I felt when Wynn sank her teeth into my arm and I had so many emotions, I wasn't sure what I was even feeling.

I drive until I reach Bakersville. The lampposts glow orange and the community is already starting to set up festivities. The hay bales are topped with pumpkins and leaves. Cornstalks and scarecrows line the main street with numbers beneath them for the competition.

As I drive through, people look up and gawk at my car, at me. I just want to be invisible right now. I don't want anyone to see me. Is that so much to ask for? I try to duck as much as I can until I reach the outskirts of the town.

A few houses are out here, but other than that, it's pretty empty.

I follow the long, winding road up to the lookout and stop in the center of an empty parking lot.

My car idles as I stare out across the small town, filled with people who probably don't know Harlow Sanctum lies only a few miles outside its walls. I look out over the vast valley and try counting to ten like our counselors tell us to.

I try thinking of things that bring me relief other than cutting into myself.

But the pull is unbearable.

There's been a hunting knife locked in my glove box since last November. It belonged to my eldest brother, Neil. I spin the knife in my hands. The black steel is clean and sharp. Sweat beads my forehead as I tell myself over and over to not do this.

Will Wynn be upset with me?

A sharp knock comes at the passenger-side door. When I look up to see who the fuck is out here this late at night, my bones chill.

His smile is crooked and all too familiar. My scars burn and my breath catches in my lungs. His eyes are as blue as my own, but altered, evil.

I will never escape him.

Chapter 21

Wynn

Lanston is already waiting for me by the greenhouse by the time I walk down the stone path leading across the field. He leans against the glass doors, smoking a cigarette with his baseball cap pulled low like he's worried someone will see him out here.

"You're early."

The embers of his cigarette fall as he lifts his head. He smiles weakly. "So are you." He looks nervous as he drops his cigarette and stomps it out. "Come on, I don't want anyone seeing us out here," he whispers as he opens the greenhouse door and waves me through.

"Why are you acting so weird? Curfew isn't until ten." *And even then, no one abides by it.* I wrap my arms around myself and step in. The greenhouse is empty; apparently, no one believes in plant therapy here. It's a shame. It's such a lovely building with an abundance of potential.

Lanston grabs my hand and leads me to the back of the greenhouse. It's dim in here, so he has to use his phone's flashlight once we reach the back. A lone door is waiting for us.

"Lanston…where are you taking me?" I shift on my feet uneasily. We're a good few hundred feet away from the mansion and unless someone is outside, I don't think anyone would be able to hear either of us if something happened.

He looks at me with an annoyed expression that betrays no aggression or danger. "Somewhere you'll understand what I'm about to tell you."

I swallow the lump in my throat. Lanston is my friend—I trust him.

He opens the door and flips a light switch on. I follow him in and he shuts the door behind us.

My stomach drops.

The room is small, maybe intended to be used as a storage room. There's a drain in the center of the floor and blood stains the cement around it.

I gasp and instinctively recoil back toward the door. Lanston grabs my hands gently.

"I know. It's terrible . . . You want to know about Crosby, right?" He closes his eyes and takes a long breath. "Are you ready to listen?"

I hesitate. I can't stand the sight of blood. This is like an X-rated horror film. My head is becoming lighter by the second. But I have to know.

I nod.

Lanston holds my hand tightly, his palm sweaty and hot.

"I didn't know Crosby was going to use this space for something so awful. He told me he wanted to make a private space where we could all sneak off and escape for a while if we needed it." He pauses and lowers his eyes to the dried blood on the floor. "So when he asked if I knew of a place like this, I didn't think anything of it. I told him."

"Crosby was Liam's old roommate, right?" My stomach is in knots and I want to throw up. If this is going where

I think it is...I don't know if I should've asked to begin with.

Lanston nods. His eyes are heavy and grim, filled with sleepless nights and regrets. "Yeah. For a few months, actually. Everything seemed fine at first, but then Liam's cuts kept getting worse. He wasn't acting the same. Every time I asked if he was okay, he'd smile and nod...He never said what was really happening to him." Tears spring to Lanston's eyes. He dips his head to hide beneath his baseball cap.

"You mean he brought Liam...here?" I cover my mouth and press my back against the cold brick wall.

"Yeah," he says on a shaky breath. "He brought Liam here and hurt him. I don't think Liam will ever tell me to what extent, but the night I found out, it was already so far out of control. There was blood everywhere. Liam was lying on the floor and he wasn't...he wasn't moving." Lanston looks at me, tears streaming down his cheeks. "Crosby was already gone—he knew he went too far. Yelina helped me get Jericho and then Liam went to the hospital for his injuries."

I stare at him bewilderedly. I couldn't force myself to speak if I tried.

"Before Jericho arrived, Liam regained consciousness and he told me about Crosby—to be careful in case he came back. He didn't want to tell anyone, so Yelina and I have been keeping his secret. I think he's afraid."

My heart shatters for Liam. "Lanston, you have to tell Jericho or somebody what really happened. We need to report this right now!" I move to open the door, panic and dread consuming my body as fear slips into my skin.

He blocks the door and grabs my shoulders. "Wynn, you can't tell anyone. Liam made me swear and I made

Yelina promise too. It's not our truth to share." He grunts as I try to shove past him.

I shake my head. "We aren't children! There's a psychopath out there and he could come back at any time. He could be here *now*. No one knows what he's done or what he's capable of doing. Liam needs us."

"You can't," Lanston begs, but I won't listen to him. I push him aside and fling the door open. "Wynn, stop! We don't know how Liam will react if you tell Jericho!" I run through the empty greenhouse and exit through the glass doors. I hear Lanston running after me but as soon as I hit the grass, I dart in the other direction and head straight for the forest.

Once I reach the tree line, I dare a glance back and see Lanston searching for me by the mansion. His distant voice calls my name over and over.

What the fuck am I supposed to do?

My heart races. Everything in the world seems so fucked-up. Because it is, right? Why else would something this horrible happen to someone as precious as Liam? I can't handle it.

I just want all the pain to stop. I don't want to hurt anymore.

My feet drag over leaves as I make my way through the forest. It's pitch black out now. I pull my phone out and check the time. Nine o'clock.

Shit.

If I'm not back by ten, James will get a phone call. If I don't go back or answer the phone, he'll probably fly out here again.

I click through our texts from earlier and frown.

★

James: Don't worry about the price. Seriously, remember that promotion I was telling you about? Well, I got it. And you never asked me about the industry I work in. Harlow is just one of our many facilities.

Wynn: You swear it's okay? I don't want to be a burden. I'm sorry I'm such a mess.

James: I swear. Love you.

Wynn: Love you too. Thank you for never giving up on me.

James: You'd do the same for me. I know it. :) Get better so we can take another trip to Ireland and get drunk.

Wynn: I'll try my best.

I don't deserve a brother as kind as James, but I appreciate him more than words could ever say.

You are lovable. You aren't a monster. You don't have to die. I drill myself with words that don't sink in very deep.

I try ones that do. *Do it for James. For Lanston and Liam. Do it . . . for yourself.*

I continue walking until I reach an opening in the forest. My eyes widen. It's the moonflower field. They're wilting from the cold now, but some are still flowering this close to death. I'm glad I got to see their last full bloom before the plummet.

I walk to the center and fall to my knees.

Then I cry.

Why did this happen to Liam? Why can't we tell anyone? Why won't he get help?

I fist the flowers, covered in a light layer of frost, and drop my head. The sky starts to cry along with me and freezing rain meets my skin.

Why is the world so cruel?

So unfair and disturbing with dark, wicked souls surrounding us.

"Wynn?"

My entire body seizes at Liam's voice. I slowly lift my head and look up at him, hoping it's too dark and wet for him to see my tears and desperate eyes.

A long cut runs from the tip of his jaw to his ear. Blood mixes with the rain and stains his white undershirt red. He looks like he's dissociating, staring long and hollowly at me. The kind of stare one has when not a single thought is fluttering through their mind.

"Liam?" I choke out his name. I can't manage any more words. My heart hurts. My soul hurts. His brows pull together more as he focuses back on me, back from wherever his mind whisked him away to.

He hurt himself again, and it's my fault. I yelled at him and bit him and acted like a psychopath.

"Hey, what're you doing out here?" he says wearily, sinking to his knees in front of me. His eyes are dark and sunken. I've never seen him look this physically poor. He doesn't give me a chance to reply before he wraps his arms around me and squeezes me tightly, desperation pulling at his tone like a broken man. "You're not leaving, are you?"

Is he asking literally or figuratively? Leaving, as in packing my shit and running? Or as in killing myself?

I shake my head, realizing in this moment that I don't want either of those endings. Tears spill down my cheeks as I hug him back.

"Thank God," he whispers.

"What happened to you, Liam?"

He squeezes me tighter and hushes me, stroking his hand down my head. "I don't want to talk about it right now, sunshine. *Please*. Not now."

I push him away. His brows pull together as I stand on shaky legs, my clothes now burdensome with the rain and mud. "Then when? I can't stand to see you this way, Liam," I say, a little more hostile than I intended. His eyes widen and I can't help but look at the blood dripping down his neck again, turning our wilted white moonflowers crimson. I start walking back toward the manor.

He's at my back in a few moments, gripping my wrist tightly. My scar stings and I whirl on him. "*Stop*, Liam. If you're not going to tell me, then I don't want to talk at all."

"So don't talk." He pushes me against a tree and presses his forehead against mine. His breath curls in the cold air. My bones ache from the chill but heat sparks in my chest.

"What's wrong with you?" I struggle against him and manage to shake his hold. I run toward the manor, Liam's footsteps close behind me. The rain stings my eyes and makes it hard to see.

I make it to the east-wing door and throw it open, running down the hallway and making it to the dark lobby just as Liam reaches me again.

The only light is that of the fireplace. It's so quiet you could hear a pin drop.

Liam breathes heavily as he stares at me. Longing and torment mix in his eyes as he backs me onto one of the sofas. I sit back and watch him carefully.

"Tell me," he mutters, dropping to his knees before me. "You tell me first. Then I'll tell you."

Is he testing me? I can't stand him when he's like this.

"Tell you what?" I ask carefully.

He grabs my arm and runs his finger down the long cut that was supposed to be the end of my story. There's something so painful about the way his eyes have dulled since this morning. Blood continues to trickle down his neck and it makes my stomach curl.

Can I do this?

"I—I don't want to be this character anymore." I press my hand to my chest. "I can't keep waking up and being disappointed with who I see in the mirror. I don't want to be me."

"That's all it takes?" he murmurs cruelly.

My lower lip quivers and I bite my cheek to keep the tears away. Anger storms behind my eyes and a list of furious responses spills out of me. "I don't have any friends in the real world. Everyone hates me. *I* hate me. My only family left is my brother. The person I called Mother hurt me her entire fucking life and then she died. I have a bad heart. All I do is hurt people. I hurt everyone. *Is that enough for you?*" I say the last bit louder than I should have, but God, does it feel fucking good to say it. To shout it.

"That's a long list," he says, not unkindly. His eyes soften.

"Your turn." I take a steadying breath. That was actually a lot easier to say than I thought. The weight that's been looming over me for so long has stopped festering.

"I cut my face because I felt guilty for earlier…and because I ditched Yelina on the highway. To be fair, I told her to shut up and she wouldn't," he says nonchalantly, a slight smirk pulling at the corner of his lips. I don't smile. He needs to stop trying to be funny when it's clearly anything but.

I don't believe that's the entire story…but at least he's trying.

His brows pinch and he rests his face on my leg. "Can we stop spiraling? I want to numb your pain, Wynn. I want to be star-crossed lovers again."

I smile wearily. "Star-crossed lovers? You read too many romance novels."

He peeks up at me and gives me a boyish grin. "Only the ones I read on your Kindle while you sleep."

"*Traitor.*"

The walk back to our room is quiet. We pass Lanston's room and then Yelina's. Both lights are on, so I suppose we know they're both okay and safe. I feel bad for running on Lanston like that. He must be worried I'll tell Liam everything…or tell someone else. I make a mental note to apologize to him in the morning.

Liam heads into the bathroom. I stop in the doorway and watch as he pulls his soaked hoodie off. The white shirt beneath is drenched in blood. His scars are long, some too awful to linger on. His tattoos cover his entire chest: skulls, forests, upside-down cities, and an astronaut floating in the space between. The dark ink tells stories I crave to hear from him.

"Come here," he mutters as he pulls down his pants, taking the underwear with them. He didn't ask; it's a command. My blood warms with lust at his deep, dangerous tone. "Let me numb you."

His body is perfect, sculpted just for me, with all his imperfections and flaws. His dick is already at half-mast and taking my mind off today's burdens.

The bathroom is empty and dark. He walks over to the shower in the far corner, turns on the faucet, and tests the water until it's warm enough to move under. His skin steams and relief rolls across his expression.

Liam's eyes burn as he watches me strip out of my clothes. My nipples harden against the cold air; I didn't realize how chilled to the bone I was. He beckons for me to come to him. His eyes linger on my bare pussy and his swollen cock only grows bigger with each step I take closer to him.

His dark hair is wet and slicked to his forehead, steam billows around him and I want to be consumed by his warmth.

I straighten my back and try to push any insecurities about my naked body away. He's already seen every inch of me. His eyes lock with mine as I gently brush the cut on his jaw with my thumb to wipe the blood under the stream of hot water. He winces, but desire and pleasure flare in his eyes.

"Make me numb, Wynn," he whispers against the shell of my ear.

A shudder runs through me as his fingers coast my breasts.

I skim my fingers down his neck, his flesh still cold beneath the warm, rushing water. My lips press softly against his shoulder. We've fucked so many times already, yet this feels more than that.

More than fucking and numbing. More than filthy sex and loose words.

This is intimate.

He wraps his hand around mine and lifts my wrist to his lips, dotting my cut with kisses and leaning his head into my hand. "Can you make me forget, Wynn? Even if it's just for tonight?" His voice is somber and hushed, sad and heartbreaking.

"Make you forget what?" I rest my cheek against his chest and listen to the pattering of his heart as warm water spills over us.

"Everything that isn't you. My life before you. Make me forget all the tragedies so that I can—" He cuts himself off and grits his teeth.

"So you can what?"

He guides me to the wall. The tiles are like ice against my back, but his taut chest presses against mine and sends heat throughout my body as his dick presses between my thighs.

Liam's lips brush against mine. The soft tingling of his words reverberates through me.

"So that I can love you the way you deserve to be loved."

Then he kisses me. He kisses me like he'll die if he pulls away. His hands hold the sides of my head and caress me as if I'll break if he's not careful. Everything I thought I knew, or didn't know, goes out the window. Nothing matters except us. Not when he's kissing me so sweetly and professing his heart.

"I can't get you out of my head, Wynn," he rasps between deep kisses. "I hated being away from you tonight. I hated the thought of Lanston being near you. You're meant for me, no one else."

My heart leaps in my chest like a wild thing, so starkly unlike its usual lifeless and heavy self. He won't even let me get a word in, he's so ravenous. All I can do is moan with each confession and unyielding kiss.

"I wanted to pull Yelina's hair when she forced you to take her to town," I admit with a small grin.

He chuckles and brings his lips to mine. "Such a vicious little creature."

His mouth is on mine again and the sound of the shower fades out as I get lost in him. Our tongues brush against one another with hunger. His hands are greedy and pull me close, his swollen cock pumping between my thighs and stroking my clit over and over.

I moan with each thrust. Heat pools in my core as I reach down and fist his shaft, squeezing his girth and guiding his tip to my entrance.

"I want to tear you apart. I want you screaming my name and crying for more." He groans as he slowly pushes inside me. I moan so loud I'm sure half the hall hears it. His teeth edge my jaw and he stops at my ear. "I love you, Wynn."

"You'll lose your mind," I say, pushing him back enough to look into his eyes as my lips curl into a sad smile. "You'll lose your mind if you follow me into the dark, Liam."

"Already there, baby."

He remains still inside me. We're connected and one and...and...

"I love you too."

He dips his head down and rests it on my shoulder. His hands grip my skin bruisingly as he starts to move his hips, pulling his dick in and out.

"You'll lose your mind," he echoes me and I can't help but laugh. He groans as my muscles squeeze his dick tighter and he thrusts into me harder.

"Liam," I moan as he brings his mouth back to mine. I've never kissed lips as cold and soft as his. As crushing and all-consuming as his kisses are, I love every inch of him, every joke and snarky remark.

"Never let me go," he says between our kisses.

"Never," I murmur back.

He pulls out of me and motions for me to bend over. I set both hands on the cold tiled wall and jut out my ass for him. The hot water warms my back. He crowns my entrance and shoves in again. "Oh fuck, Wynn. You're so fucking tight." He lets his head tilt back and groans as he grips my hips and fucks me.

I moan and pant as he works my pussy toward climax. My entire body is on fire, numb, and my weary mind full of his confessions of love. I look back at him, watch him take me, watch as his thrusts slow and pleasure pulls his brows together. His eyes are hooded with those beautiful long lashes, but that doesn't keep the hunger from shining through.

He circles my clit with his talented fingers and it sends me over the edge. His thrusts are brutal and demanding.

My lips part and I cry out, "Liam, oh God, don't stop. Don't stop."

"Come for me, Wynn. Wash my dick with your precious come."

I do. I come and everything in my body ignites with ecstasy. Liam pumps my sensitive flesh a few more times before he comes, spilling himself into me and groaning as his dick throbs. His pumps slow and he presses kisses up along my back.

I straighten and his arms wrap around me possessively, lovingly. He grips my chin and guides my lips to his.

"Wynn...you're fucking perfect," he whispers into my mouth and I bask in each and every word he gives me. "You're my cure."

"Holy *shit,* that was hot."

I squeal and cover my breasts at the sound of someone else's voice. I can't believe I forgot this was a communal bathroom and the entrance is never locked. Oh my God, was someone watching us fuck? My cheeks flush and I feel dizzy. How the other patients fuck in here in broad daylight is beyond me.

Liam's eyes turn cold and he swings around, blocking my body. "Who's there?" he snaps.

The light flicks on. Yelina and Lanston stand in the doorway with amused looks while our entire hall stands behind them, standing on their tiptoes and trying to get peeks at us.

"Oh my God!" I shout, keeping my breasts covered as I make a beeline to the towel racks. I grab two, wrapping myself and then handing Liam one. He takes it and covers his lower half before stalking toward the doorway.

"You guys are *dead,*" he says in a voice so low and sinister that even I believe it. Yelina laughs, but before she takes off running like everyone else, she gives me a hard stare.

She's hurt. I know she likes Liam...Is she the one that brought everyone here to watch? Out of spite? I mean, he *did* leave her on the highway.

Lanston doesn't run away like everyone else does. He only shrugs. "Don't get mad at me, I just got here. I didn't see anything. Well, except for the end." He winks at me. I don't miss how red his cheeks are.

I cover my face with my palms. Lanston really watched Liam fuck me and make me come? *Oh my God.*

Liam tousles his wet hair with frustration and groans. "I'm so sorry, Wynn. Are you okay?" His blue eyes inspect me carefully. I can't help but laugh about this whole thing.

"Yeah—I am, actually."

Lanston looks relieved too. He must realize I didn't tell Liam about what he showed me tonight in the greenhouse. Also that I'm not too upset about him seeing his two best friends fuck in the shower.

"Don't worry, I'll give Yelina hell for inviting us all to the *show*." He puffs out his chest before nudging Liam and leaving the bathroom.

Liam dips his head and sighs. "I hate this place sometimes."

I pick up our wet clothes from the floor and put them in our laundry bin. "It's not so bad. I mean, it's where I met you and Lanston." I take his hand and lead him back to our room.

He doesn't say anything, but his hand squeezes mine tightly, and I think that says enough.

Chapter 22

Liam

No man has the right to feel as weightless as I do in this moment.

Wynn grips my hand tightly as we hurry back to our room with our towels feebly wrapped around us. I feel like a criminal with the way she's acting; it's exhilarating.

The second we get to our room she shuts the door and locks it.

The grin that crests my lips makes the cut on my jaw sting. "You know people fuck in there all the time. You walked in several times just this week." I laugh as I pull open a drawer and fish for a pair of boxers. She grabs one of her nightshirts, but I have a different plan.

There's a large black shirt lying at the bottom of my drawer that she'd look perfect in. My cheeks warm at the thought of her wearing it.

"Hey...you should try this on."

I toss the shirt at her and she barely catches it. Her brown eyes are wide and warm when she unfolds it.

"You're giving me this?" she says cautiously, eyeing me like it might be a prank.

"Yeah. I mean, it doesn't suit me, you know?" I lie, hoping she won't catch on to the sentiment behind that shirt.

It was a gift from Neil and I cherish it. Even if I never see her again after our time here. But my heart tells me that Wynn won't be going anywhere anytime soon, at least not anywhere I'm not.

She pulls the shirt on and it falls to her mid-thigh. Her cheeks blush and she looks up at me shyly. "How does it look?"

I walk over to her and brush her wet pink hair over her shoulder. "Perfect."

She fake scowls at me, and God, her smile is enough to ruin me.

"Do you think they'll tell the counselors what we were doing in there?"

I think it's cute that she's so innocent. She thinks they give a shit what we do once they're off the clock? Or even on the clock, for that matter.

"Wynn, we're roommates. I think they know what people do behind closed doors. I kind of think they expect it, to be honest. Part of the *treatment*."

She wrinkles her nose like she's in complete disbelief at this place.

"Well, let's get your jaw patched up. It finally stopped bleeding," she says with a bit of a sting.

She's mad at me, and I don't blame her.

Her fingers are soft and gentle as she applies the ointment to my cut. The burning slowly fades, leaving that incessant itch in the back of my mind that wants more of it.

She makes quick work of my jaw, and then we slip into my bed and I hold her. I run my fingers through her hair and press kisses to her forehead.

"*Remedium meum*," I whisper with my lips coasting her skin. Her hair smells like lilacs. I pull her against my bare chest. Her legs are warm. I can't remember the last time my heart was this full, and my mind this at peace.

She scoots in closer and kisses my throat gently. "Dream of me." Her voice is low and sleepy.

I hold her tighter. "Only you."

Saturdays are my favorite. Sleep in, take a walk, drive aimlessly. Who knows what the day holds.

But we have plans today: Tattoos.

My phone vibrates relentlessly and I groan as I roll over to snatch it off the nightstand. Who the fuck is texting me this early?

> Mom:
> Your brother is visiting.
> Be nice to him. He loves
> you.

Jesus Christ.

I toss my phone back to the nightstand and take a deep breath. It's okay. I'm not going to let this ruin my day. Perry visits too often lately. I wonder if everything is all right at home... He couldn't possibly be getting worse. It's not like my mother will tell me either way. She only ever says the same three things. *He's coming. Be nice. He loves you.*

She might be fucking crazy, but she's my mom. That has to mean something, doesn't it?

I sit up and stretch, remembering I'm not alone in bed, and look down at Wynn. She's wrapped up in the blanket and still fast asleep. We had a late night. I shouldn't wake her. We still have plenty of time before our appointment in Bakersville.

My shoes are still wet, so I slip on the rehab-issued slippers and throw on sweats and a hoodie before heading out of the room. I check my phone again; it's only seven a.m. I'm never the early bird around here. Does *anyone* get up at this hour?

I head toward Lanston's room. He's one of the few people here that isn't required to have a roommate, probably because he's basically done with his program. I don't want him to leave though. He's my only friend besides Wynn.

The light under his door is on. I quirk a brow and knock a few times. It takes him a few seconds before the door cracks open and he peers out. He smiles with surprise.

"Hey, man, get in here," he whisper-shouts cheerfully like he's already fully awake.

I step in and the aroma of coffee hits me like a brick wall. I take a seat at his small bistro table and point at the pot of bitter, black soul nectar.

"Please and thank you."

Lanston laughs and pats me on the back. He scoops his baseball cap up off his bed and puts it on backward as he grabs two mugs.

"Are you always up this early? You look like shit," he says more seriously as he looks over at me, worry tugging in his eyes.

I run my hand over my face and shake my head. "No, I'm usually deceased until about noon on Saturdays." I give him a weary grin. "You know that."

Lanston chuckles and nods. "Yeah, that's why we made the appointment for late afternoon. God forbid someone wakes you on a Saturday morning."

He sets both mugs on the table with a bottle of creamer on the side. I take the mug and drink my coffee straight black. I hate bitter coffee, but it eases the itch in my mind having it this way.

"Okay, so are you going to tell me what's wrong?" He stares at me with that knowing look of his.

Part of me really doesn't want to talk about it, but I wouldn't have walked my sorry ass here if I didn't intend to. Still...I can't bring myself to do it.

I set the mug back down. "You think me and Wynn could work out? Like after we get out of this place?"

Everything is controlled here. The environment, our schedules, our food. The real world isn't like that. And that scares the fucking shit out of me.

Lanston's eyes widen and he sets his mug down too. "Like as a couple?"

It's weird to talk about it with him, with anyone, but if there's anything I've learned from counseling, it's that you have to talk shit out. "Yeah."

"I mean...maybe. You two are so different though. She's like the girl version of me—sad, hopeless, and pretty." I scowl at him and he shrugs innocently. "I'm just pointing out the obvious. You're always so callous and broody. Have you asked her what she thinks?"

Fear dips deep into my chest. No, I haven't. I can't handle rejection. I'd rather ignore things and avoid them than ever deal with them outright. "Of course not."

Lanston smirks, takes a long sip of coffee, and exhales slowly. "She's special, Liam. I know you like her, but be careful. Her mind is her worst enemy and love might be too overbearing on fabric as thin as hers."

My brows pull together. "Fabric as thin as hers?"

"Yeah, her soul is like chiffon, with plenty of tattered rips and tears. The fabric of our souls is thin and worn.

We must be gentle and love tirelessly." He leans back in his chair and threads his fingers together. A warm smile spreads across his face and I know then that he loves her too. "Hers is so beautifully torn that even wolves like us are drawn to it."

His hazel eyes stare distantly at his mug. I'm not sure how to respond—not sure if I should.

"Anyway, just be careful with her, okay?" He grabs both mugs and sets them in the sink. His shoulders slump with his thoughts.

"I know how you feel about her," I murmur, my eyes low.

He turns, not quite looking at me. "Yeah?"

"And I don't care. I love you, brother."

"Love you too, man."

Chapter 23

Wynn

I sit by myself in the cafeteria.

Liam wasn't in bed when I woke up and I couldn't find him anywhere. I stare down at the ham sandwich wrapped in clear plastic, unenthusiastically reaching into the bag of potato chips and popping one in my mouth as I wait.

The chair next to me screeches as someone sits down. I lift my head and meet Lanston's warm gaze. His hazel eyes are soft and comforting, his smile even more so.

"Good morning, Wynn. How'd you sleep?" He looks as tired as I feel. He hands me a paper cup of coffee and the biggest smile forms on my lips. We're kindred souls, he and I.

"You're the best. I slept okay, I guess. How about you? Have you seen Liam?"

Lanston takes off his baseball cap and sets it on the table. His shiny light-brown hair falls perfectly over his forehead in small waves.

"Yeah, he stopped by my room this morning. He didn't go back to yours?" His brows pinch with worry and he searches my eyes for reassurance.

I shake my head. "No, he didn't. Do you think he's okay?"

He looks down at his hands as if in deep thought. Then he snaps back up. "I bet he already took off to town. Our appointment is in a few hours."

★

The underground garage is cleaner than I expected it to be. The cement is uncracked and smooth. Every vehicle down here costs more than what I made in a year at my old corporate job. Sad.

I sold my soul at that job and what did it get me? More depression and more heart pills.

Lanston wears his black leather jacket. His crisp scent is earthy and pleasant. He glances back at me with a boyish grin.

"You ride, right?" He nods over to two black crotch rockets. One is mine; I can tell by the silver handles and the small, pink heart-shaped sticker on the side. The other must be his.

"You have the exact same model I do." I laugh. It's been ages since I've taken my motorcycle for a drive. Lanston picks up my black helmet off the seat and hands it to me, but when I try to take it from him, he doesn't let go. I quirk a brow at him.

"Think you can keep up with me?"

I yank the helmet from his hands and smile. "We'll see who's keeping up with who."

He laughs, and it actually reaches his eyes. He looks at me for a few moments before murmuring, "You're going to be the end of me."

We secure our helmets and he tosses me a pair of spare gloves. His helmet is black too, but a white line runs down the center. He revs his engine, flips me off, and peels out of the garage.

I smile beneath my helmet and giddiness fills my entire body. I haven't felt this excited in a long time. My bike purrs between my thighs and when I jerk the throttle, my tires squeal as I tear down the runway after Lanston.

Laughter that no one else can hear pours from me and the cold air welcomes me entirely, breathing new life into my exhausted soul.

Lanston circles the driveway a few times until I pass him, then he hits his gas and races after me. I squeal and speed up to stay in front of him.

These are the perfect roads to fuck around on, long and free of traffic. I turn right once I reach the highway. We head toward Bakersville with our throttles pulled toward us, accelerating to dangerous levels. Lanston has his choked as far as it will go and flies by me at a reckless speed, putting his hand up to his helmet and motioning it like he's blowing me a kiss.

Cocky asshole. My cheeks hurt from smiling.

I've needed a person like him in my life for a really long time. Him *and* Liam.

We reach the town and pull over at a small shop off the main street. I pull my helmet off and set it on the seat of my bike. Lanston dismounts his motorcycle and when he pulls his helmet off, he flashes me a bright smile as he mutters, "Damn, Wynn. You drive like a fucking psychopath."

"Shut up, you're the one who raced by me going like a hundred!"

He chuckles and wraps an arm around my shoulder. "Now, now, let's not get into the nitty-gritty details." We both laugh as we walk down the sidewalk of this enchanted little storybook town. I'm shocked it's not a huge tourist spot. Every lamppost and shop window has fall decor strung up. Leaves, pumpkins, witch hats, hay bales.

This place beckons me, makes me want to sit and watch people for a bit. Curl up next to a roaring fire and sip coffee as I watch the leaves fall and hear people share laughter. Lanston glances down at me and must catch on.

"You wanna grab a croissant and sit? We sorta didn't eat our breakfast, huh?" He lets go of my shoulder and points across the street at a cute café that's snug between a bookstore and a pub.

"You read my mind. Should we find Liam first, though? I think he'd like that too." I look around the shops to see if I can spot Liam.

Lanston sighs and gives me a forlorn grin. "Yeah, I know exactly where he is."

He leads us down a few alleys before we come up to the base of a hill. We take our time climbing the cement stairs that wind up the slope to the top.

It's a lookout over Bakersville.

When we reach the small parking at the summit, we find a white Camaro parked in the center with someone sitting on the hood, facing out toward the valley.

"Is that Liam?" I ask, not sure because the guy has his hood pulled up.

"Yep," Lanston chirps. "Our sad little Liam."

My chest sinks. Why is he sad? We had a great night, I thought. Is something bothering him?

"Liam?" I call over to him as I trot over to the car. He turns his head and doesn't seem surprised to see the two of us.

"Hey," he mutters. His eyes are sunken like he hasn't slept for days.

Lanston sits on the hood beside him and puts his arm over his shoulder. "What's up? You ready to head to the tat shop?" Liam doesn't shrug our friend off like he usually does. He just remains slumped. The sight of him feeling this down carves out a piece of my heart.

"It itches bad today."

"What does?" I say without thinking. Instantly feeling stupid, I mutter, "Oh."

He wants to hurt himself.

But...why? I can't help but feel this has something to do with last night. Does he regret telling me he loves me? The sting of being unwanted scorches within me.

"Is it because of me?" I flat-out ask him.

Lanston's eyes widen at me but Liam just looks at me with disinterested, cruel eyes.

"Yeah, I guess in a way."

Tears well in my eyes, and I fist my hands tightly to try to keep them there.

"Why are you acting like this? I thought—"

"Acting like what, Wynn? I'm fucking *sick*. Some days I just need to be alone, okay?" he snaps at me. I flinch and stare at him in disbelief. "You two should just leave. I'm not feeling like myself today."

Lanston shoves Liam off the hood of the Camaro. His ass hits the ground and he doesn't bother trying to get back up.

"Fuck you, Liam. Don't come back until you're going to man the fuck up and apologize. You don't talk to friends like that. You don't talk to *her* like that. I don't care what your fucking excuse is," he says in a low voice that sends chills up my spine.

Liam keeps his chin close to his chest, unwilling to look up at us.

"Come on, Wynn. Let's get out of here." Lanston grabs my hand and pulls me back toward the stairs.

My eyes linger on Liam for a few moments before I follow Lanston. The wind stirs up leaves around us. This hill creates a pocket of sorts for the current. The view is breathtaking, but my insides are tearing themselves apart.

"Lanston?"

"Yeah?"

We both keep our eyes on the steps ahead. It's taking everything I have not to break down and cry.

"I think I'll ride back by myself. It'll be nice to get some air."

His hazel eyes flick over to me and he squeezes my hand. I leave out that I'm unsure if I'll be returning. One phone call to James and I could be on a plane out of here tonight. Or I could ride until I end up in some random-ass town. Anywhere but here...

"Okay, but you want to grab a bite first? Let's get a cup of coffee and hit the bookstore. Then, if you still want, you can ride back alone." He stops as we reach the bottom and zips up my coat more. Lanston has a kindness about him like no one else in the world. His cinnamon scent and lingering smile are so infectious that even the coldest heart would thaw.

"That does sound pretty nice." I manage a half-assed, heartbroken grin. "What genre do you like?"

He winks at me. "Dark romance where the heroine gets fucked by the psychopaths."

I burst out laughing and he cracks a wide smile too.

"Me too. I'll give you recs if you give me yours."

"Deal."

Chapter 24
Wynn

The coffee shop had everything from fancy matcha tea to iced americanos, but Lanston and I instantly decided we wanted pumpkin spice lattes. We talked about Boston. Lanston's dream is to move there someday, and the more he spoke of it, the more it became my dream too.

Kindred souls and all.

We each have five books in our bags by the time we leave the bookstore. He thought it'd be fun to pick for one another, so I chose some I liked and a few new ones I haven't read yet.

We swore not to look at the books until we got back to our rooms, so our bags are tied shut and the anticipation is killing me. I set mine in the bag attached to the back of my bike. "Thank you."

Lanston beams at me and pulls his helmet on. "For what?"

"For not letting my day suck. Liam hurt me...and I was ready to just run away from everything."

He lowers his head, and though I can't see his face, I know he's got that sweet grin pulling at his lips. "I know...and it's okay if you still want to. I just wanted to give you a nice afternoon and see you smile. I had more fun with you today than I have in years." His voice is vulnerable and my heart flutters. "Are you riding back alone or are you down to come to the tattoo shop? Liam might be there," he warns but his tone is smooth.

We both know Liam has a heart of gold. He's dealing with demons that I can't even fathom.

"Lead the way."

The tattoo shop is a few blocks down and when I see Liam's white Camaro parked out front, my stomach twists.

Lanston gives me a sympathetic look and offers me his arm. "If he's here, then he's ready to apologize. Did you see the way I pushed him? You don't come back from that unless you're ready to say sorry," he says sarcastically.

I smile hopefully with him. But I'm still hurt from what Liam did earlier.

When we enter the shop I'm relieved to find it empty. Someone calls out from the rear for us to head back and Lanston comfortably leads the way.

I wonder how many times he's been here. Lanston always wears hoodies and sweaters with long pants so I'm not even sure how many tattoos he has. Liam, on the other hand—I've scoured his body obsessively for weeks. I don't think there's one I wouldn't be able to remember.

The tattoo gun purrs as a man leans over Liam's head. He's tattooing something behind his ear. I grimace. It looks incredibly painful, but Liam's face is impassive, at least until he looks up and sees the two of us.

Lanston crosses his arms. "Started without us?"

Liam grins but doesn't respond. We take a seat while we wait, not wanting to disrupt the tattoo artist. He does a few more strokes of ink before wiping Liam's skin and putting on a clear cover.

I try not to focus on Liam. I'm not ready to look at him and find that cold stare he gave me earlier.

"All right, Nevers, you're next."

Lanston gets up and switches spots with Liam.

I avert my eyes as Liam sits next to me and I try not to think about anything involving this afternoon except the bookstore and coffee shop.

He sets his hand on top of mine and I'm half about to cry and half about to lay into him about being a fucking asshole. But when my head turns and our eyes meet, he has an apologetic grin and weary eyes.

"I'm sorry about earlier, Wynn."

My gut instinct is to forgive him instantly and never talk about it again. But he looks like he has more to say, so I don't interrupt him.

"I lost myself for a bit. I'm much clearer now...I'm sorry for looking at you like that and saying what I did." His eyes don't leave mine for a second.

"Thanks for apologizing," I say half-heartedly. It still hurts and I'm confused about where his heart lies.

We sit quietly for about fifteen minutes as Lanston gets his tattoo. It's a Roman numeral III, just above the elbow crease on the inside of his arm. He already had a numeral two there.

They wrap up talking to the tattoo artist and pay him. By the time we walk out the door, I feel like I could sleep for the rest of the evening.

Liam walks ahead of me and I see his tattoo has changed to the same as Lanston's. A three instead of the two.

"Are you guys going to tell me what's with the number three?" I ask, looking at each of them.

"How about we race back and if you beat us, we'll tell you." Lanston smiles wickedly at me.

Liam starts his engine and laughs. "Like Coldfox could beat *us* in a race."

"I'll mop the floor with you two." I pull my helmet on and take off.

Lanston shouts something with a laugh deep in his chest and Liam just revs his engine and chases after me in his Camaro.

We ride irresponsibly fast down the highway and the three of us all get tickets. The police officer even taps his pen on Lanston's helmet while scolding us, he's so pissed.

Once the cop pulls away and we're certain no other vehicles are coming, we take off again. I'm laughing so hard that tears spill over my cheeks. I know Lanston's laughing too beneath the roar of our bikes. I can't say for Liam because he's so far ahead of us.

We make it safely back to the garage, *by the grace of God*, and park in the designated spots. Liam's white Camaro is parked across from us, empty, but the engine still makes crinkling sounds, so at least we weren't too far back in the dust.

"That cop actually let us off pretty easy." Lanston shoves his speeding ticket in his pocket after rereading it. "Still an asshole though."

"He could've arrested us," I mutter as I pull my bag of books from the luggage bag. "He's a *saint*."

"Only because you batted your pretty eyes at him! If not for you, he would've cuffed me and Liam on the asphalt." Lanston feigns being sad as he places both his wrists behind his back.

I throw my helmet at him and he barely moves his hands quick enough to catch it. "You're welcome." I smirk and run toward the stairs with my book bag.

"Oh no you don't!" he shouts after me, but I'm already swinging around the corner and taking two steps at a time. When I reach the first floor, I shove the door open and crash into someone.

My books break free of the plastic bag and scatter across the floor. I gasp and pray to God that I didn't just run over our little old receptionist, Mrs. Abett, but thankfully, it's just Liam.

He rubs his head and laughs. "Jesus, I was coming down there because you two were taking forever. I thought you'd gotten in a wreck or some—"

Lanston comes bursting through the doors behind us, trips over my feet, and lands beside Liam, groaning.

The three of us are sprawled out like idiots on the floor.

"Is this you groveling?" Lanston jests, punching Liam in the arm weakly.

"Liam? Groveling?" I roll my eyes, standing up and brushing off my pants. Lanston sits up and his eyes get big, frantically looking up at me and then back to the ground.

I raise a brow and mouth *What?* But it's too late.

Liam picks up one of the books and my soul leaves my body when I see the cover. It's of two damn-near naked people, and they are *not* fucking cuddling.

"Oh my God." I rush to pick up the rest and Lanston can't help but laugh at me as I scramble to get them all.

Liam smiles criminally and passes me the book in his hands. "You really let Lanston pick books for you to read?" My jaw drops and Lanston laughs harder.

"How'd you know?" I say as I look down at the other books, all similar to the first. My cheeks are as hot as when we got caught fucking in the showers last night.

"Because I have the same book gifted by the same jackass."

Lanston shrugs, still trying to cease his laughter. "It's a good book, okay? I can't be silenced."

The three of us look at one another with mixed expressions before bursting out with laughter. We gather our books and Liam insists on carrying my bag back to our room.

Lanston joins us and sits on my bed as he unties his plastic bag. He tosses his hat on my pillow and sets the pile down between us. Liam lies on his bed, propping his head up with amusement as he waits to see what I picked out.

"What are these?" Lanston says with pinched brows, flipping through some pages and reading the back of a few with interest.

"Murder mystery and dark romance. They will keep you up *all* night. I could hardly sleep after this one." I pass him one with a skull on the cover and his eyes fill with horror.

"Wynn, I hate murder mystery." Lanston groans and leans back to grab the stack he picked for me.

"And I'm supposed to love *these*?"

"Just try them."

"Right back at you," I say with a pointed look. Liam smirks devilishly.

We stay up way too late.

I haven't had a night like this in a long time. Why did it take me coming to a rehabilitation institute to finally find people like me? People who hurt and understand the same way I do. People I cherish more than anything.

Liam suggests a movie and pops in a thriller. We act like complete children and throw all the pillows and blankets on one bed so we can all sit together. Lanston brings popcorn and coffee in paper cups from his room while I sneak into the kitchen to snag a bag of chips.

By the time the movie is playing, I'm sitting between the two of them and smiling so easily it feels like a dream. Can being happy truly be this simple? I hope so. I want this forever.

Lanston scoots in much closer than he needs to, but I guess he's pretty freaked out by horror movies. It's sort of cute to see him hide his face beneath his hands.

On the other hand, Liam and I are on the same page. Our eyes are wide open and we smile at every jump scare and gory scene. He nudges me and nods toward Lanston. I glance over and see his head completely covered with the blanket.

"You chicken." I grab his side to scare him and he yelps.

"You're so cruel!" he jests and falls over my lap laughing.

Liam cracks up and covers his mouth in an attempt to hide his gorgeous smile. "Dude, it's just a movie. None of this shit is real."

"It says *based on a true story*." Lanston finds the DVD case and holds it up for us to see. It *does* say that. But don't most movies say something along those lines?

When you're in your mid-twenties, coffee can go two ways. Either you are buzzing all hours of the night or you have an outrageous amount of energy for an hour and then crash.

Lanston leans against my shoulder, completely passed out, while Liam is wide awake. He puts in another movie and checks his phone, frowning at another message—his mom, I'm guessing.

"Hope you like slasher films too." He smiles as he scoots in close. His eyes linger on Lanston's head resting on my shoulder but he keeps the cheerful mood up anyway.

"Are you kidding? I live for them."

His grin grows and he presses play. We watch silently for about ten minutes before Lanston topples over and lies down on my pillow.

"He's such an idiot," Liam says with a sarcastic tone.

"You really freaked me out today...I didn't know what was going on with you, and Lanston was worried too. You're all we have, Liam."

His blue eyes lower to my hand and he murmurs, "I just really got in my head...Do you have any idea how hard it is to have the two closest people in your life want to die?"

My eyes instantly burn. I know he isn't being mean, but it's horrible to hear out loud. The truth is unbearable.

"That's why we're here, isn't it? To get better." I brush my hand across his cheek and try to urge him to meet my eyes, but he won't.

"And what if you don't get better, Wynn? What if—" His jaw tightens. "What if I can't save you two? Then what? You know I'll be here every day when you wake up. But with you two...I have to keep my heart guarded because I don't know if you'll be here tomorrow."

My chest curls into a painful knot.

I didn't think of any of this from Liam's perspective.

Lanston sleeps heavily, his soft snores the only sound between us until the victim in the movie screams. What if I woke up tomorrow and learned that Lanston had died by suicide? It's the worst feeling in the entire world. It's so painful I can't even think about it.

I hate it.

But that's who we were before the three of us crashed into one another, right?

"I'm not saying I'm fixed or Lanston is either." I brush his light-brown hair from Lanston's forehead and admire the sweet smile on his lips before looking back at Liam. He stares at me with pain tugging the darkest parts of his heart. "But I'm no longer the broken person you found in the hospital by chance. And Lanston isn't the lost man he was when you saved him in the showers. Our chemistry has changed. And it's because we all met here. Even if Harlow sucks, it's where I met the two people I cherish more than anything."

His eyes soften and a relieved breath passes his lips.

"You're saying our cure had a secret ingredient named *Nevers*?"

I laugh and lean in close to Liam, letting my head fall on his shoulder as I say, "Yeah, I am, I guess. Nevers, Coldfox, and Waters." I shut my eyes as he combs his fingers through my pale-pink hair. He's so warm and his touch makes my heart flutter.

"You know he loves you, right?"

My cheeks heat. I don't say anything. What would I say? I do know...How could I not?

"You know I do too." His eyes search mine, looking for answers that my lips refuse to speak. In a perfect world, it'd be us three against everything, living our best lives. But this is reality—of course, he wants me to choose.

He wants to know where my heart is, truly.

It's not even a question.

"Liam." I angle his head and pull him in for a kiss. His lips are soft and when he wraps his hand behind my neck my entire being melds into him. We kiss for only a moment, but it feels like perfect, endless heart-pounding adrenaline that you get from jumping off a cliff or screaming atop a mountain. He's the only person I'll ever want. "I love you both completely, but in different ways. It's only ever been *you*."

Liam runs his thumb over my bottom lip and says, "The tattoo is for the three of us. It was just me and Lanston before, but you're a part of our healing as well, so we decided to add you."

I softly gasp and look from Lanston's arm to the skin behind Liam's ear. Have I really been able to mean that much to them?

"There's nothing I wouldn't do for you, Wynn. *Nothing.*"

Chapter 25

Liam

Wynn stares at the cold keys of the piano.

It's Sunday morning and we're indulging in the coffee Lanston brought us. He sits slouched over on the sofa, looking out the bay windows at the dreary view. The rain hasn't stopped since early this morning.

A smile coasts my lips as I think about how Wynn kissed me sweetly before falling asleep last night. We didn't talk much after her admission. We didn't need to. I was more than happy to have her just curled up in my arms and falling asleep to the horror movie.

She looks so at peace when she sleeps.

Not at all like how she looks now. Her eyes are tormented, her jaw set with a distant wound she refuses to extinguish.

"All right, show me one more time."

She sighs and places her fingers in position again, perfectly straining her fingers to each key as if she's been beaten into remembering this posture.

"Wait, stop." I raise my hands to the keys in the lower section and show her a relaxed position. "Try it like this. Playing should be relaxed and natural. Let the music flow through your soul, through every fiber of your being, and then let your fingers glide over the keys." I tap on the keys lightly and the music that reverberates from the piano is light and somber.

"Listen to him, Wynn. I can hear your inner demons from how hard you're hitting the keys. When Liam plays, it tickles my insides." Lanston grins, leaning over a pillow and throwing back his coffee like he'll die without it.

Wynn groans and shakes her hands out a few times before placing them back on the keys. Still strained. This might be harder than I thought.

"It's not as easy for me since my hands aren't as big as yours. I can't reach the keys I need."

My brows pull together as I try to think of a way to help.

"Okay, let's try this. Play as you normally would and I'll play a couple octaves lower. Try to match the airiness of the sound and don't be afraid to let your imagination take over. If you feel like adding a few keys, then do it. If you fuck up, who cares."

Her light-brown eyes meet mine uncertainly before she nods.

I start playing, and after a verse, she joins in. At first, it's a bit rough. She's still pressing the keys too hard and she's hell-bent on executing each stroke perfectly.

All right, time for a curve ball.

I add a few notes at the end of each chord and her eyes flash at me.

"That's not—"

"Shh, feel the music, Wynn." I grin and shut my eyes to let the sound of this beautiful melody take me. "For the Damaged Coda," what a masterpiece. I'm embarrassed to admit how much I practiced this tune just for this very moment.

She plays in the way she knows for another verse and then something magical happens.

Her chords are an octave higher than she normally plays and she embellishes each verse with some improvisation. The sound is precious and for the first time, I feel like I'm truly hearing her soul song.

My eyes open slowly as my fingers keep up their dance across the keys. The bay windows have raindrops scattered across their panes. Clouds are low and heavy through the forest, the tips of the pine trees just peeking out the tops.

"Holy shit," Lanston mutters, then I hear him get up from the sofa to stand behind us.

My hands slow and I let them drop into my lap as the song comes to an end. Wynn finishes it out and then looks at me with cheeks so red it makes my heart beat faster.

"There's our Wynn." I sweep her pink hair behind her ear, but instead of smiling like I hoped she would, her lips quiver into a frown. Big tears brim in her eyes before she lets them spill over onto the keys.

Lanston shares a concerned look with me but then she murmurs:

"Thank you for helping me remember why I loved playing."

My fingers curl against my knees uneasily. The itch has been gone since yesterday, and it makes me uncomfortable.

But her weightless smile makes that new discomfort so welcome.

Chapter 26

Wynn

Lazy afternoons and evenings with Liam and Lanston make life feel cozy.

I wonder what will happen once we leave this place. Will we fall out of touch and go about our lives until we inevitably get sick again? Or will we remain intertwined and stay sane?

I wonder.

Jericho looks particularly relaxed today. He's been grumpy and stressed out all week leading up to the Fall Festival.

"Is everyone ready? Get with your partners and meet in the south parking lot. I need a full head count by six p.m., so don't be fucking late," the counselor snipes, but he looks really excited.

"Damn, Jericho, got a date meeting you tonight or something?" Liam jests, raising a brow like he's genuinely interested in knowing our counselor's business.

"It's no concern of yours," Jericho responds without looking up from his clipboard, but I don't miss the red blooming across his cheeks.

Lanston throws his arm over my shoulder and pulls me in close. He has a big smile and a glimmer in his eyes. "Are we going to race to town again?"

Liam shoots him a dirty look as he grumbles, "Wynn's my partner. Aren't you going with Yelina?"

Lanston fidgets with his baseball hat before groaning and sliding his hands down his neck. "Yeah, I was hoping I could get out of it though."

I shove his shoulder. "That's terrible."

"She's such a bitch sometimes." He avoids my eyes.

Liam shoves him playfully too. "You're an asshole. Go meet her before she goes on a manhunt."

Lanston lowers his shoulders, defeat and dread visibly pulling his spirit down.

"Liam and I will be there too. We're all going to hang out anyway," I tell him.

His hazel eyes rise to mine. "Promise me a dance?"

I smile and hold out my pinky. "Promise."

Liam glowers and grumbles, "One dance. The rest are mine."

It's enough to lighten Lanston's mood. That handsome smile returns to his lips and he heads back to the mansion to meet with Yelina.

Liam takes my hand and pulls me toward the garage. He punches in the code for the door and my heart leaps when he looks back at me. His blue eyes are bright and weightless today. "You like going fast in cars too, or just motorcycles?" He swings his car keys around his forefinger and raises a curious brow. He's teasing me.

I shrug. "Let me drive and you'll find out."

"Yeah, right."

The Camaro's lights flash as he unlocks it and opens the passenger door for me.

"You scared, Waters?" I brush his cheek with my hand as I pass him and take my seat.

He chuckles and lowers his head. "No. But you will be, sunshine."

Jesus fucking Christ.

I *am* scared.

Liam floors it with a maniacal grin on his face that I've yet to see. He cranks the music up and blares "Thunderclouds" by LSD. He glances at me, that adrenaline-pumping energy filling his eyes, and I squeal when he takes the turn onto the highway like a speed racer. The engine roars and the wheels scream against the asphalt.

"Liam!"

He laugh-shouts above the music, "I thought you liked going fast?"

"Not when you're driving like a complete psychopath!" I cling desperately to the handle above the door. Liam's grin only grows and he finally slows down to an appropriate speed. I take a deep breath but my heart still races inside my chest.

The euphoria of fear still pulses through my veins. It's a good feeling to get high on.

"All right, sorry for freaking you out." He spreads his hand over my thigh and keeps the other relaxed on the steering wheel. "It was pretty fun though, right?" His blue eyes are steady on the road ahead and I can't help but study him in this moment. He's perfect, heart-stopping. The setting sun outlines his sharp features and the tattoos on his neck and wrists stand out in contrast to the heather-gray sweater he's wearing tonight. His black rings glisten, reminding me of my own. My thumb smooths over the matte ring around my index finger. Besides Lanston, Liam is the only person that makes me feel alive.

"Yes, it was." I lean over and kiss his cheek.

Bakersville is so busy we have to park a few blocks away from the meeting spot where Jericho and the others are. The scents of pumpkin spice, cinnamon, freshly fallen leaves, and coffee fill the air. All my favorite things are in one place and the crisp chill in the air makes it all the more cozy.

Liam notices my giddiness and grins. "That much of an autumn girl, huh?"

"Don't you love it too?"

"Yeah, I do. But I enjoy seeing how much you like it better."

My cheeks warm and I stuff my hands into the pockets of my black sweater as we walk down the street to the gathering site. Liam's arm is wrapped around me and for a delusional moment, this feels like a date. Happy, full of smiles and love.

"There you two are." Jericho marks something off on his clipboard. The lampposts and the hanging lights that connect the buildings on the main street light up.

I'm so eager for the night of activities. Getting out last weekend for tattoos was fun. We could use this reprieve from the sessions, away from the rumors and secrets left hidden away at Harlow. I've long-since stopped pestering Liam about the missing people. After discovering that Crosby is somehow linked to them, I thought it best to leave it in the basement, though I still often think of them.

Lanston and Yelina spot us from across the road. We meet them in the center of the blocked-off street. Lanston wears his baseball hat and black leather coat as usual. Yelina frowns at us as we walk up and crosses her arms. Her slouchy burgundy sweater looks really good paired with her black skinny jeans.

"Hey, how was the ride over?" Liam pats Lanston on the back.

"Horrible." Yelina scowls as she brings out some lip gloss from her purse and coats her lips with a fresh layer of red.

Lanston's face is hysterical. His brows are pulled so close together it looks like he has a unibrow and his frown is that of a man who's had his dick punched.

I can't keep the laugh from my voice when I ask, "What the fuck happened?"

"Yelina swerved off the road to avoid a bird and went straight into the cornfield. There are corn husks in my soul now and the whole ordeal took *at least* ten years off my life." Lanston dramatically slumps his shoulders and moves to stand behind me as if I'll protect him from her.

"The maze cornfield? Oh my God, you're lucky you didn't hit anyone!" I try to turn and grab Lanston but he keeps circling behind me.

Men.

Yelina scoffs at us. "If your *friend* drove a car instead of a fucking motorcycle, then we could've avoided all this."

"I would've lent you my helmet," I murmur and she narrows her eyes at me.

"Come on, guys, let's regroup and just have fun tonight." Liam throws his arms over me and Lanston, guiding us back toward Jericho. Yelina stomps ahead of us and I don't miss her cold glance back at me.

"Can I just stick with you two tonight? She suuuucks." Lanston pouts but Liam ignores him.

The night air has a way of calming me. Jericho orders everyone around with ease; he was born to be bossy, and he thrives with the results. We help set up free-standing bar tables with black tablecloths and candles. More people start to show up, which didn't seem possible, but I think this festival is sort of popular for this remote place. Apparently, people from all over come just to experience it.

I pass out brochures with the night's agenda and Liam hands out alcohol wristbands to adults.

It's hard not to stare at him. His heather-gray sweater hides most of his tattoos but I can still see some reaching past his wrists. The onyx rings he wears on his thumb and middle finger are lovely in the amber glow. His eyes lift to mine and instead of looking away like I usually do, I hold his gaze.

He mouths, *"Having fun?"*

I shrug and mouth back, *"I guess so."*

Life here isn't so bad. It's a place far from the city and bustle. I think if I lived somewhere like this, I could be happy. Find myself with nature and step away from the unrealistic standards of the buzzing world.

This is the sort of life I was meant for.

And that's okay. It's okay to be small and hidden away. Most gems are.

Self-affirmations.

Jericho claps his hands and our group assembles around him. He raises a fresh beer over his head. "Great job tonight, everyone. Now go enjoy the festival and stick with your partners. I'll be doing a head count before we head back at midnight. If you want to leave before then, you need to come find me and I'll mark you off."

Lanston and Yelina saunter over to us. At least they look like they've cheered up a little. I'm not sure why Yelina isn't interested in Lanston. He's handsome, funny, and charming. Maybe she's just into broody, dark-haired guys.

Aren't we all?

"Well, the autumn dance starts in twenty—you guys want to check out the night market first and see what they have?" Liam asks. Yelina and I light up instantly.

She's not so bad; I think she just feels outcast because the three of us are so close. I link arms with her, an act of good will, and her eyes widen with surprise. She doesn't say anything, but a relieved and thankful smile crosses her lips.

"Come on, boys!" She flips her blonde hair and pulls me close like we're sisters. "Wynn and I will need someone to hold our bags."

Liam and Lanston both look perplexed by my sudden warmth toward Yelina. But they shake it fast and chase behind us with glimmers of excitement in their eyes.

The night market is wondrous.

Little booths line the street. Orange, yellow, and brown banners hang above wooden stands and fairy lights over-head cast enough light to redden the bricks of the build-ings. Musicians play their ambient, heartfelt songs and the warmth of people's laughter melts my cold heart.

My chest curls with nostalgic emotions as I look at the handmade jewelry and paintings, sweaters and blankets knitted by the sweetest elderly women in town. But my favorite stand is the one selling bundles of dried flowers. Yelina quickly loses interest and drags Lanston with her to look at some purses.

Liam lingers around the dried baby's-breath bundles. By the awed look on his face, I don't think he's seen dried bouquets before. The peonies have always been my favorite. They hold their faded colors so preciously.

"Why do you like these so much?" Liam asks, his chest pressed against my back, sending heat through my spine.

"It is a bit morbid, isn't it?" I say as I caress one of the dry petals. "I think it's because it makes me happy to see something that was once so beautiful in life be just as pretty, if not more so, in death. Forever beautiful."

"You're right. That is fucking morbid." I turn to look at him and he catches my chin gently between his cold fingers. "But you wouldn't be Wynn Coldfox if your mind wasn't such a dark, lovely, wicked thing."

Chapter 27

Wynn

Liam Waters.

Who is he really? Outside of all this. He's only sparingly mentioned things about his past. Corporate jobs, college, his broken family. But who are we once we're *cured*?

I don't even know myself anymore.

But I've become comfortable with the idea of reacquainting with myself—listening to my innermost thoughts and taking care of the damaged and bruised part of me.

Liam carries a bundle of peonies and baby's breath back to his car. They look tragically alluring together. He insisted on the pair. I'm pleased that my morbid love of dead flowers has captivated him as well.

We make beautiful things together.

"I could've carried them around tonight. We didn't need to walk all the way back to the car." Guilt tugs at my chest. It's a few blocks out and the autumn dance is starting in a matter of minutes.

"No, you wouldn't be able to dance holding these. And don't forget about the maze. Knowing you, they'd get crushed in a matter of seconds," he says nonchalantly as he opens the passenger door and tosses the bouquet in the back seat.

He looks past me and his eyes grow wide. He sits down in the passenger seat and pulls me in his lap before shutting the door and locking his car. His labored breaths instill fear in me.

"What's wrong?" I swing my head to look out the window.

A lone man walks slowly down the sidewalk. He wears a baseball cap and a black coat. At first, I think it's Lanston, but the hat is too dark and under the dim light of the street lamp I see that the man's hair is blonde. It's nothing particularly scary, but then I recall what Lanston told me about Crosby.

The man continues down the sidewalk, minding his own business, and Liam's shoulders relax. He holds me close to his chest and fists my sweater as he dips his head and breathes in my scent. The warmth between us scorches my heart. As the fear slips away, he loosens his grip.

"Are you okay?" I ask, pulling back and looking up into his blue eyes.

"Not really," he admits, glancing down at my lips. "Wynn, I don't know if you're safe being around me." His hand threads into my hair and he presses his forehead against mine.

My heart beats rapidly, my mind blurry with the brush of his lips on mine.

"But I still want you—I can't stay away." He kisses me possessively, fisting my hair in one hand as his other glides down my back and grips my ass. My thighs are on either side of him, my shirt pulled up from the scuffle.

"Why wouldn't I be safe?" I ask. I already know the answer, thanks to Lanston, but I want Liam to open up to me. I want him to tell me why.

His tongue enters my mouth and I moan as he pushes down on my ass so I feel his hard boner beneath his jeans. He groans as I grind into him, my hands exploring beneath his gray sweater and running over each groove on his taut chest.

"Because I have a sinister past."

My breath catches and I lean back to look into his eyes. "Tell me."

Liam's eyes search mine for a moment before he clenches his jaw. "I'll tell you tonight when we get back to our room. We can make some coffee and stay up talking. How does that sound?"

"There's nothing I'd love more," I whisper against his lips. "We're going to miss the dance if we keep this up though." My hips grind into him, his hard cock rubbing my pussy.

He gives me a deep groan and slides his hand down the front of my pants. His fingers are cold, making me flinch and cry out when he unapologetically rubs them over my soaked clit.

"Oh fuck, you're already so wet and hot for me, Wynn." He bites my shoulder and slides one finger inside me. I fist his hair and quiver as he pumps me a few times before pulling his finger out and putting it in his mouth.

My cheeks heat with embarrassment. I've never been with a man who acts like Liam does, so cruel and hungry, remorseless. Unholy.

I'm drawn to him like a moth to fire.

"You taste so fucking good." He sucks on his finger and leans forward to take my lips again. I moan with the flavor of myself in his mouth.

He lifts me and unbuttons his pants, pulling them down quickly. His dick springs free and I swallow hard when it comes up to my belly button. He's fucking lethal in this position.

A drug I'll always chase.

His eyes meet mine and we stare at one another for a few seconds, panting and fogging up the windows. He lifts me and presses his dick into my pussy. I wrap my arms around his shoulders as he grabs my hips and lowers me until he's completely buried inside me.

I bite his shoulder to silence the cry that rings from my throat and he groans in my ear.

"You're mine, Wynn. I won't ever let you go," he whispers darkly, pumping into me like a crazed man. His dick hits my cervix with each thrust.

It's impossible to keep quiet with the way he's worshipping my flesh. I hold onto him tightly and breathe in his scent as he pushes down on my ass and helps me grind on his dick.

"Even though I'm sick?" I whisper.

He slows his thrusts, but every motion of him inside me is euphoric.

"I'm sick too, remember? And together, we're not as sick as we were before." He pauses as he pulls back to look into my eyes. "*Remedium meum*," he says and a vulnerable smile crosses his lips.

"My cure," I murmur back to him and then our lips are crashing into one another again. He fucks me passionately— well, as passionately as one can in a car. His lips are soft as he presses kisses on my breasts and strokes his tongue gently against my flesh.

"I'm going to come inside you, sunshine. I hope you're still taking your pills."

I laugh and kiss him deeply, our tongues exploring one another before I whisper, "I've had an IUD since I was twenty."

"Have you ever had one pulled out of you?" he asks darkly. I shake my head, dizzy and drunk with lust. His teeth brush against my tender nipple and he breathes against it. "I can do that someday for you, if you ever crave to swell with my child. I'll pull it out slow and then I'll fuck you until you're screaming. I'll fuck you until you're pregnant with my baby." He takes my lips again.

Holy fucking shit.

"Liam," I moan. I can't even conjure something to say to that. His mouth is filthy and dirty and the things he says make me so fucking hot and bothered.

"You like that, Wynn? You like it when I talk about knocking you up?"

"Yeah," I cry out.

He pumps me harder and faster, rubbing my clit with his fingers as he takes me to the edge and I come so hard my vision blurs and my entire body vibrates.

I let my head fall back and moan as I ride out the last of my orgasm. Liam comes shortly after, his dick throbbing inside me, and his brows pull together as he groans like a dying man.

I slump against his chest and we sit here for a blissful moment, panting and letting our hearts beat together.

"Do you think we still have time for a dance?" he asks innocently, his blue eyes full of promises and affection.

I laugh and kiss him. "Yes, I think we do."

Chapter 28

Liam

We walk shamelessly back to the glow of the festival. I know loving Wynn is dangerous, but I can't stop myself from yearning for her every breath.

My phone buzzes. A chill runs down my spine but I ignore it the best I can. *Not tonight. I'm not going to let that bother me tonight.*

Lanston calls out to us as we reemerge from the shadows.

"Where'd you guys go?" He studies our faces and frowns. "And why do you look like you just got done fucking in your car?"

Wynn covers her mouth with a short gasp and shoves his shoulder.

They both laugh but I don't miss the pain in Lanston's eyes.

This is a shitty situation.

These two people mean more to me than anything else, but whatever I do hurts one of them. Guilt ebbs into me and the itch to hurt myself sends goosebumps up my arms.

"You promised me a dance." Lanston grabs Wynn's hand and she throws me an apologetic smile before running out into the street with him among the other couples. He whispers something to her and she laughs. His eyes shine at her with affection. I take a seat on the bench next to Yelina.

I see many others from Harlow dancing here tonight. Staff, patients. Jericho has a beautiful young woman in his arms and a flush across his cheeks that makes me grin.

I watch Lanston and Wynn dance in slow movements. They smile, completely engrossed in the moment.

"That bad, huh?"

"What?"

Yelina pulls out a cigarette and lights it. Her eyes are dull and she looks like she's had enough of tonight already. "You're in love with her," she states nonchalantly, as sure as the smoke she breathes in.

"Yeah...I am." Lanston's hands are low on her waist and Wynn's arms are wrapped around his shoulders like she'll never let him go. My heart twists uncertainly.

"Well, isn't *she* lucky? Are you both fucking her?"

I cast Yelina a cold, warning stare. "No."

She laughs cruelly. "We'll see about that."

In my heart, I know Lanston would never do that. But my eyes and brain tell me differently. They hold one another so casually, affectionately. Yelina isn't helping the dark whispers in my head.

Just like that, the seed of doubt has been planted.

And the darkness inside me itches.

Chapter 29
Wynn

Lanston's hands are warm, his endearing eyes more so.

The song is slow and nostalgic. One of my favorites. "The Night We Met" by Lord Huron.

Lanston pulls me close and whispers, "I remember the night we met," his voice and eyes melancholic.

"Me too. It was like a month ago and under the influence of a counselor." I grin and raise a brow in an attempt to lighten the mood.

His eyes soften and he nods. "Yeah. I guess that's what made it so different. You, the girl with pink hair and sorrow in her eyes. *You*, the person who was broken like I was."

My heart sinks.

I know what he's trying to say. Liam's words from the other night turn in my head. *You know he loves you, right?* It's an incurable ache, to know that you'd love a man without a shadow of a doubt if perhaps you'd met him first. But Liam has that part of my soul. I love them both viciously—but I love them differently.

"I don't think anyone in this world understands me more than you do, Lanston." I rest my head on his chest and he caresses me delicately. His embrace is like being wrapped in a warm blanket under the stars.

"But it will always be him, won't it?" he whispers.

I tighten my jaw and nod. "But you'll always be a part of our cure."

He lets out a short, low chuckle. "Your *what*?"

"Our cure. The three of us. Always the three of us." I beam at him and the sadness in his eyes brightens until it fades away.

"So, he told you about the tattoos then, huh? Come to think of it, you two have cured me in ways I never thought possible. Because of you two, I want to live. Every single day." He presses a kiss to my forehead and I cup his cheek with my palm.

"Because of you two, I want to live too."

We stare into each other's eyes until the song ends and everyone starts switching partners. I see Liam walking toward us in the corner of my eye and mutter, "Let's race again tomorrow?"

"There's nothing I'd enjoy more." He turns and smiles brightly at Liam.

"Care if I catch the next dance?" Liam's blue eyes are soft and my cheeks warm as he takes my hand.

"She's all yours," Lanston says with a false smile.

Liam takes position, bowing and kissing my hand like a gentleman as the next song picks up. "9 Crimes" by Damien Rice. He straightens and pulls me to his chest, our feet moving in time together.

"Such a violent song to dance to," he murmurs as he presses his lips to my forehead. He spins and dips me back. Our eyes connect. I long to kiss him, tangled in the bedsheets until the sun rises.

"Liam?"

"Hm?" His eyes are hooded with those beautiful dark lashes. He dips closer until our noses touch.

"Why did you come into my room that day at the hospital?"

Liam stares into my soul like he's searching for doubt. "To be honest, I'm not entirely sure. I wanted to see you. I'd heard the nurses and doctors fussing over you for a few days while I was lying in bed, and the more I heard, the more curious I grew. I *had* to see you. And when I did— God. I was so mad. I was mad because you were perfect, Wynn. You were beautiful and you had pink hair, you had the softest frown on your face, and the moment your eyes met mine I wanted to shake you. I wanted you to live, and the thought of you dying . . ." He takes a deep breath to reset his composure. "I came to you that day because I wanted you to live. And I wanted to help you find a reason to. I didn't know we'd be roommates here, but fuck, am I glad fate worked out that way."

He lifts me back up and we finish the dance, standing still. Everyone else moves fluidly around us as if only he and I are trapped in a time bubble. He curls strands of my hair around his finger and grins.

No one else has experienced a love like Liam's. It is chaotic. It is pure. It is love in its simplest, most cathartic form.

Liam presses a kiss to my lips. "Thank you for the happiest moments of my life."

The man on staff takes Lanston and Yelina's tickets before nodding for them to head into the maze.

Excitement and fear twist in the air and my skin itches with anticipation. Who doesn't love a good scare in a haunted maze?

Lanston screams almost immediately, followed by Yelina shouting at him that he's an idiot. Liam snorts and I elbow him with a wide grin.

"He can't help it." I try to keep the laughter from my voice but fail horribly.

"All right, you two ready?" The staff member holds out his hand for our tickets and we pass them over. He nods us through. Liam takes the lead, even though I offered since I don't mind being scared shitless first.

The maze is dark, only lit by cellphone flashlights and lanterns scattered sporadically throughout. It's impressive that this town puts on such a big festival. The atmosphere is perfect and the screams and laughter only add to it.

"You can cling to my arm if you're scared." Liam grins sarcastically.

"Says the man who almost peed himself going into an abandoned basement."

He narrows his eyes at me and wraps his arms around my chest. "Such cruel words from lovely lips."

We make our way through the maze, screaming and running from masked staff chasing us, wielding fake knives and axes. Liam's initial courage has turned into belligerent laughing and shouts at every jump scare.

"Fucking run, Wynn!" He cackles as he charges ahead of me, leaving me to die at the hands of the slasher-movie villain Jason and his machete.

"You asshole!" I laugh-scream as I run from Jason. I quickly look back to see if he's gaining on me, but the masked man stands still, ominously so, with his head tilted just enough to send eerie tendrils of fear through my bones. Liam pops out from around a corner of the maze and I squeal as he grabs me. He kisses my neck before he pulls me with him.

"Like I'd actually just leave you behind."

A gust of wind sweeps his black hair to the side and the warm glow of a lantern halos his figure. I find myself memorizing this moment. The way his gray sweater lifts to showcase his stomach, his oak scent consuming every last piece of me.

Then I hear Lanston scream.

"Wrong way, wrong way! Turn around!" He snatches me from Liam and I laugh as I run along beside him. Liam's right behind us, followed by Yelina, who looks pissed that she's been left behind. *I know the feeling.*

The four of us head toward the dark center of the maze. Our phones are the only light sources here. We hide behind a crate covered with pumpkins and hay bales and shut our flashlights off. Minutes tick by silently before we hear rustling.

One of the staff ghouls runs past the crate and then it's eerily quiet. It's too dark and I can't tell whose lap I'm sitting in. The four of us are packed in tight and it's not until Yelina stands that we start to untangle ourselves.

"That was terrible. This isn't fun anymore and I think we're lost," she whispers.

My cheeks warm as Lanston speaks up behind me, his arms holding me. "Shit, well, let's just keep walking back the way we came. We'll find our way out eventually," he murmurs.

"Okay, but which way did we come through?" Yelina tuts. She's right—with only our flashlights and nothing else to guide us, we're fucking lost.

Liam taps his screen and tries to pull up our location. "I'm not getting good bars out here, so I can't really tell where we are on the map app." His eyes linger on me and Lanston. I stand up next to Yelina and cross my arms against the night's chill.

"Let's just call Jericho and head back that way," I suggest, turning on my flashlight and helping Lanston up. He still looks scared shitless.

"Where are the town lights? The festival can't be over already—what time is it?" Yelina sounds panicked.

All of our heads lift to the sky.

No town lights.

"What?" Liam mutters, his breath curling in the cold air.

"Did the power go out?" Lanston shifts uncomfortably.

I shrug. Okay, this is getting weird. "Let's just walk back. I'm sure it's fine."

We walk silently through the maze. There's not a soul left in the cornfield, or at least none we can hear. The screams and laughter from before are long gone and our nervous energy permeates the air.

Liam dials Jericho and on the third ring, he picks up. We all audibly sigh in relief.

"Where is everyone? It's dark as hell out here." Liam's voice is sharp and irritated.

Jericho is loud enough that we can all hear him. "*The power went out in town; a drunk driver or something hit a powerline. The festival shut down early, so everyone is heading home. Where are you? Who's with you?*"

"Yelina, Lanston, and Wynn. We're all in the cornfield still."

"*Well, find your way out and text me when you get to the café. I'll wait for you guys.*"

Liam ends the call, looks up at us, and shrugs. "Power went out."

"We heard," Lanston grumbles.

A cornstalk snaps behind us and the four of us go deathly silent.

Someone steps out from the row and holds up a machete. I hold my phone flashlight up and reveal it's the guy wearing a Jason costume from earlier. His head still tilted in that creepy, unsettling way.

"The festival is over, buddy. Mind helping us find the way back?" Yelina snaps more bite in her voice than required. Lanston takes a step back and grips my hand tightly. His flesh is cold, and all the blood is drained from his face.

Jason takes a step toward us and swings his machete at the cornstalks, slicing a clean line through five of them easily.

"Stop it! We aren't participating in the maze anymore— we want to leave. *Now*," Liam snaps at the man. He steps forward and tries to take the machete away, but Jason moves his hand back and elbows Liam in the face. He falls and we all gasp in unison.

Liam lifts his head, blood dripping from his brow. Jason leans down close to him and chuckles, a sound so dark and wicked it sends a shudder up my spine.

Jason whispers in a low, distorted voice, "Come on, Liam. *Let me play with them.*"

Yelina chokes out a fearful sound, a terrified, open-mouthed sound that crawls from your stomach.

The masked man jerks his head toward her and lunges at her, slicing her arm. Screams and panic consume my blood like a narcotic.

"Oh my God," Liam says so absently that it sends goose-bumps up my arms. His eyes are wide and my heart instantly drops to my stomach. "It's *Crosby*."

Chapter 30
Wynn

Cornhusks shake violently as we crash through the field.

Fuck the maze.

We run blindly through the stalks, taking the brunt of the whipping husks.

I don't know how we got separated so quickly. After Liam said Crosby's name, everything happened so fast. We all darted instinctively into the corn. Lanston, thankfully, had a death grip on my wrist, but we lost Yelina and Liam.

When your blood is pumping erratically through your veins, you can't hear anything except the beating drum that tells you to not look back.

We're going to die. We're going to die.

I'm unsure if Liam is behind us or Crosby is, but someone is trailing us. Their footsteps are clumsier and louder than ours.

"Keep running," Lanston orders. He lets go of my wrist and before I can say *no*, he stops abruptly. His hazel eyes flash at me, telling me to listen to him.

And I do.

I fucking hate myself for it.

But I keep running.

After a few minutes, I break free of the cornfield, unsure what to do next. My first instinct is to call the police.

My hands tremble; I can hardly force my fingers to press the buttons. My breaths are labored and a dizzy spell falls over me. Pressure weighs down on my chest and pain twists in my heart. I know if I don't calm the fuck down, I'll pass out. My blood pressure is surely out of control and my medication is at the institute. I take a long, shaky breath and hold it for three seconds, breathing out slowly as I dial 911.

I have to lean over as the dizzy spell turns into horrible spins. I hold the phone to my ear as it rings and watch the thick wall of the corn maze with unblinking eyes.

Yelina bursts from the other entrance, her eyes painfully wide and her breaths raspy and labored. Her face is riddled with cuts and scratches from the stalks. She keeps running until she disappears behind the first building on the main street, where I hope Jericho will find her.

"911, what's your emergency?"

"A m-masked man is trying to h-hurt my friends," I say in a hushed, wheezing voice. "H-he has a machete and is trying to kill us."

"Ma'am, are you at the cornfield?"

"Y-yes."

"We've had multiple calls tonight. You are aware it's a part of the festivities, right?"

"No! This isn't a staff member. Please send someone out here immediately!" I scream into the phone so loud that my voice cracks. My body shakes violently with rage and fear.

The dispatcher pauses and then tells me they'll send someone out, but I can tell they don't believe me.

I tighten my jaw uneasily as I wait for Liam and Lanston to emerge from the corn.

My phone vibrates in my hand. Liam. I take a deep breath of relief and answer it immediately.

"*Liam*? Where are you?" My voice is raspy from screaming.

The line is eerily quiet.

My stomach twists and everything in my chest feels like it stops working. My lungs. My heart.

"*Crosby*," I whisper.

"*Where'd you go, little bunny? Come plaaaay.*" His voice is distorted and gurgly.

Despair unlike any I've ever felt takes hold of me. All I can do is stand here like a fool and tremble.

"*He's mine to punish.*" His voice is disturbingly lower all of a sudden—and angry. "*Mine to hurt.*"

He hangs up and the phone drops out of my hand.

Corn rustles a few feet to my left and Liam limps out with Lanston's arm over his shoulder. They fall to their knees, and as they do, all the lights turn back on.

Horror crawls through my conscience like poison.

Lanston's hair is wet and matted down with blood. Liam's thigh has a long cut down the front of it—his shoe is red and blood spills to the dirt beneath him.

I can't muster any words.

I only manage to fall next to them and pull them both in tightly before the sirens start. Lanston's eyes remain closed. I'm unsure if he's conscious, but I gently cup his bloody cheek and try to comfort him. Liam's labored breaths are shaky, each one curling in the frigid air. He looks at me with terror and my heart breaks. It breaks for all of us.

Because I don't think we'll ever be the same.

Red and blue flashing lights illuminate the shroud of cornstalks, and I see Jason standing with that awful tilt of his head. He points his machete at me and then puts his gloved hand up to his lips, blowing me a kiss. Then he turns and disappears into the maze.

The police officer checks with us before unholstering his gun and running into the maze where I point. A few more police officers show up and a medical team soon after.

I sit quietly as they tend to Liam and Lanston and load them both in the ambulance. Someone helps me up and guides me in as well.

Liam looks at me with dark, hollow eyes. He knows.

He's going to have to tell me everything.

Chapter 31

Liam

Wynn sits at Lanston's bedside, holding his hand and waiting for him to wake up.

They had to put a few stitches in my thigh and the pain is already throbbing through down to my bones. I deserve it; it scratches the itch and makes looking at my traumatized friends less heart-wrenching. This is my fault...I look down at my phone with heavy eyes. Three missed text messages from Mom, the same three messages she always sends.

I pull up a chair next to Wynn.

She doesn't look at me as she whispers, "What does Crosby want? No more secrets, Liam. No more lies."

I slouch back in the uncomfortable chair and run my finger over a small scratch on her neck. She flinches and looks at me with distrust flickering across her eyes. Somehow that hurts worse than the machete cutting through my leg.

"*Liam.*" She stares at me coldly, clearly not wanting anything but words.

Words I don't seem to have.

"Wynn...I can't."

She stands from her chair, pointing at the door and saying in an icy, hushed tone, "Then get the fuck out."

Lanston stirs, groaning and lifting his hand to his head slowly.

"Wynn? Oh, thank God, you're okay." He smiles as she wraps her arms around his shoulders, sobbing as he murmurs softly that he's okay.

"Why did you stay behind? We could've made it out together." Her voice cracks and guilt sets in deeper inside me with each tear that falls from her chin.

Lanston holds her tightly. "No, I don't think we could've." She sits back on the edge of the bed as he wipes away her tears. "Can you give me and Liam a few minutes, Wynn?" he asks her softly.

She glances at me hesitantly before nodding. Lanston waits until the door clicks shut behind her before speaking again.

"I thought Crosby was gone."

I lean forward in my chair and duck my head, rubbing the back of it and staring at the floor.

"He never left. He never will."

Lanston sits up, wincing. "What do you mean?"

I thread my fingers together and look up at him. "He has a grudge against me that long precedes my time at Harlow...but I'm worried he's set his eyes on someone else now—" My stomach curls at the thought of Crosby's cold hands curling around Wynn's throat.

"*No*. Not her."

I nod, not knowing what else I could possibly say.

"We need to file a police report. We're not safe anymore." Lanston throws off his blanket and tries to get out of the bed. His legs give out and I catch him before he falls. His hazel eyes are filled with anguish and it hurts to see him so afraid.

This is my fault. This is *all* my fault.

"I already did. I told them everything." I set him back in the bed.

Lanston's eyes search mine warily. "Did they catch him?"

I shake my head. "Not yet." Can a monster like him even be caught? I seriously doubt it.

There's no hope for me, but Wynn can get away with Lanston. As long as they are away from me, Crosby won't follow them. He only wants them because they're close, because they mean something to me.

They can be happy.

They can live on without me.

"I'll take care of him when he comes back...I'm sure he'll be here again in a few weeks." I lower my eyes, thinking of how I'll kill the man who's haunted me for such a long time.

Lanston's face pales. "Has he been coming back often?"

"Yeah." I keep my eyes on the floor. "Like clockwork. I never thought he'd hurt you two though...I know what I have to do now. I want you to promise you'll take care of Wynn."

Lanston's eyes widen and he fists the sheets. "No. She's in love with you, Liam. The three of us can get out of this. Let's just leave; he won't be able to find us."

I shake my head. "He'll know. He always finds me."

He's quiet for a few minutes before muttering, "I told her about Crosby."

My head snaps up in fury. "You didn't."

His hazel eyes are hard with resolve. "I did."

I shouldn't be surprised. They're so close and I've refused to tell her myself. Surely things have been odd enough for her to seek answers elsewhere.

Crosby.

Lanston is as far in the dark as she is. That's where they need to stay.

"Thanks for saving me back there." Lanston cautiously touches the wound on his head. The pain medication has probably taken most of his agony away, but I grab his hand and stop him from exploring too much of the damage. He was hit with a fucking machete; he's lucky his skull wasn't cracked clean open.

"I should've killed him," I mumble mindlessly, staring at the bloodied bandages wrapped around Lanston's head. The wound starts at his forehead and ends at the back of his skull. I don't have the heart to tell him that they had to shave part of his head in order to stitch him back up.

I make a mental note to stop at the gift shop later and get him a new hat.

"I'm sorry that I didn't...that I *couldn't*." My hands tremble against my legs. Why couldn't I force myself to do it? I had him...I could've.

"Who is he to you exactly? No more secrets, Liam. No more lies." Lanston sets his hand on top of mine and my heart aches with the kindness he's always shown me when I don't deserve it.

"He's my brother."

Chapter 32

Liam

Twelve Years Ago

Marissa sat on my lap and laughed at something I was too damn drunk to remember saying. I took another long sip from my beer and looked down at my phone.

Goddamnit.

I'd missed four calls from Neil.

I left the party and walked down the street in the dark, stumbling and cursing as I called him back.

"Liam? Where the hell have you been? Are you fucking drunk again?"

I laughed and tossed my beer can into one of the neighbor's trash bins left on the side of the street. "Sorry, Neil. Sorry. I'm walking now. Can you come—hic—pick me up?"

There was a long pause before Neil responded.

But he was a good brother.

He always came to pick me up.

I looked at the clock on the dashboard. "Fuck, it's one a.m. already?"

Neil shot me a glare and told me to buckle in. Perry gave me a dirty look from the back seat. Jesus, it was just a party. They acted like I had shit in the street or something.

"Yeah, it's fucking late and Mom is already worried. This isn't helping, Liam. I just don't understand . . ." He paused, thinking better of whatever it was he wanted to say. He was always considerate, unlike me.

My chest was hot with fury. I knew what he wanted to say. "You don't understand what?" I pressed.

Neil gritted his teeth and looked at me like I was the root cause of all our family's problems. Why Dad left. Why Mom's mental state shattered. Why he had to take responsibility for Perry and me.

"I don't understand why you're so fucking selfish. You're seventeen and I have to take care you like you're a goddamn child. Perry is younger and he's more of an adult than you!" Neil shouted at me, the vein in his forehead protruding.

I knew I was all those things. I knew I was a fuckup.

Perry tapped Neil's shoulder and murmured quietly, "Please don't yell. Liam's just sad . . . He'll try harder tomorrow, won't you, Liam?"

My chest sank. "Yeah, I will. I'm sorry."

Neil glanced over at me and then heaved a long, weary sigh. "It's okay. I'm sorry for shouting."

I didn't know what I'd do without my brothers. They were all I had—all I needed.

Mom texted me. I read the message quickly.

Mom:
Your brother is coming to
get you.
Be kind to him. He loves
you.

Great, even Mom knew I was out getting drunk and Neil was coming to the rescue.

Neil raised a brow as he turned onto the mountain pass. The shortcut was steep and narrow in places.

I didn't want him to know Mom had messaged me. We were all so worried about her mental state already. That's why I just smiled, held up my phone, and showed him a photo I snapped at the party.

"It's just a stupid picture of the party."

Neil only looked for a second.

It was only a second.

Only . . .

When I woke up, I was in the hospital room alone.

No one was holding my hand. No one was waiting for my eyes to open.

Perry? Neil?

A nurse walked in and took my vitals. She said that my mother refused to see me, that my older brother was dead and my younger brother was in critical condition. And finally, that I would be discharged in a few days.

Neil was dead.

My soul died during those days. I wanted to see my mom and tell her I was sorry. That it was my fault. But she wouldn't even visit me.

Something corrupted inside me during that time spent alone. My pain was so overwhelming, damning, like waves pushing and pushing until the floodgates opened.

And then it stopped, as if someone had clicked delete on the pain center in my head. It was gone. I felt nothing. Horrible, rotting nothingness.

Nothing except guilt.

On discharge day, they released me from the hospital and I stood at the entrance bay for six hours, waiting for my mom. She didn't come to pick me up, and Neil wasn't here anymore.

I walked to a gas station and bought a pocketknife. I thought about killing myself, but it didn't seem right.

I didn't want to die—I wanted to be punished.

I cut myself beneath a dirty bridge until my hands shook so badly that I couldn't lift the blade anymore. And I cried. I cried until some passerby called the cops and an officer came to pick me up.

He looked at me for a long time. He had a twisted, astonished look on his face.

Then he took me home. When my mom answered the door, she wouldn't look at me. I walked past her to my room. We didn't talk until Perry came home weeks later.

I walked to school. Cooked for myself. Took care of myself. Punished myself.

Perry was different.

He didn't remember the crash. Even though my mother told him Neil was dead, he acted like he didn't hear it.

It only took a few hours for his first episode to happen. He became a devil. A demon in the flesh, sent to punish me. I welcomed it.

He called himself Crosby.

That was the first time we properly met. Crosby remembered the crash and why we were all on that road to begin with. It was because of me.

For weeks he tortured me. I thought it was right. I didn't mind because it was my fault.

Mother watched and smiled when Crosby came to punish me. She'd say over and over in that cruel voice, "It's your fault." I'd nod and accept the pain. Then when Perry returned, she would go back to her room and lie in bed mindlessly again.

Perry was always confused about why I kept getting hurt. My ribs were cut, my head bashed, toes broken. He couldn't understand. He'd wrap me up and cry for me. His heart was so tender and broken.

"Why do you keep hurting yourself?" he'd ask.

I never could respond to it. Never.

He looked for Neil often. And once the school noticed his shifts in behavior, they filed a report and had him sent away. He was gone for a year.

The second I turned eighteen, I left my home without saying goodbye.

He was gone for only a year.

Then the texts started again.

Mom:
Your brother is coming to
get you.
Be kind to him. He loves
you.

At first, I didn't understand. I was only upset because this was the message that haunted me. But I soon understood.

Crosby came to find me. And find me he always did.

I didn't know he went to a mental institution. I didn't know I would end up at the same one years later.

It was nice for a few months, until I got the text again. And then my life became hell.

Crosby became my roommate. It was odd. At the sanctum, he never reverted back to Perry. He remained Crosby. Hateful and angry.

The old rumors about the missing people were suspicious to me. Lanston had that odd Clue game. I couldn't shake the feeling that it was...peculiar that they went missing at the same time Crosby was at this institution.

I collected articles about them, hoping they would turn up somewhere someday, but they never did. Jericho left his keys on the front desk one evening and I happened to notice during my nightly walk. The guard was doing his rounds and I was completely alone.

I opened the filing cabinet and searched for my brother's name. It wasn't until I came across it that I realized I'd forgotten his real one. Perry Waters. He was here. And in my heart, I knew he'd done something to them.

Maybe that's why he decided to wrap things up with me that night.

"Deeper," he hissed at me.

I shoved the knife deeper into my ribs and jerked the blade so it'd cut. My hands were trembling and the blood made the handle slick. Crosby pushed it further since I was incapable.

I thought it might be the last of my punishment. It hurt more than the rest ever had.

Then Lanston found us. Oh God, I felt my soul shatter when he did.

Crosby fled. I went to the hospital. I didn't die. My punishment would continue.

But then I saw her.

And for some reason, I thought maybe I didn't need to be punished anymore.

My cure.

Chapter 33
Liam

Lanston's eyes widen with horror.

The way he looks at me has shifted. The monster is my brother, my flesh. Born of the same damned mother and heartless father.

"But...he—" Lanston's eyes brim with tears as he glances down to my side where Crosby made me cut myself so deeply, helped push the blade in.

That night was hell and the limit I found to my punishment. I've never bled so generously in one sitting, bathed in my own blood, and felt that deep cold in my bones.

"He's sick. I'm sick too," I admit with clenched fists.

Crosby's words echo in my mind. *"You need to be punished, Liam. You survived so that you could be punished for Neil's death."*

Lanston's grip tightens around my wrist and he pulls me in for a hug.

I'm shocked for a second before I smile weakly and embrace him the same.

"You've been suffering for long enough. You're my best friend, Liam. *My brother.* We need to get away from this place, find somewhere he can't find you again. You, me, and Wynn. The three of us can make it."

I hesitate.

A vision of the three of us, happy, walking the streets of Boston like he and Wynn talk so much about draws a painful smile to my lips. We look so relieved and...fixed. Wynn's pink hair is curled and her wrists are covered with fresh tattoos, quotes from books she loves. Lanston's too, with dragons and skulls. I look happy. Weightless. We walk beneath the spring foliage and warmth spreads to the darkest chambers of my heart.

But we can't run from Crosby.

He'll find me again.

He'll kill everyone.

My smile fades, and the beautiful image of the three of us turns gray and dreadful. I stand before their graves.

"You need to take Wynn first and get somewhere safe. I'll deal with Crosby and once he's gone...I'll find you two."

Lanston pulls back and looks into my eyes. He's scared. *Fuck*, I'm scared too.

"Okay. But we have to tell her everything. I won't leave her in the dark any longer."

I nod and grip my chest.

The truth would be so much easier to say if it didn't hurt so much.

Chapter 34
Wynn

I sleep in Lanston's hospital room the night Liam opens up to me. He tells me everything. It's...painful. The three of us cry like traumatized kids, but once we pull ourselves back together, we plan how we will survive.

Lanston gets discharged after two days. When we get back to Harlow, nothing is the same.

The walls look different now. Knowing that someone as corrupt as Crosby was here ten years ago leaves a bitter taste in my mouth. The missing people...I wonder what he did to them. Where they are now. Liam seems certain that Crosby did *something* to them.

Liam insists that I stay in Lanston's room. He's keeping me as far from him as he can; while I understand why, it leaves me with such deep anguish.

Lanston holds me tightly against his chest, smoothing his hand over my head in calming strokes. He tries to comfort me. "It's going to be okay."

I shake my head. It's already well past midnight but my mind won't rest. It's filled with fear and dread and worry for Liam.

He's alone against the devil and I hate it.

★

I thought once that I knew what a broken man looked like. I thought I knew what their eyes held.

I was wrong.

I don't see Liam all morning. Lanston even skips some sessions and drives to Bakersville to see if he can find him. It isn't until the afternoon music session that we find him.

A broken man is like a dead flower.

I think I'll die, sitting as silently as I can as I stare at Liam. He sits at the piano bench with his back arched, leaning over the keys, staring hollowly at them. Both of his hands are bandaged, blood seeping from the fabric over his knuckles and staining most of it red.

"I can't play today," he says so shakily that I want to go to him and take him far, far away from everything.

Jericho narrows his eyes at Liam. "I want you to sit there for a few more minutes and think about what you did to yourself, Liam. I want you to understand why you can't play today and whose fault it is."

My chest scorches with rage and I stand abruptly.

Poppie gasps from a few chairs down. And all eyes in the room shift toward me.

"It's not his fault."

My blood is boiling so hot I can barely get the words out. My fists clench tightly at my sides. "It's *not* his fault."

Jericho looks at me and shakes his head. "Then whose is it, Coldfox? Since you're so eager to talk today. Whose fault is it? Did *you* cut his knuckles? Did *you* break his pinkies?"

My breaths come harder as the rage keeps spilling, growing inside me like a dark beast. I want to scream and throw my chair at the counselor. He doesn't understand. He doesn't know.

I look back at Liam.

He sits on the piano bench, hunched and weary. His eyes are so dull today that it shatters my heart to look at him.

I help him up.

And together we walk out of the room.

Chapter 35

Wynn

It's strange how quickly your reality changes.

Only a month ago I wanted to die. Now, I'm running for my life.

Lanston's stitches are less visible than they were earlier this week. He wears a black beanie now that the weather is getting colder. November has been cruel already.

I sit next to him and we whisper about our arrangements to leave Harlow. I feel the edge of a blade in my chest. I may not love this place, but I will miss spending time here. Surely I knew my time here was limited, but now I find myself cherishing every memory, every last moment of existing within the stones of the mansion.

Lanston leans against me and I shut my eyes with his warmth.

"You never told me you had a car here as well as your motorcycle." I chuckle as we look down at my tablet. We have the apartment we'll be moving into pulled up.

"I don't like driving the Mercedes. Makes me feel too posh."

I laugh and shake my head. "Yelina will kill you if she finds out you had one and refused to drive her to the festival."

Poor Yelina. She's so upset over the cornfield incident. That's what the police are referring to it as—*the cornfield incident.* Yelina hasn't spoken to us since, and I heard she's transferring to another institute at the end of the week. I don't blame her.

Lanston shrugs. "We'll be long gone by the time she knows."

My eyes lower to my hands and I stare at the onyx ring Liam gave me.

I understand things now that I wish I had to begin with. Liam's brother has haunted him for half his life. He's been running from him, literally and figuratively. His illness makes more sense to me now...A tragic accident like that and his environment after? I can't even imagine.

"Where'd you go?"

"Huh?" My head tilts up toward Lanston.

"You went somewhere just now. What're you thinking about?"

My head feels so heavy, my chest more so. "The crazy guy who's tormenting us." My fingers brush against the ring. I look up at the door to Jericho's office. Liam's in there right now discussing his departure from Harlow.

One week.

We're leaving. Lanston and I are moving to Boston, while Liam will remain at Harlow to keep Crosby here until either he's caught...or Liam *takes care* of him.

It's not murder, I tell myself. Liam didn't explicitly say he was going to kill him...but I think it's implied.

I tell myself this over and over. Crosby will hurt us, *has* hurt us. He's trying to kill us...Liam is only protecting us from him.

"I'll protect you, Wynn." Lanston rubs my arm soothingly. "Always."

My eyes shift to the fireplace and I slump into the couch. "Well, who will protect you then?"

He barks out a laugh and I glance at him with a raised brow.

"Isn't it obvious? Liam, of course."

Chapter 36

Wynn

My last counseling session is traumatic. All the cards are on the table.

"Can you tell us what made you dissociate? What hurt you?"

I stare at Jericho with cold eyes. Dr. Prestin sits next to him with his legs crossed.

"*I* know. But I want you to say it and feel the words come out of your mouth. Admitting the things that hurt is important, Wynn. Especially since your time with us is ending."

What made me dissociate?

Is it fair to point fingers? Whether it's fair or not, I suppose it's real for me.

"Words."

"Words hurt you? Can you elaborate?" Dr. Prestin presses me. His white eyebrows are drawn low. His eyes focus on his clipboard, not the people in the room.

I look hesitantly across the circle at Lanston. His hazel eyes are warm and reassuring. Liam isn't here today, and I'm sort of glad he isn't.

"Words that convinced me to die."

"And who said these words? What were these words?" Dr. Prestin asks matter-of-factly.

"Everyone who ever claimed they loved me." Every word lodges deep in my throat like a knife. *Betrayal by those who were meant to care for me in the darkest of times.* "They acted innocent and coy, drawing me in like fresh air. Wishing to know what ailed me. And the only thing I *ever* learned from opening up to people was that they desired to know exactly what would hurt me, only to turn the blade back and inflict riotous, irrevocable damage themselves."

Everyone remains quiet, even Jericho and Dr. Prestin, who now looks up and meets my gaze. The counselor lowers the clipboard and removes his glasses. I force myself to look at Jericho and the part of my heart that was frozen over thaws a bit as I watch him wipe tears from his eyes.

And somehow, a great weight has been sloughed from my shoulders. The tear that rolls down my cheek isn't filled with rage or hot with disdain for the world.

It's sadness for myself.

The first grief I'll allow myself to feel for the sins against me.

Why is it so hard to show ourselves mercy? Did a part of me believe that I deserved what I endured, just as Liam does? Why didn't anyone help me? Didn't I ask more than once? Didn't my eyes scream loud enough for those that observed me so callously to stop?

"Coldfox, what hurt the most and how have you come to reject this disbelief?" Jericho clears his throat and returns his glasses to the arch of his nose. His green eyes are significantly softer on me, filled with sympathy and grief.

He has a hard job. Taxing on a soul, I'm sure.

I have to think for a moment. There are so many that hurt for so long. *Monster. Demon. Evil. Insufferable child. Miserable bitch.* Though they all hurt and damaged me in unique ways, I think one was worse. One broke me, unlike the rest. One made me realize that perhaps death would be the only cry loud enough to be heard.

No one heard me. No one *ever* fucking heard me.

"Being told that I was, inevitably, going to kill people. Being told that they could see the sinister evil inside my soul. That looking at me made them *sick*." I choke on tears and swallow hard, blinking past the emotions and fighting all my inner safety walls to get the words out. "That I was better off dead. Because all my existence did was make them wish to die."

Lanston stands from his chair and walks to me, tears streaming down his cheeks as he lowers to my level. Words evade him; his mouth opens and closes but he cannot find the right ones to speak. He pulls me into a tight hug, and it says everything he can't.

I break, wrapping my arms around his torso and sobbing into his shirt.

Finally, Lanston finds the words he was trying to conjure. He speaks so low I know only I can hear him. "You wanted to die so they didn't feel like they had to."

Hearing someone else say it...

It saves me.

"Thank you," I whisper.

Chapter 37

Wynn

Lanston tosses my black duffel bag in his trunk. His smile is loose and hopeful.

Mine is as well, oddly enough.

Our bags don't hold much, but there's something exciting about that.

We can start new lives in Boston. It's so far away and different from here. Buying new clothes and furniture, starting fresh—it's like a token to a new world.

Liam stands behind us with a blank expression.

He's been so broken up preparing himself for our departure this last week, but it's more than that. It feels like he's pulling away emotionally for our sake. So we don't see how much it hurts him.

We begged him to reconsider, to just come with us to Boston. Liam, in all his stubbornness, declined.

There's no way Crosby can be all-knowing. He wouldn't be able to find us that far away, would he?

I'm not so sure anymore.

"You two drive safely. No racing or any of that shit," Liam mutters like a father would to his children. "Don't text me the address until you hear from me that it's okay. We can't be too careful."

Lanston stretches his hand out and Liam clasps it. "We'll

be careful. And we'll see you soon." They pull each other into a brotherly hug and my heart aches with the way Liam's brows pull together in anguish.

None of this was ever fair.

Liam holds me so fiercely it makes me think he's changed his mind, but he loosens his hug, kisses me softly, and lets me go.

Lanston leans forward in the driver's seat and looks at the rearview mirror with excitement and anxiety flashing in his eyes. The windows are rolled down halfway; the chill in the air skips across my forearm and raises goosebumps.

"I feel like shit for lying to him," Lanston says reluctantly, glancing over at me. I nod. Lying makes me feel like a traitor. Even if it's to help the man I love.

What else were we supposed to do though? We couldn't just let him face Crosby alone. He refused to let us stay. So we had to sneak behind his back and make plans without him. Plans that don't include Boston and being on the East Coast.

"So do I. But it's only temporary," I say, more to reassure myself than him but it seems to work by the way Lanston's shoulders relax.

We drive into Bakersville and park in the alley behind the studio house we were able to rent last-minute.

It's not like everything we told Liam was a lie. We do have the apartment in Boston ready. Our motorcycles are on their way there, along with all our things from our storage units. My brother is seeing to it that our apartment is furnished with a bed for our arrival, which James is under the impression is this week. We had to lie to more people than I'd like, but if Crosby is truly keeping an eye on us, we need everyone fooled.

Lanston puts his Mercedes in park and frowns at the small space allotted for his car in the alley. I pat his shoulder as I walk past him to retrieve my bag from the trunk.

"It will be fine out here."

"Says you." He pouts, but the hint of a smile hides behind his lips.

I grin and toss his bag to him. He barely catches it. "Says me." I laugh and brush past him.

The studio is more like a garage that's been converted into a rental space. Actually, I'm positive that's what it is. Not a shroud of a doubt. The walls are bare, tanned with years of someone chain-smoking cigarettes. Pretty gross, given that this is a furnished rental. The curtains are stained and the carpet has burn holes riddled throughout.

Lanston drops his bag on the couch and looks around with a frown. "Change of plans. Let's go to Boston," he quips and walks back toward the door.

I laugh, setting my bag down next to his. "And let Liam deal with his brother alone?"

He groans dramatically before winking at me.

I don't know what I'd do without Lanston. He's become a rock in the void of my existence. He tethers me to the ground and I can breathe so freely in his presence. The world isn't so scary and hopeless with him lighting up everything around us.

We spend the rest of the afternoon unpacking what little we have on hand. The bed is at least clean. I'm not so sure about the couch. Lanston plugs in his phone charger and checks the calendar.

Our plan is pretty shit. But it's all we've got.

Today is Tuesday. Liam is meeting Crosby in the greenhouse in two days, like he did last week...when his hands were so terribly damaged. We are going to be lying in wait with weapons. We'll call the police anonymously so they will arrive, but should things not go as planned, then we'll improvise. There's no way that night ends without Crosby being caught or *taken care of.*

We eat microwave noodles for dinner and huddle in the twin-size bed at midnight. It's absurdly cold in this house. Neither of us could figure out how to work the stupid ancient heater and we gave up after a few hours of trying to Google instructions with no success.

"Hey, you asleep?" Lanston murmurs close to my ear, his arms wrapped around me.

"Not yet," I whisper softly, brushing my thumb over his warm hands. They're always so warm.

He takes a deep breath. "I keep thinking about what you said."

I hesitate. My brain instantly jumps to the worst thing. He's talking about our therapy session.

When I don't respond, he continues. "I will never fully endure what you have, but I think I understand it. My father was always really mean to me. I couldn't cognitively bring myself to accept why though. He hated me. More than hated me, he wanted me gone." I swallow hard and my hands tighten around his. "I didn't understand it...and I'll never be okay. It hurts to admit. It hurts to say out loud. I will never be okay. And it *is* his fault. For a long time, I blamed myself. I would tell myself, 'If I was just a better son. If I wasn't so unbearable. If I tried harder.' It took me a really fucking long time to realize. *Fuck,* I was just a kid."

Tears fall from my eyes and wet my pillow. His voice breaks with emotion as he continues:

"All I wanted was for him to love me. I was just a *kid*. But he judged me like an adult for everything he blamed me for...So no, I don't think I will ever understand exactly what you've felt, but God, did it hurt to hear you say it. Because I know the burden of wanting to die. To die, just so they can live without the weight of your existence."

My jaw trembles and I shift in the bed to look at Lanston. His hazel eyes are watery and glisten with misery I feel down to my bones. My eyes trace the stitches that reach down to his forehead.

His fingers caress my cheek softly. "No one looks at me like you do, Wynn. When you look at me, I feel like I can shatter into a thousand birds and just...fly. You set my soul free from the chains I keep wrapped around my shoulders." Lanston smiles wearily. He looks so tired. I wonder if that horrid man he calls father haunts him in his dreams too. I hate him. I've never hated someone I've never met so vehemently. Lanston is the gentlest soul I've ever known. One that would never hurt me.

Not like the others. Not like so many.

"You're my best friend, Lanston. The closest soul I'll know to my own. How rare that we'd find one another in this life. How beautiful that our illnesses would allow us to meet in such a horrible place. I love you. I'll always love you dearly."

His eyes close and a sad smile crosses his lips as he presses a kiss to my forehead. "You're mine too, Wynn. There's nothing I wouldn't do for you. Liam knows that; I think that's the only reason he trusts me with you. My love for you two...It's endless. Like a sea that just keeps lowering the depths to make more room for the life we three have ahead."

We fall asleep crying, hands clasped and hearts full.
Full of dreams.
Full of all our life not yet lived.

Chapter 38

Liam

My room has never felt so cold. Unwelcome.

I stare at Wynn's empty bed and try to smother the ache that throbs in my chest. All I've ever sought is pain. I loved pain.

Or at least I thought I did. Now it only festers.

I hate the sting of it. I despise the scars left behind by every foolish thing I've ever done. Most of all, I regret my hands. My eyes linger on the scabbed cuts on my knuckles and fingers. The purple bruises that keep getting darker.

I hurt more than myself that day. I hurt her. So terribly I hurt her. I've never seen her eyes so consumed with pain and suffering. I'm certain with everything in my heart that I will never do that again.

My bed creaks as I sit up and set my feet on the cold floor, rubbing my hands together to try and bring some heat back to them. They're always so icy, much like my demeanor.

I lower my head and anxiously rest my hands on the nape of my neck.

My phone *dings*, drawing my eyes to the lit-up screen.

It's four a.m. Another text from Mom. I eye the phone. Not quite sure how she got my new number, but I'm sure Crosby has his ways.

Mom:
Your brother is coming to
get you.
Please be nice to him. He
loves you.

I scoff and toss the phone on the bed. She always chose him, didn't she? It was always Crosby who needed protection from the world because he was her last son alive. I was dead to her. After Neil, after everything, I was dead to her.

He murdered five of the neighborhood cats and tortured me. Then came here and probably killed those missing patients too. He's a monster.

The door shuts quietly behind me as I slip from my room. Crosby shouldn't be coming until tomorrow, but Mom's text warrants a look. I clench the knife in my hand, preparing myself to kill him once and for all.

The lights are dimmed throughout the estate. Only the guard at the front entrance stays awake through the night. He's been on high alert since the police haven't been able to find Crosby. I walk past the guard and he nods at me.

"Out for your nightly walk, Waters?"

I let out a tired chuckle. "Yeah."

There's a span of time in which you can learn someone's name. After that window, if you don't know their name but they know yours, it's unspeakable to ask for it. Or at least that's my own personal rule. I've been hoping to get a glimpse of his name tag but I keep forgetting to look.

The grounds are cold. The temperature is well below freezing. November in Montana is more gray and dead than most places are in fall. It's basically winter already. Frost coats the grass and the dark, naked trees in the distance are eerie.

246

I take my time walking through the forest. The moon-flowers have long since shriveled away into their deep slumber for the winter months and now it's just an empty field that a sick man visits each night.

Haunted, in a way. By me. That's an unsettling thought.

It's easy to lose time when you're trapped in your past. I think of Neil and Perry and wonder where they would be in life right now if that night had turned out differently. Sometimes I hope if I close my eyes and wish desperately enough, I'll wake up and this will all have been a dream.

But, of course, I inevitably open my eyes, and I'm still standing in the field.

Still haunting it.

I take a deep breath and walk back through the forest to the greenhouse.

It's more difficult tonight than I thought it'd be, forcing myself to walk through the familiar hedge pathway and down the stones to the glass cage. How much blood have I spilled in that broom closet? How much more will be enough for Crosby? I've decided to not find out. I'll be putting an end to his reign of horror.

From down by the greenhouse, large hedges block the view of Harlow. Someone must have woken up and turned all the lights on in the recreation room, because just above the bushes, a warm light shines bright.

The stale, mildewy scent of the greenhouse invades my nose. This building was wasted in its disuse. Dust and wet cement floors are all that this place offers now. My soul tires as I drag my body to the back room. The light beneath the door glows amber.

He's already here.

I tighten my grip on the pocketknife. I take staggered breaths and my forehead beads with a cold sweat as I force my hand to twist the doorknob. Everything in my head screams for me to run. To stop and leave with Lanston and Wynn.

I ignore it.

The door swings open and I hastily step inside, knife drawn and adrenaline pumping a mile a minute.

But the room is empty.

My heart sinks and my eyes land on a small sticky note lying in the center of the floor, atop the steel drain.

My head feels light and dizzy as I bend down to inspect the note.

It's a smiley face with a single word beneath it. As I read it, the blood leaves my face. My lips are numb and my fingers scorch with the onset of an anxiety attack.

I turn and leave the room. The glass walls of the greenhouse are a bright orange, lit from outside.

No. No, he wouldn't do this.

I burst through the door and fall to the frozen ground the second I witness the flames licking the sky in angry throws of orange, red, and yellow.

The sticky note falls from my hand.

:) Burn

Chapter 39

Wynn

Sirens ring through the streets.

Lanston hands me a cup of coffee as we head outside, blankets wrapped around our shoulders, to see what the hell is burning down at four thirty in the morning.

A bright warm glow lights the sky toward the south end of town.

Lanston sits on the hood of his car and sips his drink. "Think it's the cornfield? Kind of late in the season for a brush fire though."

I shrug. "Maybe someone set it intentionally."

My cup stops before it reaches my lips as one name comes to mind.

Our eyes meet and Lanston pales as we mutter at the same time:

"*Crosby.*"

The entire town is awake and watching with horrified faces as we race down Main Street. The fire is much too far away to be the cornfield. My heart pumps erratically inside my chest and my throat feels dry.

Lanston hasn't uttered a word since we got in the car. Fear tantalizes the air around us.

Please don't be Harlow...please.

I repeat the thought over and over until we're speeding down the long stretch of road leading to the institute.

249

My heart drops to my lap as we break the forest line and see firetrucks lined up, spraying water relentlessly at Harlow Sanctum. The entire building is lashing with angry flames, reaching higher into the sky than I've ever seen fire climb. A guttural, animalistic cry leaves my lips.

Lanston slams on the brakes and stares at the inferno like he's been shot in the chest. His eyes are wide and his jaw shakes uncontrollably.

My body acts of its own volition. I throw the door open and sprint toward the burning building. The heat is unbearable, even from twenty feet away. Firefighters' heads turn as I run past them, some dropping their hoses and chasing after me in their full gear.

"Stop!" one calls out.

But I can't stop.

Nothing can stop me from reaching Liam.

One moment I'm charging straight for the front doors. The next, I'm on the ground, staring up at Lanston's anguished face.

He tackled me.

It takes a few seconds for my wits to return to me before I struggle against him and fight with every ounce of strength I have.

His grip tightens and he doesn't let up.

I scream furiously at him, "Liam's inside! What are you doing? Lanston, you're killing him! Let me go! Let me go! LET. ME. GO."

I thrash something feral in his strong arms until the energy of the adrenaline pulses out of me and tears berate my eyes. The initial shock becomes a sense of loss I've never experienced before, a crushing, hopeless weight that burrows into your very soul.

The wail that crawls from my chest is the worst sound I've ever heard anything make, heartbreaking. Lanston cries with me. A few firefighters kneel beside us and urge us to move back to the ambulances.

How Lanston finds the strength to stand and carry me is beyond me. Medical staff lay out tarps and stretchers, anticipating to fill them with injured people, but as the hysteria fades from my shaky mind, I realize they've not extracted a single person yet.

Jericho, Yelina, Poppie, Liam, Dr. Prestin, Mrs. Abett, all the other patients and staff inside...There are easily fifty souls inside Harlow. And not a single one has been saved yet?

I lean over and vomit off the back of the ambulance. Lanston holds me desperately and rubs smooth motions over my back in an attempt to calm my whimpers.

How could this happen? Why did this happen?

A man limps from the building with two others on his shoulders. Everyone animates and a team of emergency personnel run stretchers over. I watch as they try resuscitating one. The other they set on a stretcher for immediate treatment and transportation. I break free of Lanston's hold and run to the stretcher.

It's not Liam. They're much smaller than him, but that's all I can tell. Despair and shock consume me as I stare at the burned human before me. Their skin is gone. All the hair has been singed from their body.

I don't know who this was.

All I know...is death would be kinder than this cruel fate.

My eyes trace back to the other two. Lanston is at my side, sobbing as he stares down at the person I just verified isn't Liam. The putrid smell of burned flesh stings my eyes but I blink past the urge to vomit again.

We walk uneasily to the man who carried the two people out. He kneels, mainly unscathed, but covered in soot and coughing horribly. I recognize him as the night guard. An ambulance takes him off site immediately.

The paramedics cover the person they were trying to resuscitate with a white sheet.

I stare at the body before us with hazy eyes—whether it be from shock, smoke, or tears, I'm uncertain.

Lanston grabs my hands and shakes his head. "No," he whispers, the sound so raspy I know my voice will sound the same.

I don't listen. Foolishly I don't listen.

The white sheet has already turned red from the blood. I carefully peel back the corner. A twisted and severely burned woman lies on the stretcher. Unlike the other person, she still has her hair. And I instantly know who she is. The skin on her face is mostly unscathed but the rest of her...

"*Yelina*?" Lanston asks with an absent, heartbroken tone.

My stomach churns and tears fall unwarranted. My lips are numb and my fingertips sting. My chest hurts from the shock, the pain of loss, and my illness. I take staggered, wheezing breaths and shake uncontrollably.

"Hey, stop fucking around," Lanston says softly, as if she is sleeping. "You're transferring to a different treatment center tomorrow, remember? You can't... You can't—" He chokes and sobs.

I pull Lanston close to my chest and cry with him.

"Wynn, you're pale. Hey, what's wrong? *Wynn*?" Lanston jostles me by the shoulders.

"My h-heart." I barely manage to get the words out. My hands clench and grab viciously at my chest of their own accord. It hurts. *It hurts.*

He lifts me in his arms so effortlessly, even though I know it's no easy feat. His warm scent wraps around me and instills warmth through my veins. He murmurs soft, comforting words that are empty of fear, calm and reassuring. The physical pain starts to fade in my chest, but heartbreak is a distinctly different type.

Lanston takes me to the ambulance staff and they check my vitals. They insist on taking me to the hospital due to my blood pressure, but I refuse to leave until they extract more people from the building. They agree, only because I've calmed enough for my levels to lower.

But as the minutes pass, as the hours do, we realize no one else is coming out.

We cry together, wrapped in a tight embrace, until no more tears are left.

We sit like ghosts on the blackened lawn of Harlow until the sun rises. Until the firefighters have extinguished the fire, and all that remains are the stones that framed the building.

Police have long since taped off the area. A few detectives tried speaking with us only to receive hollowed eyes and raspy breaths.

They transport us to the hospital without another word.

"Did you catch the arsonist?" Lanston asks the officer tasked to watch us. The man shakes his head. "It was Crosby," Lanston says in a low, hateful tone. His beautiful hazel eyes are sunken and dark. They don't shine like they did last night. He looks like an entirely different person. Part of me wonders if I do too.

"The same guy from the cornfield?" the officer asks, noting something down on his notepad.

Lanston nods, keeping his eyes lowered.

He hasn't looked at me since we arrived here.

The nurse stops in and gives me something that makes me drowsy. I'm reluctant to sleep with Crosby somewhere out there. I refuse to believe Liam is gone. He can't be. *He can't—*

Chapter 40

Wynn

The view from the hospital window is depressing, barren trees and sad, long stretches of empty field. Lanston sets a cup of coffee down next to me and frowns as he leans back in the chair.

We've been here all day and we still know nothing. We don't know the body count. We don't know if they've caught Crosby.

My stomach sinks.

"You should try some...it's not so bad." Lanston urges me to take a sip of the coffee. I shake my head and lower my chin.

He's quiet for a few minutes before he scoots in closer and sets his hand on mine. I dredge up the will to look at him and he feigns a weak smile.

"It will help. We'll hear something soon." His hand trembles and he pulls it back, gripping it himself to stop the shaking.

I swallow the lump in my throat and look at Lanston in defeat. "Why did *we* get away? Why didn't we burn with them?"

The guilt tears at my soul unlike anything I've ever endured. Why do we, the two who desperately wished to die, get to live?

Lanston's lower lip quivers as he mutters, "I don't know, Wynn. But I wish it was me...So Yelina could live...So anyone else who perished could live." His head dips and the sobbing shakes his entire body.

I have no tears left; my eyes won't bear them. So I crawl into his lap and we hold each other.

"I'm so happy it wasn't you," I say selfishly, burying my face into his shirt.

A few hours pass and we get discharged, sent away with sleeping pills and the detective's phone number. When we call, he asks us to stop by the investigation site.

We drive to Harlow.

Smoke still billows from the ashes. The stones I once cherished are blackened with death.

We sit quietly in the car. It takes thirty minutes before Lanston opens his door. He patiently waits another ten minutes for me to follow.

He holds out his hand and I thread my fingers through his.

The gravel sounds so much louder than it ever did before. We walk around the perimeter of the building, taking in just how much damage was unleashed here. The detective asks us questions and we tell him everything we know. The basement, the greenhouse, and how Crosby seemed to have easy access to both. The detective mentions that all the windows had been nailed down, and though the investigation is early, they suspect that carbon monoxide was used prior to the fire, since most of the bodies were found in their beds.

The greenhouse comes into view, untouched by the flames.

Lanston looks at it and shakes his head.

"I'll just be a minute," I say as I make my way slowly to the glass enclosure. Lanston and the detective continue up the slope. It's not that I believe Liam will be in there. I just want to have something...a last memory of this place other than the fire.

I make my way quickly through the greenhouse, stopping briefly at the door in the back before opening it.

I don't find anything. It's the same horrible, bloodstained room it was my first time here. Memorizing the small space takes but a minute, and then I slowly shut the door and walk back outside.

The detective gives us a grave look before we get back to Lanston's car. He hands us a report and dips his head.

Only two survived the tragic fire at Harlow Sanctum, Roman Bear and Sydney Lawsen. Over fifty-six bodies, including staff and patients, were recovered. Police are still looking for the arsonist.

We stay silent. No tears. No screaming.

Nothing.

I've never wanted to die more than I do at this moment. *Liam. I'm so sorry.*

Roman Bear, the night guard, and Sydney Lawsen, one of the patients. That's it.

We leave as the sun starts to set, silent and tired. We're both reluctant to return to that rental so we stop at the café to grab coffee and maybe dinner if we can stomach it.

Crosby showed up a day early. And that one day took everything from us.

"It was always supposed to be the three of us," I say.

Lanston parks the car and stares at me with darkened eyes. "I know." That is the only thing he says before turning the engine off. *"I know."*

Chapter 41

Liam

Something sharp pierces my thigh.

My eyes shoot open, fear and adrenaline instantly igniting in my bloodstream. I can't move my arms or legs—am I tied up? Where the fuck am I?

"*Finally*. I thought I was going to have to kill your friends without you watching."

My spine straightens and every hair on my neck rises.

"Crosby? Where are we?"

He unties the blindfold slowly. The light stings my eyes and I wince past the pain of the intrusion before he comes into view. My head throbs and my limbs ache.

I've never seen my brother so disheveled. He looks worse than he ever has before. His dark-brown hair is messy, and his light-blue eyes are almost silver in the dim light. What has he done?

"Crosby, what are you doing?" I tug against my restraints but it's futile. He has me tied like an animal awaiting slaughter.

He tilts his head back and groans like he's annoyed. "I *just* told you. Aren't you listening? I'm going to kill your friends. Since they magically weren't at Harlow as I was expecting them to be." He *tsks* and lowers his head to look me straight in the eyes.

Sweat beads down my forehead and dread fills my chest. Memories of the fire resurface, twisting my insides.

"You didn't."

Crosby's eyes light with his sinister smile and he laughs in my face. "Oh, but I did."

Horror befalls me. I don't have the courage to ask how many people survived. I doubt he cares.

He wants the people I love—and he can't have them. The only thing he's ever wanted since Neil's death is to torment me.

"How could you... When did your punishment for me turn into murder? Do you have any idea what you've done?" I pull against the restraints to no avail.

Crosby shrugs. His black hoodie is a size too big on him. "It's not like they were my first."

I hesitate momentarily before lowering my voice. "The missing patients."

"*Ding ding ding*! Took you long enough."

My heart tears more with each breath I take. "Where did you put them?" I don't think I'll survive the night, but even if I don't, at least someone will have known.

Crosby levels his eyes with mine. Ice flickers through his cold gaze as he grins sinisterly. "A place you've been way too many times. Some might say you danced on their graves."

My eyes widen. "The moonflowers . . ."

He taps my forehead and nods manically. "All of them but one. *Monica* got away. That one was smart and witty—she changed everything about herself so fast I never was able to find her. She's the one that planted those fucking night flowers out there."

Perry... how did you devolve into this monster? I stare at him with new eyes. A part of me wanted to believe he

259

was still in there, deep, deep down, but Perry is dead. He died with Neil that night. Something else came back in his stead.

"Where are we?" I gnash my teeth together, desperately trying to formulate any sort of plan that could stall him. Lanston and Wynn should be halfway to Boston by now.

They're safe. They have to be safe.

"In Bakersville. You didn't think you could hide them, did you? They fucking showed up at Harlow and waited to see your sorry ass dragged out of the fire." He laughs cruelly.

In Bakersville? No, they were on their way to Boston... "I hate to ruin your fun, but they are far from here," I say resolutely.

Crosby stops laughing and leans forward, eyeing me like I'm messing with him. When he doesn't see any wavering in my eyes, he questions himself. Anger flashes across his icy eyes and he grips his hair, talking to himself in hushed whispers. "He's lying. He's lying. There's no way I mistook them. Or maybe...did I? No. No. No. No. This messes up everything. Everything."

I try to block out his deranged voice as he speaks to himself. My eyes skirt around the small room we're in—a bathroom. Not one I've been in before. *Focus, Liam.* I take a deep breath and try to think rationally.

My eyes open and I softly say, "Crosby, Mom let me know you and Neil were coming to pick me up."

Crosby freezes. He turns slowly, his eyes manic and feral as he assesses me.

"Mom told me to be nice to you. You love me, remember?" As much as I resent my mother, at least she always tips me off before he comes. Reminds me of his trigger words. My trigger words too.

Sometimes it works, and I'm really fucking hoping that this is one of those times.

Crosby's eyes lower to the floor before his demeanor noticeably shifts. A wave of calm and steadiness replaces his crazed, demented side.

I love him dearly, but he's going to die tonight. He's not going to hurt anyone ever again. I'll make sure of it.

Perry tilts his head and smiles normally at me. "Liam, what kind of game is this?" he asks jovially as he unties me.

I only manage a tight, weary smile.

The adrenaline is fading from my bloodstream and the knife wound in my thigh is now throbbing with agony. "A stupid game the seniors were playing. You know them, Perry," I lie, and he nods easily, believing his older brother like he always has.

This is his true self, Perry Waters, my dear younger brother, who's stuck in his sophomore year of high school in his head. The one that was in the car with Neil and me when the accident happened. The normal boy who suffered significant brain injuries and couldn't accept the reality that his eldest brother was dead. The innocent brother I tried to hold onto.

I lost them both that night.

Perry looks at me with confused, frightened eyes as he inspects the odd bathroom. He notices my bloody leg and panics. "*Liam*, your leg."

It never gets easier hearing him talk in his childish voice. Looking at an adult man's face and hearing the innocence he tries to imbue into his tone is chilling.

"I'm okay. Let's get out of here and find Neil." It stings, pretending he's alive and waiting for us. But I'd like to think he's waiting somewhere for Perry.

He animates and helps me leave the bathroom. It's a small studio apartment. My heart skips a beat. The pounding in my head is so loud I don't hear anything else.

That's Wynn's duffel bag. Lanston's baseball cap.

They didn't leave for Boston.

My breaths are so labored that Perry raises a concerned brow at me. "What's wrong?" His eyes are bright blue.

It's already been a few minutes since he phased into Perry. He usually changes back after five or ten minutes—sometimes not for days, but in this escalated environment with me panicking, who knows what will trigger him.

I thank God that the two of them aren't here. I motion toward the door and we hobble out. Lanston's Mercedes isn't here. Momentary relief floods me and my thigh starts throbbing again, reminding me that I'm potentially bleeding out.

"Oh, I parked up there." I point down the alley toward the lookout. It's secluded up there; the only people who visit there regularly are me and Jericho...I try to shake the fear that he might not be alive anymore.

Perry laughs. "Why did you park so far?"

I feign a lighthearted shrug and bend over to pretend to tie my shoe. Perry stares out toward town, smiling, indifferent to anything around him.

I look over his belt, finding the revolver I knew he'd have saddled in the holster. He carries it everywhere.

As I stand, I bump into him and grab the gun, shoving it in the band of my pants. Perry looks at me like I'm acting weird and shakes his head disapprovingly.

"You can't keep getting drunk like this, Liam. Neil's covered for you so many times. You're breaking Mom's heart, you know...following right in Dad's footsteps."

That was a low blow I wasn't expecting.

I was a careless teenager—perhaps I did deserve everything Crosby did to me. It certainly felt earned.

"I know," I say in a hushed tone. "I promise I'll stop."

He smiles. "Good."

Does it make me a monster if kill him? My heart wavers. He doesn't mean to be Crosby. He doesn't...

I stop hobbling as we reach the base of the stairs and ask him for his phone. He rolls his eyes like he can't believe I lost my phone too.

I dial 911 and wait patiently as the phone rings. Calmly and discreetly, I tell the operator to come to the corner of Berry Street and Tallsaid. When they press me on why, I simply hang up.

"A taxi was probably smart. You shouldn't be driving when you've been drinking," Perry scolds me.

I flinch. Talking about drunk driving usually triggers him.

He stands placidly for a few seconds and then darkness shrouds his features. His eyes flame with icy fire and that deranged anger takes over again.

I don't waste a second.

Taking the stairs two at a time sends shock waves through my stabbed leg, but as my fear has reignited, so has a fresh wave of adrenaline.

Crosby watches me with cold, daunting eyes before he sprints up the stairs after me.

I just need to lead him away from them.

Chapter 42

Wynn

We drive slowly down the alleyway. Police lights are flashing and an officer is taking photos of something at the base of the cement stairs leading to the lookout.

Lanston shares an uneasy look with me.

We were at the coffee shop for a little over an hour. I'm tired and just want to lie in bed and mope. One look at Lanston tells me he feels the same way.

The officer waves at us to stop.

"We got a phone call from a man asking to meet him here. Have you two seen anything unusual?"

My heart sinks when I catch sight of blood at the base of the stairs. The only trouble this town has seen has been at the hands of Crosby. Call it whatever you want, but I know it in my bones.

Liam.

Lanston speaks up from behind me when I don't say anything. "No, we haven't. But we'll keep an eye out." The officer nods and returns to the lower step, where the blood is.

I turn in my seat. "Lanston, I think Liam was here."

He keeps his eyes forward as he parks and unbuckles his seatbelt. The circles under his eyes make my heart ache.

"I know you want to believe that, Wynn. But I don't think so. He's...dead."

Tears spring to my eyes. Lanston frowns like he's sorry to say such a cruel thing, but I know he's weary. Tired of having a thing as silly as hope.

He gets out of the car and heads inside. I remain sitting for several minutes before deciding to pursue the inkling I have pulling in the back of my mind.

"Sorry, Lanston," I mutter to myself as I navigate over the center console and into the driver's seat. I start the engine and take off down the road to the lookout. He really needs to stop leaving his keys in the car; we're not in Harlow anymore.

The parking lot is empty.

I park the car and get out, listening, but it's silent. The only sounds are those of the wind and crisp leaves blowing around on the ground.

I knew it was stupid to look into this. Lanston knew it too. But I can't give up...not until I'm sure he's really gone. I won't give up.

Deep breaths. I inhale and exhale slowly.

A flash of color catches my attention.

I look at the ground closer and see a drop of blood, still wet and glistening in the cold air, not yet frozen.

My surprised breath curls in the air and hope pulses through me. I'm hesitant to call out Liam's name. If it is him, he's bleeding and running from something.

From someone.

A gunshot pops off and I don't think. I thoughtlessly run toward the sound.

It was muffled with distance, so I know he's close enough but I can't decipher where.

Another shot goes off, closer. I run straight into the forest beyond the parking lot. It's inclined, and after about twenty paces up, an expansive golden field stretches out as far as I can see.

Two bloodied people are struggling over a gun.

"Liam!" I scream and run toward the two men.

I know it's irrational. I know I should call for help. If I were in a rational state of mind, maybe I would do that and risk Liam dying.

But I'm not rational right now.

I'm blindly in love, and each second I waste means his life on the line.

Both men snap their heads toward me and Liam's beautiful face comes into view. His eyes are fearful and he's bleeding. He's yelling at me to turn around and run.

But he's alive.

He's not covered in those indescribable burns or in the morgue with a tag around his big toe. He's breathing and screaming and looking at me.

He's here. And so is Crosby.

I don't hear anything except the pounding of my heart as I tackle Crosby to the ground. He's as tall as Liam and I register it quickly as he throws me off of him easily and pins me to the ground.

His eyes are ruthless and filled with malice. He pulls his gun and aims it at me.

I've never stared at the muzzle of a gun before. It's paralyzing—your brain doesn't know if it should beg or scream. So I do neither and look past the muzzle, locking eyes with Crosby.

His stare hollows my soul. He murdered everyone at Harlow Sanctum, potentially those before us too.

Liam stands behind Crosby, a rock the size of my head in his hand. He cries out as he brings the rock down.

Everything slows, like a movie, except I'm watching from the worst seat in the theater.

The rock cracks against Crosby's skull so hard that the sound reverberates in my chest, so loud my ears hurt.

I watch Crosby's eyes roll to the back of his head and he falls to his side. Liam crawls to me, groaning painfully with each breath. He collapses next to me and tears stream down his face.

"I thought...I'd never...never s-see you again," I rasp. I flinch and knit my brows at the deep, harrowing pain that throbs in my chest. Something's wrong.

Why am I wet? It's warm.

Liam's eyes are calm and reassuring. He presses his hand down on my chest and it hurts. I try to squirm beneath the weight he's administering there but he holds firm.

"I love you, Wynn. I'm so sorry—sorry for everything." He coughs and blood coats his shoulder from the spray.

My eyes widen; he's hurt worse than I thought. "Liam— *ahh,* it...it hurts." *It's getting colder.*

"Listen to me, Wynn. You need to stay awake, baby. Can you do that for me?"

"Huh?" I mutter. It's becoming hard to focus. I'm dizzy and cold. "I'm so c-cold, Liam. Why...am I s-so cold?"

I'm so tired and...it hurts. I'm hurt.

"It hurts," I cry.

"Shhh...It's okay, Wynn. We're okay. I love you so much—please hold on. It's okay, baby. We're going to make it. All three of us are going to make it. You, me, and Lanston, remember? I promise nothing's going to happen. I love you—"

Chapter 43

Lanston

She ran off without telling me. Of course she did.

My chest heaves as I reach the top of the lookout. Those steps are way too steep for anyone's good. Well, there's my Mercedes...

Pop.

My head jerks toward the hill. A gunshot?!

I sprint up the hill and see three bodies lying in the golden field.

Oh God. No.

I reach them in a matter of seconds. A gun and a bloody rock are on the ground. Crosby looks either dead or knocked out cold. His head is bashed in, covered in blood.

That's when I see them.

They lie still, holding each other like only death could possibly tear them apart. Their eyes are closed and tears and blood mix on their faces.

There's a bullet hole in Wynn's chest. Two in Liam's.

Panic surges through me but I have to keep my head. Everything I do right now matters. Every second counts.

I pull out my phone and call the police, telling them where we are and who the culprit is, all on speaker as I go into survival mode. I tear Liam's shirt open and examine where the bullets are. They've missed his heart and aorta. Relief floods me as I dip down and hear his breaths.

I move to Wynn.

My heart shatters as I stare down at her. Her pale-pink hair is covered in blood and mud; her face is scratched and dusted with dirt and red. A dry trail of tears runs over her nose and down her cheek.

Why didn't I go with her? Why didn't I? I drill myself. Her shirt tears easily and all the pain in the world couldn't describe the mind-numbing agony that rips through me as I look down at her chest.

The bullet found her heart.

I hold my breath and press my index and middle finger to her carotid artery. There's a faint pulse but it's fading fast.

I take my sweater off and press the fabric onto her chest, praying to a God I don't believe in and crying as I stare, unblinking, at her.

"Please don't go, Wynn. You hear that? The sirens are getting close. We're going to be okay now. We're going to—"

Pain pierces my back. My legs instantly lose all feeling. I glance up with clouded vision and see Crosby staring at me, blood running down his face and the gun in his hand.

He shot me. I don't feel anything...but I know he shot me.

The sirens get closer and despite my own wound and shaking body, I keep the fabric pressed down on Wynn's chest. *It's okay. We're safe. We're going to be fine.* Sweat covers my entire body as I watch a police officer rise above the hill and shoot at Crosby.

He tries to stagger away but his head injury slows him down. He falls close to Liam and I watch as the evil light in Crosby's eyes shifts into that of a softer soul.

His eyes round as he stares at Liam's face. He looks so innocent and scared it almost breaks my heart. Then he starts crying. "Liam? Oh my God, what happened? Liam? Neil, help us! Help us, please!" he shrieks. The sound makes me sick to my stomach.

This is all so fucked-up.

Police are yelling and running toward us. Crosby is screaming and crying like a child. The world is too loud right now. My insides are starting to burn.

Keep the pressure on her. Just focus on the pressure.

Liam's eyes crack open—he heard his brother's plea. Crosby quiets down, tears still running down his face. He looks at his big brother with large, pleading eyes.

Liam smiles faintly, reassuring him, as he chokes out, "I'll always love you, Perry."

Pop. Pop. Pop.

Crosby's eyes widen only for a moment before they go dull and distant. Liam sets the gun behind himself and then tries to pull his brother in close for a hug, but he's too weak, lost too much blood. He keeps his bandaged hand atop Crosby's shoulder.

"Liam," I cry. My insides hurt so bad. My back and legs have lost all feeling. "Liam, I'm here."

"Lanston," he rasps, taking a wheezing breath. "T-take care of her."

The officers reach us and hurry to move Liam.

I shake my head and tremble, trying to force my body to keep the weight on her chest until they reach us.

I stare down at Wynn, brushing her hair from her forehead and pressing a kiss to her lips.

"You have to pull through, Wynn. You will always have my heart. Always."

Chapter 44

Wynn

I wake up in a cold room.

My chest hurts. And I'm alone.

Tubes are attached to me. Before I can make much sense of it, I drift back into a listless sleep.

The next time I wake up, I'm in a warmer room. There aren't as many tubes attached to me. There are other beds, but they're empty.

They are all empty.

I know this is wrong. Part of my mind is telling me something is wrong.

Where am I?

I'm . . . looking for someone. More than one person.

My eyes close. I'm so tired.

I'm so very tired.

Chapter 45

Wynn

I'm walking down the streets of Boston.

It's a cold, dreary day, but that's okay—we like the cold days.

Lanston smiles at me, his beanie pulled down over his ears. Liam rolls his eyes at our friend but grins too. We walk down our favorite street, which has a bookstore and a coffee shop. It's just down the road from our apartment. It's what we dreamed of together. What we always wanted.

I've never been so happy in my entire life.

"Wynn, do you remember the first time we met?" Lanston asks gleefully.

I tilt my head. "Of course. Jericho's counseling session."

He nods. "That's right. I saw your pink hair and how broken you were, and just like that, I knew."

I grin and press him, "Knew what?"

"Knew that I loved you. Always you." He brings me in for a tight hug.

It starts trickling rain as I look up at him. He's crying, but his smile is endearing.

"I love you too. You know that." I glance back at Liam, who is still walking ahead and getting further away from us. "Come on, we need to catch up or we'll get left behind."

Lanston shakes his head. "Not this time, baby. Go on ahead without me. I'll see you two later."

I hesitate. Our hands are clasped tight. I never want to let go. "Are you sure?" I ask, tracing his cheek with my forefinger and memorizing his lovely features, those kind hazel eyes and high cheekbones.

"Yeah. I'm sure."

My eyes open. The familiar ceiling of the hospital welcomes me back into the cruel world.

I sit up.

No tubes are attached to me now, only an IV drip in my arm. James sits in the corner, slouched over and resting.

My chest still hurts. And unlike in my blurry, drug-induced state, I remember why.

Crosby shot us.

I look at the other beds in the room. All empty.

"*Liam?*" I call out, my voice hoarse from disuse. I have no idea how long it's been, but my heart beats faster as despair takes hold of me.

"Lanston?"

James wakes up to my shouts and the beeping of my heart monitor. He hurries to my side and whispers soft words that I can't hear, because I'm screaming.

"*Liam! Lanston!*"

Nurses rush in to tend to me. One pulls out a syringe, but someone calls out for her to stop.

Everyone stops fussing as I cover my mouth and still.

His eyes find me first, then he runs to me and embraces me so tightly that I squeak from the pressure.

"Not so hard," James snaps furiously from my side.

"Sorry," Liam mutters as he unwraps his arms from me and caresses my cheek adoringly. Tears fill his blue eyes and he presses a long kiss to my forehead. "I thought I'd never look into your eyes again." He starts sobbing and shock unfurls inside me. I've never seen Liam cry like this.

"Where's Lanston?" I ask, expecting him to walk through the door any second. I want to tell him about everything he missed. I'm so fucking relieved he wasn't there.

Liam's eyes widen and he cries harder, shaking his head. His hands tremble so violently that one of the nurses braces him and tries to coerce him to calm down.

Why is he upset about Lanston? He wasn't there. He wasn't...

James takes my hand and looks me in the eyes. He blinks away tears as he shakes his head.

"*No,*" I say, convinced they're wrong. "No, he wasn't there. He didn't come with me."

Liam reins in his sobs and shakes his head.

"H-he s-s-saved us." Fresh tears fall from his eyes and he grits his teeth as he forces himself to continue. "C-Crosby shot h-him."

My world ends with those words.

My kindred soul cannot be gone. Surely I would feel the shift in the universe. I would feel the weight crashing in on me like the pressure deep in the sea, wouldn't I? Wouldn't my heart and soul just...know?

No, they're wrong. I still feel him. He's still here.

James frowns and holds my hands firmly, taking on the burden of telling me the news Liam cannot bear to speak. "He was shot in the spine, instantly paralyzing him from the waist down. Somehow, he miraculously remained upright and held his sweatshirt over your heart to stanch the bleeding. You all arrived here alive. Both your conditions worsened. Without a heart transplant, you were going to die. He didn't pull through." James lets his tears fall as he clears his throat. "His last request was that you receive his heart."

I was born with a bad heart—literally and figuratively.

But you gave your heart to me, and because of you, I will live.

Because of you, I will never take my life for granted ever again.

Chapter 46
Wynn

One year after the fire

Snow falls outside the café windows like little puffs of cotton, soft and slow. Boston is a lot warmer than Montana. I rest my head on my palm as I watch people pass, wrapped in warm clothes, their breaths curling in the air as they laugh.

Liam sets a plate down, then two coffees. He presses a kiss to my cheek before he sits down across from me.

"Where do you want to start today?" He grins and reaches his hands across the table for mine.

I intertwine my fingers with his and smile back. "Well, we'll need to stop by the office and pick up the new floorplans, and then we're pretty much free until the flights tomorrow."

He nods and raises a brow with a hint of trouble. "How much free time are we talking, Wynn?"

I laugh. "Probably enough for whatever your wicked mind has planned."

We walk to James's new office down the street. That's what I love about the city—you can just walk a block or two and be where you need to be most of the time. It also helps that my brother wanted to relocate to be closer to me.

I grab the memorial blueprints and let tears fall silently. The moonflower field will become a memorial park, with a path circling it and tall stone pillars with the names of those we lost etched into them. They found the missing people there beneath the flowers and finally put them to rest, but we never did find Monica.

We look over the floor plans for the new institute, Never Haven, to be built in place of Harlow. It stings my heart to replace it with a new building. The memories of the people and the healing I experienced there can never be succeeded, but perhaps, with love and time, we can create a new rehabilitation institute that will be home to many like us. Many like Liam, Lanston, and me. The ones that come after.

I look at Liam adoringly. He studies the new building specs with excitement and tells James how great it looks. His blue eyes flash up to me, giving me a simple smile, one that tells me he still fights the battles inside, just like I'm sure mine does. But we've grown so much together.

The three of us were the cure. In our darkest hours, in the darkest of nights, we are the light.

By the time we reach our condo, the sun is already setting outside. Liam sets down the grocery bags from our little pit stop—movie snacks for tonight.

"Popcorn, my dear?" Liam asks. I'm not sure why though; he's already putting the bag in the microwave and he knows my answer will be yes.

"I love you." I smile giddily as I wrap my arms around his wide chest.

He turns and scoops me up in his arms. I squeal as he takes me to the couch, pressing kisses on my neck and lips, only stopping momentarily to whisper, *"Remedium meum."*

The words bring tears to my eyes each time he says them, always with the same warmth and devotion as the first moment I heard it.

I kiss him deeply. His tongue strokes mine fervently as his hand slides beneath my leggings and starts circling my clit. I moan and writhe beneath him as he teases me. His dick is already tenting his sweatpants and I know movie night is going to turn into an all-night fucking session while we watch people run from ghosts and figure out mysteries.

The microwave dings and I reluctantly pull from his ravenous lips. "It will go cold if we don't get it," I warn him.

He shoves a finger inside my pussy and pumps into me, making me throw my head back and cry out.

"Fuck the popcorn, Wynn. I want you," he murmurs as he pulls my pants off and lowers his lips to my needy clit. He strokes me a few times with his hot tongue before looking up at me with heat and vulnerability in his eyes.

I watch him, quirking a brow when he stops and lifts his head.

"You know what else I want?"

My breaths are short. "What, my love?" I press my hand to his cheek and he leans into it, shutting his eyes for a moment.

He brings his hands up to my stomach and looks at me with somber, hopeful eyes. "The final part of our cure."

Tears spring to my eyes and I bite my lip to keep the cry in my chest. Him tearing up too sends me over the edge.

He pulls me up and holds me tightly. "If you don't—"

"*No.* I do." I sob into his shoulder. "I want there to be three of us again."

He brings my face to his, kissing away the warm tears as they fall. Our cries slowly transform—happiness for our future, and sadness for the past.

Liam brushes his finger across the tattoo on my arm, in the same spot Lanston had his.

III

Epilogue
Liam

Two years after the fire

Never Haven stands tall and magnificent against the morning sunlight.

It's beautiful, everything Harlow was and more.

Gray bricks contrast the freshly planted mums and marigolds lining the driveway. *Some of my darkest ghosts live here*, I think to myself as I take in a deep breath of the crisp scent of autumn. *But some of my most cherished moments were born here as well.*

Wynn tucks into my chest and I pull her close.

James flew us out here ahead of the ribbon-cutting ceremony so that we could stand where everything ended once more before the new beginning. I don't miss the middle-aged woman walking down the path toward the memorial site, moonflowers in her hands as she walks nostalgically through the grounds.

Monica, I'd like to think. But I'm not sure I'll ever know.

"It's perfect," Wynn mutters as she wipes away silent tears. "Lanston would've loved this place. What we did. He'd—" She chokes up and tightens her jaw.

"He'd be smiling from ear to ear. Asking us to freshen the driveway with a race." I laugh and try to fight back my own tears.

She looks up at me and smiles, tears running down her face and as beautiful as the day I first laid eyes on her. I set my hand gently on her stomach, swollen with our child. Her hand meets mine.

This is what I want for the rest of my life. Us three.

My wife, who's loved me through the dark, the wicked, and the cruel. My child, who will know the stories of those who are no longer here. Those who came before him.

And myself.

I've learned to forgive myself. I've learned to love *me*.

"*Remedium meum*," I murmur as I press a long, adoring kiss to Wynn's forehead. "Let's make sure the greenhouse is filled with flowers before everyone arrives. Then we'll visit Lanston and make sure he's got a new hat this year."

Wynn wipes the last of her tears and lights up with the promise of flowers and visiting our dear friend.

"Let's bring him a bundle of baby's breath and peonies. And I still plan on dancing at the autumn festival tonight." She winks at me.

"I'll dance until I die if it's for you, sunshine. But fuck the cornfield."

Lanston Nevers
"The Fabric of our Souls is thin and worn. We must be gentle and love tirelessly."

Acknowledgments

Thank you for reading this morbid, depressing book and letting your soul wander a while with me.

I would like to thank my readers for enduring my sad stories and still loving them. I appreciate you more than words could ever depict.

Thank you to my ARC readers for your wonderful reviews! I always stay up late reading them and crying because, my god, you all have such a way with words.

Thank you to my editor, Leanne. You are wise, kind, smart, and so insightful. I couldn't make these stories shine without you.

I'd like to thank my beta reader, Jay, for always giving me the reassurance I need. You believe in my stories even when I lose faith.

Thank you to my proofreader, Cierra! You are my rock. You do so much more than proofread and I will forever shower you with love.

Thank you to my husband and the close friends who endure my dreary, weeping mind.

Finally, I'd like to thank me. If there's anything I've learned from writing this story, it's that you have to love yourself. So, I thank me, for putting the heart and soul into this story and being brave enough to share it.

About the Author

K. M. Moronova has always loved telling stories. She adores reading and writing dark fantasy with a helping of dread and romance. Often, she is found drying flowers and drinking coffee while relaxing in her garden. She loves spending time with her partner exploring the forest and envisioning more devastating stories to tell. Visit her at KMMoronova.com.